THE
DISVARIANTS

to the ones whose art and stories inspired me to create my own

THE
DISVARIANTS

PROLOGUE

The struggles faced by the average teenager make life complicated enough. You're bombarded with loneliness, anxiety, school, the pressure of figuring out who you are and everything you want to do with your life in only a few years, and the expectations from adults for you to have it already figured out.

Life was already immeasurably difficult, but even the seemingly infinite struggles managed to be multiplied the day Julie died.

Being frantically woken up at 6^{AM} by your panicked and terror-stricken parents to be told the news that your best friend is dead is not the best way to start your day, and undeniably not the best way to start the first day of the rest of your life.

'They found Julie, in a ditch. They don't know how she got there. They think she was murdered," my mom spoke to me in a soft, but shaky voice as she caressed my face in her cold hand.

At first, I refused to believe it. My mind frantically sorted through various series of events where someone would start a false rumor about Julie's death just to mess with people. But not long after that, it hit me all at once that this wasn't a lie or a prank, and I began to shut down. I couldn't even convince myself to shed a tear, because no matter what I did, it didn't feel real. None of it felt real, until I saw her parents.

My parents and I had went over to their house to help them make funeral arrangements over tear-soaked coffee and the sound of the phone ringing nonstop with halfhearted condolences and empty promises to help out in whatever way they could.

I ditched them and hid in their guest bathroom and cried so hard I couldn't breathe, until finally my parents forced me to leave.

I was excused from school for several days to prepare for the funeral and to mourn Julie. I spent most of that time lying in my bed, unable to move. Everything, even my own ability to walk, was stripped from me, as if the electrical impulses in my brain died, just as Julie had, before they ever reached my hands and feet.

Two days after I watched her body lowered into the ground, I was, once again, lying in my bed, schoolwork piled up on my desk, wishing it all merely a cruel nightmare, and dreading having to go back to school — to life — the next day. Then someone knocked on our door. A knock that ensured I would never again have to go back to high school.

It was the police who had come to arrest me, because they thought I, of all people, had murdered Julie. The cops spent hours interrogating and intimidating me, trying to get me to confess.

"We have overwhelming physical evidence to prove you did it! Your fingerprints were found on her neck, your skin was found caked in blood under her fingernails. 'Fess up now and maybe the DA'll go easy on you," shouted a tall, bulky cop, with skin so pale he appeared sickly.

"That's not true. I wouldn't hurt her. She was my best friend!" I said furiously. "I would... I would *never* want her dead."

They interrogated me for hours — despite my reluctance to talk and insistence of my innocence — trying to get me to confess, in order to make the trial easier on their part. They only stopped when I vomited on the floor of the interrogation room.

I never confessed, they found more "evidence" against me, and took me to trial. As hard as they tried they could never prove motive (probably because there wasn't one. A gaping plot hole in their fictional version of events that they merrily overlooked). Their case rested on wringing the falsified evidence for all it was worth (which was a lot, apparently), and the testimony of a few witnesses. No one actually saw me anywhere near her that awful night, but having those who found her body sit on the stand and describe how beaten up she was, through watery eyes, is enough to turn a jury against you.

The trial was, for the most part, a complete daze. I hardly remember what happened, except when I cried after they gave gruesome details of her death; how she was dragged out of her bed in the middle of the night, her neck was snapped after she was suffocated by choking, her skull was crushed, and she was sprawled out in a ditch for several hours before any passing cars bothered to notice she was there. I remember that last part far too well.

I also remember my attorney telling me to plead guilty for a deal of "only 25 years" in prison. I had considered it, the odds being completely stacked against me and a conviction imminent, but then I remembered if I confessed that I would have to tell the court exactly how I killed her. I couldn't do that. I didn't kill her and I couldn't pretend that I did. It's not in me to lie and it's not in me to murder.

Last week, I was found guilty of murder and kidnapping in the first degree.

Yesterday, I was sentenced to life in prison. I was shown no leniency because I'm a minor.

Today, I am being moved from a jail cell to a high security prison upstate, where I will spend the rest of my life for a crime I never committed.

ONE

In the distance I hear the rattling of the gate as it slides open to let us through into the yard of the place I will reside at for all my days to come.

The driver parks the truck I'm in, and two guards the size of bodybuilders escort me out of the vehicle. I step out onto the pale pavement surrounded by the giant, perfectly mowed front lawn; the vivid green clashing against the dull color of the colossal fortress up ahead.

Both of the guards hold tightly onto each of my arms and guide me along the cement pathway to the front doors, where I'm afraid of what I will see inside.

When the doors slowly open, all I see are long, gray hallways and metal doors, with labels that used to indicate what each room was. They have long since worn off.

A tall woman with white-blonde hair, smudged glasses, and a face worn from too many years at this job, is there to meet me when I walk in. She looks down at me, at my small body and childish face, as if she knows exactly who I am. Her stare suggests she sees through my innocent appearance and knows me for the killer she thinks I am.

The woman eyes me suspiciously as she runs a metal detector over me and pats me down to check that I haven't smuggled in any potential weapons, then unlocks my handcuffs.

Afterwards, the guards take me by my shoulders and guide me down the halls. I pass a room with only "s" and "p" remaining on the label.

A walk down the long stretch of hallways leads us to the cells, which are a stark contrast to the ones where I was previously being kept. Instead of metal bars, they have heavy metal doors that must be two inches thick, with small, barred windows in them. Several inmates glance at me through their tiny windows with looks of excitement and others with anger. Both expressions make me very nervous.

As we draw closer to my cell, it comes to my attention that all of the inmates staring at me were men. I was under the impression that I would be in an all women's prison, since I am a woman, or better said: A girl. I'm not a legal adult, though I will be in only a few months time, yet I'm in an adult prison. And to go along with that, they seem to have had the genius idea of putting me in a prison with grown men in it as well.

"Is this a prison for both genders?" I inquire of one of the guards death gripping me.

"Yes," he answers, without so much as glancing at me.

"So, I will be in a cell with a girl, right, or will I be alone?" I ask. The chance of being put in my own personal cell is very high because of how *heinous* of a crime I have committed.

"No," the other guard responds.

"No? To which part?" I ask, but I receive no reply. In their silence, my heart drops into my stomach, and I'm sure both the guards could hear it shattering.

No to both? I won't be in a cell by myself or with another girl? I can't be in a cell with a man! As if they had not already ruined my life enough, now I could be roomed with a man, and not just any man — a convicted felon.

The thought of sharing a cell with a female convict already had me worried, but given the notoriously bad reputation men have, especially with women, I am terrified to be left alone with one who has a track record of bad behavior. What if I get stuck with a pervert who is twice my size? (A very likely fear since I am only 5'2".) He could rape me, but even if he doesn't, how am I supposed to change clothes in front of him? How am I supposed to sleep in the same room with him?

No, Anna. Calm down. There's no way they would do that to you. There's no way the people who falsely convicted you of murder would do you any wrong.

We reach my cell and my heart is beating a million times a minute. The guard on my left, who has been keeping an extra firm grip on my arm, pulls the door open. I'm forcibly pushed into the cell.

It's a small, perfectly square room. It's white, unlike the dull gray of the hallways. To my right is an empty, twin sized bed that looks no more comfortable than a futon without cushions. I assume this bed will be mine.

I examine the plain room and see someone lying on a bed opposite of mine — a man. He has curly, light brown hair, deep brown eyes, and light skin. His eyes are fixed upon me and he stares curiously, without blinking.

I hastily spin around to face the guards.

"I can't stay in a room with a man!" I protest, not caring that the man can clearly hear my objection.

"You don't have a choice," the taller one chortles, with a malicious grin protruding across his face. "The women's side is full!"

"No, please!" I beg as I try to push through them and run away, but they both gang up on me, shove me onto the floor, and slam the door shut behind them.

"Don't be such a prude!" One of them yells from the other side of the door, then they both break into laughter as their heavy footsteps disappear into the distance.

I stand to my feet and peer over my shoulder at the man laying on the bed. He appears completely unfazed by the whole ordeal that just took place in front of him, and unbothered by my demand to not be here with him.

I can't entirely tell since he's lying down, but my guess would be that he's six feet tall. If he stood up, he would tower above my small frame, which terrifies me. They could have at least stuck me with someone small enough for me to stand a chance against.

He is not as old as I was expecting, though. He looks to be in his twenties, far too young to be here — same as me. But he is not the same as me. He is a man and a criminal. My chest pounds and my mind flashes with ideas of the various crimes he would have to commit to end up here. All of them sickeningly vile and heartless. All while my mind juggles between arson, rape, and murder for his crime, his gaze remains steadily fixed on me.

"Hey," he speaks calmly.

My eyes are surely filled with fear. My whole body is shaking, and I have no doubt he can tell it, yet he speaks in a way that says, "Hello, old friend. How have you been? You look well, and definitely not like you're scared out of your mind right now."

"Hi," I reply hesitantly.

He begins to sit up and I instinctively jump back. The back of my legs hit my bed and I fall over onto it.

"I'm not going to hurt you." His voice is raspy. "I'm Thomas Nobles, by the way."

"I'm Annalise Atwood," I mutter, sitting back up after my awkward collapse. He doesn't break eye contact, so neither do I.

"Why are you in here?" he asks, as casually as he said hello, as if whatever it is that put me into a high security prison for the rest of my life is no big deal.

I take a long time before finally answering, "For something I didn't do."

I expect him to question me about what exactly it is that I didn't do, or laugh because he finds it funny that I would claim I'm innocent even after an entire jury ruled otherwise. But he doesn't.

Instead he responds, "Me too."

TWO

I've been here for a week and Thomas and I have barely spoken since my first day, but I've gone against my better judgement and decided him to be a fairly decent person, so I sit with him when all the prisoners gather to eat meals.

The cafeteria is an enormous, circular room filled with gray, rectangular tables, with stools that are screwed to the floor. The tables usually separate into cliques and gangs, so Thomas and I usually eat by ourselves, or with an ever-changing group of people, who were not deemed cool enough to sit at the other tables.

"This place reminds me too much of high school," I mention to Thomas, who nods in agreement.

He hasn't asked me again about what I have been accused of doing, and I haven't asked him either, though I can't help but wonder what it is, and if his conviction was really false or if he's a delusional liar. But since I have no other choice, I have to trust that he's telling the truth. Otherwise, I have befriended a criminal. Though he doesn't act like one, but I guess criminals don't have to act a certain way, or do any certain thing, other than commit a crime. But he isn't in a gang, he doesn't taunt the female prisoners, and he doesn't get into fights. He actually tried to break up a fight between two inmates the other day, but it didn't do any good. He ended up with a black eye and two new enemies, who automatically became my enemies, since I'm his cellmate. They would have beaten me up too, had I not yelled at the guards on my first day to put me on the women's side of the fence during our "mandatory fresh air break." Apparently, not having enough room in the women's cells gives them the right to treat me like a man in every other aspect as well.

"I thought you'd want to stick with your man," the guard chuckled, referring to Thomas. All of the other guards broke into laughter with him. This all seems to be a sick joke in their minds.

I don't know if Thomas believes that I'm innocent or if he's as skeptical of me as I am of him, but either way, he puts up with me and allows me to hang around him.

Yesterday, during our break, a tall, lanky woman with jet black hair and dark circles around her eyes, that made it seem as if she had not slept in nine years, approached me and demanded to know what I had done to get myself in here at such a young and fragile age.

I told her I didn't want to talk about it; it was too painful of a subject, but she kept insisting that I let her in on my "secret."

Her tone reeked of condescension as she leaned down until we met eye to eye. "C'mon, honey. Everyone on the outside knows what ya did. Why can't I?"

"She doesn't have to tell you anything," Thomas said from behind me. He was standing at the spot where the two fences that separate the men from the women meet each other.

"Yeah, I think she does!" said the bitter woman.

"Dude, not everyone is as proud of what they've done as you are," he retorted.

"Proud? Ya think I'm proud of what I've done?" she bellowed. Her fist was clenched and her arm was drawn back, ready to punch me.

"Whatever you do to her, I do to you," Thomas shouted.

She banged her fist up against the fence instead of my face.

"What ya gonna do to me through this?" she snickered, shaking and clanking the fence.

"Do you really think the guards would stop me," he sneered, and pointed to a couple of guards currently eyeing our quarrel with piqued interest, "if I told them I wanted to come around there and knock you out?"

She contemplated this for a moment before turning away, cursing under her breath as she stomped back to tell her gang what had just happened.

"You need to stand up for yourself," he said to me afterwards. "You're too quiet."

That was the first thing he said to me in two days, and he hasn't spoken since. *Yeah, I'm definitely the one who's too quiet.*

If I ignore the constant, unnerving sensation that some of the larger inmates are about to attack me, and the knowledge that I'm being held here against my will until the day I die, this almost seems a half decent place to live. I get three meals a day. I can earn TV and monitored internet privileges. And, unlike my jail cell, which had a silver toilet in the middle of the room, I actually get privacy when I use the restroom, although the toilets here are grossly undercleaned.

This place has separate restrooms for men and women, which I find strange considering they clearly aren't strict when separating the bedrooms by gender. The women's restroom is always filled with women smoking, usually with one of the female guards, because that's who they get their cigarettes from. None of the women want to go to the male guards for anything.

I thought rules would be very strictly enforced here, given this is where the worst criminals in the state are sent, but the only rule they care to enforce is the lunch schedule. Very few guards actually care about anything that's happening around here, and sometimes they join in on the rule breaking. That includes the male guards forcing the female prisoners to sleep with them. I've learned that from the girls always talking about it in the restroom. Some are angry as they vent, but most tell their horror stories through bouts of heavy tears. They tell of how the guards threaten to make their stays in prison longer (can they do that?) or put them in isolation, take away their privileges, or let the male prisoners mess with them if they don't agree to sleep with them.

I don't join in on the stories. I rush in and out of the bathroom as fast as I can to avoid inhaling the smoke, and because I have no idea how to comfort someone going through something that horrible. None of the guards have ever come onto me, so I, thankfully, have no story of my own to share, but I don't think the other women would take so kindly to hearing of how fortunate I am in that area while they cry about the monstrosities done to them. So, I avoid any mention of it, and often hold in my pee for several hours longer than I should so I don't have to see their darkened eyes and hollowed faces reflected in the mirror above the sink as they stare me down, urging me to say something.

I only hope I never have anything to add to that conversation, though I don't really expect to. Something about me staying on the men's side of the prison seems to make me off limits to them. Maybe they assume Thomas and I are together since we share a cell, and they have more respect for other men and what's "theirs" than they do for the women here. Once a guard lays claim to an inmate, none of the others are allowed to mess with her until he's tired of her. Maybe they are only waiting for the day they think Thomas is tired of me.

It takes everything in me to get up everyday. Even considering how uncomfortable my bed is, sleeping in and fading into nothing often seems a better alternative than waking up to the life I'm currently living. This used to happen to me every now and again, even before my life blew up in my face. Back then, it was much easier to convince myself that I had a life worth living, a day worth waking up to.

Nowadays, the only thing getting me out of my bed isn't motivation or my own pep talks, but required daily activities. Breakfast this morning is what got me out of bed today. The only thing stopping me from curling up into a ball of scratchy blankets and dreaming of a better life is my next appointment: Lunch.

I sit with Thomas, same as every day. Some female prisoners join us after getting into a fight with one of their friends, and leaving her to eat by herself as punishment.

The black haired girl, who almost punched me in the face the other day, is among those who join us. When she sits down, she acts happy, as if the confrontation between us had never happened.

The group of girls act rowdy and make a scene as they laugh loudly to each other over every little thing that's said. They try to convince Thomas and me to join in on their pointless conversation, but we both stay quiet.

"You two are a boring couple, aren't you?" shouts Elaine, a tall brunette at the edge of the table, who has mentioned her name to us both several times since she first sat down.

"We're not a thing," I mumble, then stuff my face with a forkful of spaghetti.

Thomas is nice to me, which I appreciate, but I'm not attracted to him. I'm not even sure if he's truly innocent, and I'm certainly not going to date a criminal, even though that's my only option at this point.

"The only couples in this place are the guards and their unwilling partners," another girl scoffs, and my mind flashes to when I zoomed by her in the bathroom as she told the story of her and a guard named Ronald, "but you two... always sitting together at meals, sharing a cell. How cute."

"Maybe when you two get released, you could get married," beams Elaine, and Thomas becomes visibly irritated.

"I'm in for life," I mumble.

I didn't expect such a strong reaction, as I assumed most of the people in here had received life sentences, too, but all of the girls go crazy as soon as I say it. One of them even shouts so loudly the entire room turns to stare at what's going on, but people quickly lose interest.

Thomas tries to hide it, but he, too, looks taken aback. He doesn't know what it is I've been accused

23

of, but now he knows its level of severity. No one gets life in prison for a misdemeanor.

"Maybe you two could get hitched in here. Ministers visit all the time," Elaine cackles.

"I already have a girlfriend," Thomas mutters casually, and continues eating. Rather than silence them as he had clearly hoped, they break into questions about his girlfriend.

"What's her name?"

"You really got some crazy chick waiting for you on the other side?"

"Is it someone you met in here?"

"How long have you been together?"

He refuses to answer anything they ask him, or even acknowledge that they are speaking to him.

"Still," the black haired girl insists, "you and Annalise would be way better for eachotha than whatever whore is waiting for ya. She's probably sleeping with another man by now."

Thomas, once again, offers no response, but instead throws down his fork and leaves without finishing his food. I follow right behind him. I wasn't finished eating either, but there's no way on earth I'm being left alone with these people, especially now that they have something very interesting to yell to each other about.

He rushes out of the cafeteria and I catch up with him when we reach one of the many doors only guards are allowed to open. From there we are escorted back to our cell.

"Sorry about that." I frown once the guards leave.

"It's not your fault," he assures me, and after a long silence he adds: "Can I ask... what were you accused of doing?"

His question catches me off guard. I knew, eventually, he would ask again, and if he didn't, I probably would have asked him how he got here, but I was not prepared to talk about it just yet.

But I do. I tell him everything. From the day I met Julie, sophomore year, when she was the only person who didn't ignore me, up to her murder and my conviction. I start to tear up talking about it, but I continue on. I tell him how there was false evidence against me. I tell him that her killer is still out there and there will never be justice against them, because I'm living out their sentence instead.

Then, as always, there is silence between us. However, this isn't our normal, awkward silence. This is sorrowful silence. Tears slowly stream down my face and I wipe them away, hoping Thomas won't notice, but he is staring into the distance.

I wonder, at first, if he's processing what I said, trying to decide whether or not to believe me. After a few minutes, he comes out of his daze and begins talking.

"My best friend died in a car accident. He drove off a bridge. At first they thought he'd fallen asleep at the wheel, but then the cops said," he pauses, as though the words he's about to say sting to leave his mouth, "they found evidence that his car had been

25

tampered with. And that evidence pointed toward me. They never found his body in the river, but they speculated to its whereabouts. I guess speculation is enough for a jury. I was given life in prison with no substantial evidence, only circumstance. I'm eligible for parole in twenty five years.

"I don't know what really happened, but I can promise it wasn't me who did it. His name was Caleb Rhodes. He was only seventeen — nineteen now, if he were still here — and I would never do anything to hurt him."

He doesn't tell me what he looks like, but I already know. Thomas has a picture of himself standing between a tall, dark-haired boy and a short, brunette girl, both with big, gleaming smiles.

The picture is taped crookedly above his bed. I've been looking at it since the day I got here, wondering who they were and why they matter enough to Thomas to keep the photo. Now I know. One is his girlfriend. The other is his dead best friend.

"So, we're in here for the same thing then?" I raise an eyebrow at him.

"Yeah, dude. What are the odds?" he laughs.

"I don't know, but I'd like to find out."

THREE

I never find out. I only get half an hour on a computer everyday, and I'm not going to waste it Google searching "How many people are falsely accused of murdering their best friend every year?"

I'm not entirely sure I believe Thomas's story, even as convincingly as he told it, because of the very question he posed: What are the odds?

Several days pass and, as usual, Thomas and I do not speak. We sit silently in our cells, we quietly eat meals together, and we usually end up in the computer room at the same time. Sometimes, we go to the library together, but even in prison, you're not allowed to speak in libraries, so we sit in silence while reading our books. Thomas reads much slower than me. I can finish a book a day, but three days later and he's still reading the same thing.

We spend most of our time together, but we are still separated during outdoor breaks, so I found myself spending those with the aggravating group of girls who enjoy pretending Thomas and I are a couple. But eventually they began to bother me too much, so I end up at the edge of the yard, near the fence. I sit

down as the chilly wind tingles my spine and re-
freshes the air, and I begin plucking up grass that has
grown through a crack in the cement.

I stare longingly at the limbs of trees that have
found their way into spaces of the chain link fence
that I'm surprised no one has tried to jump over.
The leaves are now turning shades of bright, happy
oranges and soft browns as a sign of autumn's arrival,
but it doesn't seem right. Nothing about smoky bath-
rooms, metal doors, and limited internet access
paints the perfect autumn picture for me. But I attempt to force it into my mind anyway. I gaze up at
the swaying trees. I breathe in the fresh, crisp air. I
want the changing of the seasons to cover me. I want
the holidays and my approaching birthday to take my
mind off the rest of my life. The birthday I'll be
spending in a cell instead of with my family — the
family that has not visited me once since my incarcer-
ation.

Staring at the trees was a bad idea. Instead of the
seasons change comforting me, my mind is now spi-
raling into thoughts about what I would be doing if I
weren't here. I would be anticipating Thanksgiving
and Christmas with no idea that my loving family
would so easily turn their backs on me. I would be
finishing up high school and preparing for college.
My parents really wanted me to go to college. I did,
too. But I never knew what to go for. I was told I had
years to make up my mind.

"This is the time in your life where you're supposed to be figuring out who you are," my aunt said to me, only a few weeks before Julie died. "It's not always the time in your life where you already know."

I'm supposed to be finding myself, experiencing the all-important epiphany of who I really am coming to light, but instead I'm spending this time in prison, being told that who I am is a dangerous criminal.

It's hard to think I went from someone so full of hope, with a bright future ahead, to a criminal with nothing but cell walls in my future. I still manage to cling onto a tiny piece of hope, though. I just know, somehow, even stuck in this prison, my life can mean something. It's just not the meaning I always thought my life would have.

I continue to sit at the edge of the yard and pluck up blades of grass during breaks, but after doing that for a few days, it started being noticed by the guards who then forced me to stop, and would no longer allow me to sit near the fence. They thought I was plotting some way to escape over it; a task that would not be hard, considering no guards stand anywhere near this edge of the fence. I could easily grab onto an overgrown limb and be in the distant woods before anyone could stop me.

Right after a guard tells me off for, once again, being suspiciously close to the fence, our fresh air break is over and I head back to my cell. Thomas arrives shortly after me and he lies down on his bed, stares up at the white ceiling, and doesn't say a word. After half an hour of this, I finally speak.

"Thomas, if we're going to be cellmates for life, I don't think we should continue this 'not talking to each other for several days at a time' thing. It's not going to work."

"Yeah, I guess so," he reluctantly admits.

"So, talk to me. Say something. Don't go quiet again."

"Fine." He sits up. "What do you want to talk about? What do you want to know about me?"

"Everything," I smile.

Over the next two months, Thomas and I tell each other everything we know about ourselves. He tells me about his girlfriend Hailee Clark, a 19 year old with dark brown hair, green eyes, and a firm belief that Thomas is innocent. She had always come to see him on visiting days until he asked her to stop. He said she needed to live her own life and not waste it waiting for someone who wasn't going to see the light of day for another twenty-five years.

No one comes to see me. We are supposed to share everything, but it hurts too much to reveal that I have yet to receive a single visit, even on my birthday — October 18th, the day I turned eighteen years old. On that day, Thomas sang "Happy Birthday" to me, which was uncomfortable for both of us, but he sang the entire song anyway.

Thomas tries the best he can to avoid talking about Caleb, but when he does I can almost see his heart break when he remembers he can no longer talk about Caleb in present tense. I share stories with him about Julie and also find myself talking about her in present tense, so I begin to avoid that subject as well.

Instead, I tell Thomas about my struggles, which I *can* talk about in present tense. I am mentally trapped in the darkest place I have ever known in my life, but I believe the light will seep back through to me somehow. It has to.

"How do you believe that?" he asks me at the place where the men's and women's fences meet.

We both sit crisscrossed on opposite sides of the fence, talking to each other as we have been the entire break. People stare, but we have both stopped caring about how the other prisoners perceive us. He stares at me through the chain links between us with a befuddled and inquisitive look as he waits for my answer.

"How can you not?" I ask in equal confusion. "If I didn't believe that, I'd go insane in here."

"Things don't always work out," he scoffs, as he absentmindedly rattles the fence. "Sometimes life just sucks and no matter how long you're alive, it still sucks, then you die, and that sucks, too."

"Just because life sucks doesn't mean that life isn't valuable. Those who do the most important work lead the most difficult lives. That's a quote, or something similar to it anyway... but it's true."

"Yes, because wasting away in a cell is important work." He rolls his eyes.

I lean in close to the fence and whisper so only he can hear me, "Listen, I don't have a clue why we're in here or how we'll find some sort of purpose in this giant piece of crap, but we are meant to be here, and we *will* find a way to make something of it."

"Well, now you've completely lost it, Annalise!" He throws his hands up in the air in protest. "Dude, do you really believe we're meant to be in here... that anything good can possibly come from this?"

"Yes, or at least I hope it will. I think —" I sigh in exasperation. I know he's going to laugh at me for these next few words. "I think there is such a thing as predestination, and things happen for a reason. So, even though I hate this with everything in my soul, I do think there's a reason for it. I also think evil can come and take over the whole world, but in the end, the good will always find a way through. If you find something truly, genuinely good and pure, and believe in it, and hold onto it with everything you've got, then no matter what happens in life, you'll be okay."

"Really, dude? Do you feel okay right now?" He begins to stand up to leave.

"No!" I yell at him before he has a chance to walk away. I'm now speaking loud enough for everyone in the vicinity to hear. "I feel like absolute crap right now, Thomas, but when I talk about "good" I'm not talking about *feel good* stuff. I'm talking about what's

32

right. Whatever happens in life, if you stick to what's right, then you will have accomplished something in life. They can trap me in this prison and take away all of my friends, but they can't take away my purpose. They can't take away what matters."

Admittedly, I don't know exactly what my purpose is here, but I know I'll find it. I refuse to die without finding it.

"I think they already did," he retorts. Not a word I said seemed to have affected him.

"No, they didn't. This situation may suck, but good things can come from tragedies." I try not to be angry at his refusal to agree.

"What good can come from this tragedy?"

"I don't know, yet," I say with much less confidence than my previous statements.

"Tell me when you find out," he mutters as he walks away.

Since then, he has still continued to listen to my "crazy" beliefs, and although he pretends to hate them, I think he secretly enjoys them. It's the only positive thing he hears all day, and I think he takes comfort in that. Although, being a positive light is exhausting. Most days I don't want to wake up in the morning, but then I do, and I have to find the strength within me to continue to say that life has meaning, which often doesn't seem truthful. But I have to make myself believe it, because I don't know what I would do if I didn't. We can't both lose hope.

After a while he stops pretending to argue alto-gether, and just listens to me. He starts to seem much more open to the idea that good can prevail. A part of me wants to believe it's because he sees it in me, but in reality, he's probably clinging to anything that will keep him sane. The idea that your life has purpose, even when you're trapped inside a cold cell, is the only thing that keeps me from losing my mind. It makes sense he, too, would want to cling to anything that helps him grip onto sanity.

FOUR

I grab a plate of eggs and bacon and sit down next to Thomas. I roll up the long sleeves on my oversized jumpsuit and pick up a greasy piece of bacon. He's almost done with his food by the time I start mine.

"You don't have to rush. No one's going to take your food away," I remind him.

Thomas continues to eat quickly, probably to avoid giving the obnoxious group of girls a chance to come by and pick on him about the girlfriend he refuses to give them any information on. I try to eat as quickly as him. Anytime he finishes his meal before me and leaves me sitting alone, one of the male inmates will always come over and sit with me. Usually, it's the same man with bleach blond hair and a tattoo that reads "eye don't care" under his right eye. He winks at me with that eye every single time. He seems to think it gives him an edge, but it's like looking at a cheesy quote I would find on a T-shirt in the sale rack of Forever 21. So, to avoid awkward conversations with the eye tattoo man, who is already staring at me from across the room, I eat at the same pace as Thomas.

I'm taking my last bite of bacon when the lights shut off. The room goes completely black, besides the small amount of light shining in through the windows above.

One person screams in the darkness, and I think someone must have been stabbed, but they were only overreacting. However, everyone else begins to panic when the lights don't immediately return. In the middle of the confusion, several other inmates start screaming and running. At first I'm unable to understand what they're yelling as all their voices collide with one another, but I finally make out a few sentences.

"I'm out of here!"

"Head for the doors!"

"Run for it!"

This is a breakout. Someone must have colluded with security to switch off the breakers during breakfast.

I sit completely still, frozen in my seat, unlike the others who are running for the exit, gladly taking this as their chance to ditch this place. No one had warned me this was coming.

The light from the windows above shine down on Thomas who is still sitting in his seat as well. With how much he talks about hating this place, I'm shocked to see he isn't gleefully running for the exit.

My mind is racing with what to do as people frantically run around me and bump into my table. I'm on the fence as to whether running with everyone else is the best option. The guards could shoot me for trying to escape, but staying here is just as much of a death sentence, so maybe taking that risk is worth it.

Next to me, Thomas is taking in all of the pandemonium that has been unleashed. As I watch him try to soak it all in, I become sure of one thing: I don't want to sit here any longer.

"I think we should probably leave. It's chaos in here," Thomas suddenly says to me. I'm surprised by his inclusion of me in his escape. I know we confide in each other, but that's only because we're strained for options. In the back of my mind, I always thought he would take the first opportunity he had to get away from me.

"I agree," I say, though I'm still not sure why he wants to leave together. He could probably run a lot faster than I can.

I slide out of my seat and stand up when someone runs past me and knocks me onto the hard floor. More people are right behind them and they walk over me, pretending I'm not here, but I'm sure they feel me under their feet and can hear me grunting in pain when they step on my abdomen, but are choosing to ignore me.

One rather large person digs the heel of their shoe into my lower left arm, something I'm certain was intentional, and I hear a loud crack in my bones. I let out a shriek of pain, and I have no doubt that stranger has just broken my arm.

"Are you okay?" Thomas asks nervously, over the sound of prisoners and infuriated guards shouting.

"Someone stepped on my left arm. I think it's broken," I mumble through gritted teeth, and he pulls me up off the floor.

As Thomas knows, I have never broken a bone before, and I'm finding it's the furthest thing from pleasant.

"Let's get out of here," he shouts hastily, and tightens his hold on my uninjured arm, pulling me swiftly towards the exit.

I let Thomas be the guide. I'm in too much pain to think clearly, and he's been walking these halls a lot longer than I have, but still we manage to run into them quite a few times.

"Dude, are you okay?" he asks, after I accidentally ram my broken arm into the frame of one of the many doorways in this building.

"Yeah," I wince. "I'm good. I'm good."

As we blindly walk further along the halls, it gets quieter. Most of the prisoners have already escaped and the guards are busy chasing them. This is good for us. They will be too busy with the other inmates to stop us from leaving.

A buzzing combination of pain and adrenaline makes me lightheaded and I rely on Thomas for balance.

We take a few more turns and finally we see an unknown light source just ahead. We turn right, towards the light, and a wave of relief rushes over me when I see the gigantic front doors that I have not laid eyes on since my first day here. Sun bursts in through the small windows on the doors and lights up the entire empty hallway.

Thomas breaks into a sprint towards it and I'm right behind him. I've barely begun moving when I become paralyzed, my body tenses up, and I collapse on the floor. I want to scream from the pain, but I make no noise, and I cannot move.

I hear the opening of the front doors up ahead and the clang as it slams shut. I find the strength to lift up my head, hoping Thomas will still be here, that I heard someone else leave, that he's standing right in front of me, waiting for me to get up. He isn't. Instead, I see the figure of a female guard running out the door after him. A taser lies on the floor directly in front of me. It must have been the one she used on me.

I sit up, which proves to be difficult when I only have one good arm to push on and my legs are still tense from the shock. I slump into a sitting position and stay here, staring at the unmanned exit only a few feet away. I would bet that no guards remain in the building to come for me. I could sit patiently, right here, and wait for the breakout to be over. I haven't left so they couldn't punish me for this, and since I would be the only one who didn't leave, they might reward me for that. Maybe they could make me eligible for parole in thirty years or so, and if I run now, I'll be on the run by myself since Thomas ditched me. Staying might be the smart choice, but I can't stay.

This is my only opportunity to leave, so I force myself to stand up, ignoring how much my trembling body and the booming voice inside my head tell me to sit back down. They want me to stay, but a quiet little voice, that is almost drowned out by everything else, is telling me to run, and I know that's the voice I need to listen to.

I inch towards the exit and lean my head out of the door to see all the commotion outside. All the guards are spread out across the lawn, too concerned with tackling other inmates to notice my little head poking out of the double doors.

Am I really about to do this? I ask myself. *Yes, I am,* I answer, and make a break for the fence in the distance. On the other side of it is a wide expanse of forest I just might be lucky enough to never get found in.

I'm sprinting through the front lawn, zooming through the chilly winter air, when I abruptly trip over a sprinkler planted in the grass. Luckily, only a few of the inmates notice. I jump right back up and run even faster the rest of the way across the lawn, down the hill, towards the fence, checking my path along the way for more sprinklers to avoid.

I reach the fence and find a large break in it that no guards are posted at. I slide through it with ease and scan the yard to make sure no one is following me when I hear a scream coming from the forest. I rush to the edge of the tree line and I see Thomas lying bloody on the ground a couple hundred yards away, with the guard who tasered me on top of him, beating him with a rod.

I stare at them in shock. My brain almost convinces me I'm watching this on a TV screen, because this can't really be happening in front of me right now, can it?

The initial shock wears off and I realize I'm not staring into a box of pixels, so I snap back into reality, but I hesitate to move in any direction. Part of me immediately wants to run far away from this. I don't want to risk a beating for the person who abandoned me only moments ago. Running away is what I *want* to do, but instead, I sprint straight for the guard and push her off of Thomas. The impact sends a pang through my whole body, especially my newly broken arm.

As soon as she hits the ground, she's back up on her feet. I'm still trying to get over the initial impact of pushing her down when she hits me square in the face. I fall backwards onto the ground, right next to Thomas who is unconscious, but hopefully not dead.

Before I have a chance to regain my composure, she sits on top of me and holds me down and begins beating me with the rod. I attempt to push her off me, but I repeatedly fail. She is stronger than me and weighs much more than I do. She swings the rod and slams it into my broken arm. I let out a wail of pain and tears immediately well in my eyes. Once she sees how much that hurt me, she continues hitting that arm with even more force. She shows no regard for actually doing her job — which would be to detain me, not beat me senseless — or any remorse for the pain she is inflicting upon me.

I see crimson red blood slinging everywhere with every strike of my arm, but I am unaware of whether it is my own, or some of Thomas's blood that was already on the rod.

I keep trying to push her off, but I don't succeed. I can hear a crack as another part of my arm breaks. I start to lose my vision and even my own screams begin to sound like a noise in the distance. My eyes regain focus, but I shut them tightly, because the sight of blood splattering everywhere is too much to bear.

I hear another distant scream, then a loud thud far away, and the weight of the guard is no longer situated on me, so I open my eyes to find that no one is there. I lift my head up, unable to convince the rest of my body to get up with it, and see the guard laying on the ground thirty feet away. Something slammed her into a tree and knocked her unconscious. I turn my head every way to see who or what hit her, but there's nothing other than more trees and a battered, unconscious Thomas. At first, he remains so still I think he's dead, but then I notice his chest moving up and down with his slowed breathing.

I want to lie here and be still forever, because every move that I make hurts my arm, every time my face flinches my cheek throbs from where she hit me, and every time I move my head the light wants to leave my eyes and never come back. But I know I cannot stay here. Either more guards will come, or the one lying unconscious, only a few feet away, will wake up, ready for vengeance. If I wanted to stay, I should have done it before I left the prison doors.

I stare dreamily up at the top of the trees, momentarily unable to convince myself to move, despite the blaring alarms sounding off in my mind, urgently telling me of the impending dangers of remaining here. I hear it all, but none of it shakes me until my actual hearing returns to normal and the sound of something hitting the chain link fence rattles me back into reality.

I painstakingly force myself to sit up, wincing the entire time. I hesitantly glance down at my arm and, as if it being broken wasn't bad enough, it has now been beaten beyond recognition. If I didn't know for a fact that it was *my* arm, I wouldn't believe it was an arm at all. The skin is broken and bruised, blood is covering every inch of it, and it hangs limp and unusable from my body. A steady stream of blood flows from the wounds and I become lightheaded and in dire need of a transfusion. The mere sight is unsettling and makes me nauseated. I may pass out just from glimpsing at it, so I turn my gaze to Thomas and try to figure out what to do with him. I cannot cary him or even drag him with the state of my arm, but I couldn't make myself leave him here either, even though he left me behind.

Thomas's eyes begin to open and he groans in pain. I slump over beside him.

"Are you awake? Are you okay?" I ask through the throbbing pain in my jaw.

"Just dandy," he murmurs.

"Can you walk?" I ask in concern.

"I think I can manage." He sits up slowly, still looking rather dazed.

"Well, we really need to hurry. We have to leave before someone else comes or she wakes up." I point to the passed out guard resting near a tree. Thomas looks to me in confusion, then suddenly notices the blood all over me.

"Are you alright?" he asks frantically. "What happened, man?"

I chuckle a little at how concerned he is for me, given the state he's in.

"I'm fine. We can have explanations later. Right now, we need to leave." I pull him onto his feet with my one good arm and he nearly falls over on top of me.

"I stood up too fast," he laughs, and blinks quickly, trying to get sight back in his eyes.

Just as we both get to our feet, the sound of gunshots break out back at the prison, along with horrifying shrieks of pain and fear.

Thomas and I both run away from the direction of gunfire as fast as we can both manage, which is more of an awkward jog than anything, but at least we are moving at a steady pace. It sounds as though most of the guards are staying and dealing with the prisoners still on the grounds, which is very good news for me. But every time a gun goes off and a scream is cut short, images of death flash through my head. I try desperately to block it out and focus on what's in front of me.

The forest ahead is thick with trees whose leaves have recently been plucked from their branches, painted vivid shades of red and orange, and left to fade. The barren trees do not offer us much cover, but all of the leaves on the ground mean less foot-prints to track, and if they can't track us, maybe they won't find us. Maybe we are free.

Every step forward aches more than the last. My legs are not even injured, but each step sends a pang through my head where the guard struck me, and every little movement of my arm causes unbearable pain shooting all the way through it.

I can only imagine Thomas's pain. As far as I know he hasn't broken anything, but he's far more battered than I am. There's no telling how many times the guard struck him, but even with all of his injuries, I can't help but be a little resentful towards Thomas. I sustained my own injuries trying to save his life, but he had abandoned me only minutes be-fore.

I am afraid and angry at the thought of him running away from me again as soon as he's given another chance. I know it must be cruel to be mad at him with the state he's in, but an explanation for why he ran off, or a "thank you" for saving his life — neither of which he has yet to offer — would be nice.

FIVE

After nearly an hour of stumbling through the woods, my body is aching and chilled to the bone, and it decides it has had enough for the day and I collapse at the foot of a tree. Thomas sits down and leans on a tree to the left of me.

"I think...we're far...enough away for...now," he breathlessly spits out, putting a hand to a giant whelp on his face that the guard left with her rod. "I don't think... they'll bother to search this... far out when they have all the other prisoners to deal with."

"Neither do I." I pause for a moment, studying my arm. Most of the blood has already stopped flowing and begun to dry and I am no longer lightheaded from it. "We need to find some water, food, and a first aid kit."

He laughs, "I think we're going to need more than a few little bandaids to fix our problems. We need to find a hospital."

"Why? They'll just turn us back into the police." I don't particularly enjoy the idea of being on the run, or breaking the law by doing so, but those guards got trigger happy way too quickly. If we go back there, I'm sure we will be shot on sight.

47

"Your arm is going to get infected if you don't get help for it, and the bone won't heal right if you don't get a cast," he says, staring at my unrecognizable arm with great concern.

"Your face could use a little help, too," I smirk at him, and to my surprise, my cheek doesn't throb when I do.

"I'm not worried about myself," he chuckles, which turns into a flinch of pain.

"You should be," I say. Why is he so worried about my health and safety when he so willingly left me behind to save himself?

We stand up and make our way in a direction we hope leads towards civilization. I try to step on as many leaves as possible to avoid leaving too many footprints in the soft dirt underneath. We walk our steady pace in silence and I try to think of small talk to fill the air, but small talk has never been our thing.

I almost ask Thomas why he left me back at the prison, but I force myself not to. I don't want to create a conflict when I need Thomas to stick with me. Besides, I'm not sure if I'm ready to hear his answer. *I don't like you. I don't want to be around you. I'm only here now because I owe you.*

"Do you think this is wrong?" I ask Thomas, although it seems as though I could be asking it to the sky, or the trees, or anyone listening.

He raises an eyebrow at me. "You'll have to be more specific."

"Running away," I elaborate. "I mean, we were sentenced by a court of law. What we're doing is illegal."

"It is, but I don't care. I couldn't stand it there and I can't go back." Thomas shrugs.

"I'm not saying we should go back," I sigh. "I'm asking if you think we should have left in the first place. We've broken the law and we were both beaten to a pulp because of it."

"I don't know if it was the right choice. I know you want me to give you some spiritual answer so you can have a clean conscience about this, but I can't do that. What we are doing is very, very illegal. If you can't deal with that and you want to turn back around, go ahead, but I can't."

He begins walking away without me, and against everything my gut is telling me, I follow him.

After about twenty more minutes of walking, and avoiding any more conversations about moral conflict, we emerge from the forest and find ourselves near a crowded roadway, with a road sign to our right, letting us know there is a town just up ahead.

Thomas and I stick to the edge of the woods to avoid being noticed by any of the drivers in the traffic jam, who may rat us out to the police.

"None of those cars are running," Thomas suddenly says after a few minutes of walking.

"What?" I ask, and begin surveying all of the unmoving vehicles I previously thought were only sitting still because of a traffic jam.

49

"They aren't running, dude. Look, no one is in these cars!" he says, running over to a nearby car and checking it for occupants, but he doesn't find any. Every car is shut off and without a driver. Some even have their doors left wide open.

"Why would all these people just abandon their cars?" I ask in utter bewilderment.

"Maybe they stopped working?" he suggests, leaning into the back seat of another car.

"Every car on the road couldn't have suddenly stopped working," I insist.

"But maybe they did," he ponders, pulling out a few jackets that were left behind. He puts one on and tosses the other to me.

I normally wouldn't accept stolen property, but I'm shaking with chills that have struck my core and have put me on the verge of freezing to death, so I wrap my extra small self in an extra large, puffy blue jacket without hesitation. Besides, the people who owned this car clearly didn't care enough about the jackets if they left them behind.

"Do you think it could have something to do with the power outage at the prison?" Thomas asks.

"I don't know." I shake my head. "I just assumed it was a planned breakout that I didn't get the memo for, but if these things are somehow related, a lot more than the prison lights and these cars have stopped working."

Thomas nods in agreement and we walk hastily next to the line of abandoned cars leading to the town up ahead.

As we get closer, we pass by a few people who haven't left their cars behind and some who are headed towards town. We don't stop to ask any of them what happened, because when they catch a glimpse of our jumpsuits and the blood splattered all over them, they walk a little bit faster.

Thomas and I are both hesitant to enter the town out of fear of getting arrested, but we decide our need for medical care and some place warm far outweighs our need to not be seen.

Once we enter the town, there are hoards of people wandering the cramped streets, and many sitting in their stalled cars all throughout the roads. Some of them are hysterical. Others are simply confused.

"Why isn't my electricity on?" one man yells furiously at a police officer on the sidewalk.

"We don't know, sir. The power all over the city is off. We are doing everything we can to fix it," he reassures the angry man who doesn't seem to be listening, because he begins shouting profanities at the cop instead.

A few more people cast us strange, wary looks because of our jumpsuits until, eventually, we attract the attention of an officer who marches towards us.

"Is this a joke? Are you guys wearing costumes at a time like this?" the cop barks. I guess news of the breakout hasn't spread to him yet. "Answer me or I'll arrest you." He spits on my face as he speaks.

"We need medical attention," I say, instead of answering his question, then point to Thomas's battered face.

"The hospital is six blocks up on the left. Have fun walking," he smiles, then struts away.

It is chaotic in the hospital from the moment we walk in. The regular smell of antiseptics is covered with the scent of rotting flesh and sweat. All the lights and machines have been shut off. Nurses are pushing ill patients from room to room, hoping to find something that's working to hook them up to, with no success. People are dying, but most are already dead.

I want to leave as soon as possible, but we have to stay for several hours, waiting on a doctor who isn't busy. As we wait, Thomas and I discuss what's happening, even though we really have no clue what's going on.

"It can't be a power surge. They can't take out cars," he says, and attempts to touch the gash on his face, only to flinch so much he scratches it and it begins bleeding again.

"What if this is widespread and it's happening everywhere?" I ask fearfully, then steal an unused hand towel off a nurses cart and hand it to Thomas.

"No, no. This can't be happening everywhere. It can't be," he sighs, expressing my exact thoughts. Everything that is going on leads me to believe this may not be a local event, but even the thought of that sends chills down my spine.

"It could," I begrudgingly admit. "Maybe this was an attack, like an EMP?" I ponder.

"A what?" Thomas asks, then winces from pressing his wound too hard.

"An electromagnetic pulse. It's a burst of electromagnetic energy that has the ability to wipe out all electricity, even in cars and other machines," I say, but Thomas squints at me, looking wildly confused. "It can be caused by a solar flare or nuclear weapons. I'm surprised you've never heard of it."

"Sorry, I didn't spend my free time studying electromagnetism," Thomas chuckles.

"It's common knowledge, loser." I roll my eyes.

"So, you think it was an EMP?"

"I hope not. Because if it was, and it was from a nuclear weapon, we have much bigger issues than getting some stitches and a cast."

A doctor finally comes to see us, only to refuse to give us any medical attention even when I show him my broken arm.

"Get out of here before I call the authorities on you!" he shouts at us.

"We need to get some new clothes," I tell Thomas as soon as we leave the building. "They draw too much attention."

"I'm not too fond of the blood stains on them, either," he adds.

We walk around the hysteric town, asking people for food, water, and clothes. We try to get their sympathy, pull on their heart strings, but no one wants to help us out. Instead, we get dirty looks and mothers holding onto their children for dear life. Luckily, no one calls the cops on us, because no one can get their phones to work and most people are too concerned with everything else happening around them to prioritize us.

After only a few hours of not having electricity, this place has become a chaotic mess. While Thomas was flirting with a pretty girl in an attempt to convince her to help us, I saw two grown men break into a convenience store across the street. No one came to arrest the robbers, and as they left, they shouted nonsensically about how it was the apocalypse and we were all doomed.

If it's already this bad after a few hours, it makes me wonder how crazy this town must have been before everything shut down, and how bad it's gotten everywhere else, if this really is widespread.

After about an hour of walking around the crowded town, Thomas and I are chilled to the bone from the dry, windy air whipping at our faces and chapping our lips.

With fair certainty that no one is going to let us persuade them for help, we both sit down on a bus stop bench, exhausted, hurting, and frostbitten. Winter should only last a few more weeks, but it's taking complete advantage of every day it has left until spring checks in.

I want to be angry at all of the people who refused to help us. We're confused and injured, but we're also convicts with labeled jumpsuits telling that to everyone we cross paths with. To be honest, I'm not sure I would have helped me, either.

"Maybe we should find another town," Thomas sighs in defeat. "We need to find a hospital that will give you a cast."

"It's pointless," I mutter. "We're not going to find anyone anywhere willing to take in convicts and we'll freeze to death before we reach another town.

Across the street, a couple in their mid-twenties is sitting nonchalantly at a patio table outside a restaurant that is currently closed. Their outfits scream of abundant riches, something you wouldn't expect to see in this small town. The man's Gucci coat and dress shoes are undeniably more expensive than anything I have ever owned. Both of them keep glancing over at us curiously, instead of fearfully, as most people here have been.

"Unless you're willing to help us, quit staring," I yell over to them. They give each other a calculating look and then walk over to us.

"We might be able to help," says the woman, a tall blonde with a naturally bitter expression on her face. "What do you need?"

Thomas looks at me suspiciously before answering, "Food, water, clean clothes, and medical supplies."

I expect them to suddenly realize they don't really want to help us that much and be on their way, but that's not what happens.

"Alright. Do y'all need a place t' stay?" the man inquires. "We have a big house on the other side of town."

I don't respond. I only stare at them warily, because they seem far too eager to shelter fugitives.

"That would be great," Thomas beams in delight and I shoot him a look that he ignores.

"Great, but it might take a while t' get there since we have t' walk. Our car died, same as everyone else's," the man says with suspicious elation.

"That's not a problem," Thomas says. Then, the woman grabs his face without warning and examines it.

"I can stitch that right up," she says, squinting at the gash on his left cheek.

"Perfect," he says, and sighs with relief when she finally lets him go. "Can you get a cast for Anna?"

"Sure thing!" the man says. "Oh, by the way, I'm Mark Traile and this is my wife, Katherine."

"I'm Thomas and this is Annalise," he smiles.

"Are you sure we should stay with them?" I whisper to Thomas on the walk to their house. "Didn't they seem too willing to help us?"

"Maybe they're being good people. Aren't you the one who believes in good prevailing and whatnot?"

"Good people don't harbor fugitives."

"We're not actually criminals, Anna!" he whispers angrily.

"But they don't know that!" I match his tone, and he rolls his eyes at me.

Thomas and I give each other the silent treatment until we arrive at their house on the outskirts of town, away from most of the commotion. It's a mansion compared to the tiny houses lined up next to it. It has two stories, five bedrooms, high ceilings, and a large open living room. A chandelier, that isn't working, hangs in the dining room, which is filled with recreations of famous paintings.

Mark opens the curtains, covering all of the over-sized windows, to bring light into the gigantic house, and I see all of their expensive knick-knacks with much more clarity. A small, golden statue sits on an end table in the living room, and given the lavishness in which they live, I think it might be made of solid gold.

Katherine shows me up the curved staircase to a room on the second floor that she said I could stay in for as long as I want. It is twice the size of the biggest bedroom I have ever had. Its walls are decorated in more famous paintings that I'm beginning to believe might be real. A vase covered in gold flecks sits on the nightstand, holding withering sunflowers that match the floral painting right next to it.

As she leads me back downstairs, I am beginning to become suspicious of how a young couple could afford all these nice things, and why they would allow two sketchy characters into their home when they have so many valuable items to keep safe.

I follow Katherine past the enormous living room with an oversized leather couch in the middle of the floor, and a supposedly fake Van Gogh and a very real flat screen TV both hanging on the wall. I step into their large kitchen, covered in shiny tile floors and granite countertops. Thomas and Mark are having a conversation over the island in the middle of the room while eating a bag of sour cream and onion potato chips.

"Help yourself to any food we have. I'm going out to find you both something decent to wear, and a cast for that ugly arm," Katherine says, eyeing Thomas and me up and down, and lingering on my blood covered arm, before marching out the door.

Thomas offers me a few chips, seeming to be over the silent treatment. I take a few and join their conversation. Mark is already making plans to survive the next few months, in case the power never comes back on. He talks of food, water, and bathing arrangements. I shudder at the thought of never taking another hot shower, though that's the least of my worries.

Mark says if things get too bad within society, laying low will be crucial, but he seems to be overlooking the part of his plan where he wants to lay low in a mansion that sticks out like a sore thumb.

Half an hour later Katherine returns with two carts full of water, canned foods, and piles of high-end clothes that still have tags on them. I don't dare to ask her how she acquired all of this, because something in my gut is telling me I don't want to know. I haven't been with them long, but I can tell something is very off about them.

I stand in front of the full length mirror in my new personal bathroom. I'm wearing some of the clothes Katherine brought back for me; a plain white T-shirt paired with a green bomber jacket, high waisted skinny jeans, and black boots that add a few inches to my height. The outfit was surprisingly easy to put on, considering I have a broken arm, or at least, I'm supposed to, but it barely hurts anymore. Katherine found a sling for me, though I don't think I need it, but was unable to acquire plaster to form a cast.

To go along with my arm that is healing unusually well, when I look in the mirror I can see that my face bears no significant bruises or swelling from where the guard repeatedly hit me.

Downstairs, Thomas wears a black button up shirt with blue jeans and a dark trench coat. His hair is frizzy from where he attempted to comb it, but only upset his curls. His face is bruised from where the guard repeatedly hit him. As he laughs at a joke Mark made, he twinges from the pain in his cheek, and I instinctively touch mine and feel nothing. If it weren't for the blood splatter that still remains, you wouldn't be able to tell anything had happened to me at all.

"How's your arm?" Thomas asks when he sees the sling.

"Oh, it's fine," I say, a little embarrassed to admit how fine it really is. "You know, it may not even be broken. I think it's only sprained."

"That's great!" Thomas says.

"You'll still need t' wear that sling for about two to three weeks t' get that arm all fixed up," Mark says, but I don't think I would even need it for two to three more hours.

In the middle of Mark and Katherine's perfectly mowed backyard sits a wide fire pit that Mark uses to heat up the water that Katherine brought back for baths.

The yard is covered in stone walkways and flowers that somehow survived the winter frost. The back patio is decked out with expensive looking outdoor furniture that will only get ruined the next time it rains.

After a couple of hours, everyone else has taken a bath and I go last. Mark fills the downstairs bathtub with steaming water and I wait for it to cool enough to step in.

I wash the caked up blood off of my supposedly broken arm to reveal not so much as a bruise underneath. I shake my head because of how ridiculous I am. If my arm had really been broken, it wouldn't have magically healed after a few hours. The truth is that it was never broken and I'm an overreactive weakling.

I take an extra long time scrubbing myself to make sure I am completely clean of everything that happened today, then I take out the plug and watch the pink water go down the drain, gone forever. I dry myself off with a towel and stare at what little I can see of myself in the foggy bathroom mirror. I am an unidentifiable, blurry mass and I prefer it this way. If I could see myself, I would have to face the fact that I don't recognize the person in the mirror, and I haven't since Julie died, but today has only further detached me from who I really am.

I leave the bathroom and find everyone else is already heading off to bed. It is not late, but the sun has gone down, and there is no sense in wandering around a dark house.

Katherine says she will go out tomorrow to find candles and lanterns. She will "find" them in the same place she "found" all the water and designer clothes, I presume.

I take a pair of pajamas that Katherine brought back for me and curl up in the most comfortable bed sheets I have ever felt. But even though I am exhausted, I cannot fall asleep.

My mind steadily races with scenarios of how and why everything shut off, and how widespread the damage is, with occasional vivid flashbacks of the breakout.

I try to change my thoughts, and end up paranoid about Mark and Katherine. Nothing is normal about two people letting total strangers, and known convicts, into their luxurious house, providing them with food and clothes, whilst having genuine paintings hanging on the wall and showing up with a suspicious amount of fresh water from an unknown source.

Somewhere between imagining the complete destruction of society and being suspicious of Mark and Katherine, I fall asleep.

I wake to the sun shining down on the dusty room, through the windows, directly into my eyes. In this moment, I think that I may have never felt a more comfortable bed in my entire existence. My body is still exhausted, but my bones surprisingly do not ache from all the running or the injuries supposedly inflicted upon them, though I still do not want to move for at least three more hours, or three more years... but Katherine is knocking on the door.

"Breakfast is ready," she says from the other side of the door.

I throw on the outfit I wore yesterday, along with the sling I don't need. I'm too afraid to admit to everyone that I overreacted to a minor injury. I head downstairs where Mark is bringing in hot food from a fire he started outside. He hands everyone a finely decorated plate piled high with eggs, bacon, and unevenly burnt toast.

Thomas eagerly takes his plate, but has trouble chewing, because he now has several stitches in a vertical line across his cheek from where Katherine must have stitched him up before I woke up.

Thomas sees me staring at his cheek. "Do you need any stitches? Your arm looked pretty rough yesterday."

"Oh no... it's fine. A few small cuts, but nothing bad enough for stitches... Won't all of the food in your fridge go bad since there's no power?" I ask to change the focus from my perfectly healed arm.

"No. I filled the refrigerator and freezer with bags of ice to keep everything chilled," Katherine says.

"Where did you get all that ice?" I inquire.

Katherine's smile gets noticeably smaller. "I just picked it up from a friend."

Her tone is firm and assures me that I don't want to go digging into any corner of their lives. If they obtain their ice through suspect ways, I have no desire to know how anything of greater value in this house ended up here.

There's so much food on my plate that I can barely eat half of it before I'm so full I can't stomach another bite. Everyone, including myself, is surprised by how little I eat. I haven't had a meal since breakfast yesterday, but when your current predicament is this nauseating, it can be a little hard to eat.

I dump my excess food into the trash, rush back into my borrowed room, and close the door behind me. I lie back down on the bed that doesn't seem quite as comfortable now.

Assess the situation, I tell myself. I broke out of prison and I can't go back. I can't go home. I can't leave Thomas. The only options are to stay here in a place I don't feel right in, or convince Thomas to abandon a roof over our heads to enter into a chaotic world neither of us are prepared for.

As if on cue, Thomas opens my door. "Are you okay?" he asks.

"I'm fine," I answer without hesitation.

"Are you sure?" he asks. Concern surfaces in his voice, but he pretends to act casual by leaning nonchalantly on the doorframe.

"I don't trust Katherine and Mark," I admit bluntly.

"Why not?" he asks, shutting the door behind him so they don't hear what I'm saying.

"Why would I?" I sit straight up in the bed and glare at him. "Everything they've done is shady; harboring fugitives, refusing to answer simple questions about *ice* —"

"Maybe they're nice people. Aren't you the one who believes good can come from bad things, or something? Maybe they're the good that has come from this bad," he sighs.

"Stop saying that. They're not good, Thomas. I get a really bad vibe from them."

"A bad vibe?" Thomas chuckles. "Dude, I'm not going to leave this place because of a *vibe*."

"Well, I can't make it out there on my own."

"So, we both stay here. Please?"

I pause for a moment. A question is bouncing around in my head, but I don't know if I should take the risk of asking it.

"Why can't we go find Hailee? She would take you in."

He takes a great step back. If the door wasn't closed he would've backed right out of the room, but instead he stays pressed up against the door.

"I can't do that. I don't even know where she lives now. She probably —" He can't finish his sentence.

"Well, can't we check the last place she lived?" I stand up and walk towards him.

"No, we can't do that. She might not even take you in. She knows I'm innocent, but she's never met you."

His eyes beg for me to stop this conversation, but I can't.

"Shouldn't we at least *try?*" I sigh in frustration.

"No, Anna. We can't. I can't take the risk of losing this place, traveling all that way —" his voice cracks, and tears begin forming in his eyes, but I pretend I don't notice. "Only to find that she's not there anymore."

"Alright. We'll stay," I give in before he has a chance to start bawling, "but only for a little while, until we can figure out a plan. When a better, safer option presents itself, we take it."

Staying here is a monumentally terrible idea, but sometimes, bad ideas are all we have. Braving the lightless world on my own, when the police are searching for me, seems a worse idea than staying with two people I get a bad vibe from, or at least, I hope it is.

SIX

Two and a half weeks later, we are still living with Katherine and Mark, and the electricity is still gone with no signs of ever returning. Katherine has since made several more suspicious trips to get water and other supplies, though she now takes a handgun with her every time she leaves the house. Thomas and I haven't left this street since we first arrived, but Katherine says there is still plenty of violence and looting taking place, and the police are failing to maintain any order amongst the angry and confused people who still have no explanation for their lack of electricity.

When I built up the nerve to ask Katherine about where she was getting all of her supplies from, she said she was friends with a "prepper" — a person who spends their life preparing for the apocalypse — who had stockpiled all of it and was willing to share. Any further questioning into who the prepper was or *why* they would share with us resulted in more glares and short answers. I am still very skeptical of both of them, but they have made no attempt to harm us, ditch us, or sell us out to the police, *yet.*

Four days after we arrived, I finally, and pathetic-ally, admitted my arm was fine and I no longer needed to wear the sling. I would have kept it up for longer, but the sling was irritating and scratched my arm. Not to mention, Thomas and Katherine would both overreact anytime they came close to rubbing up against it and apologize profusely for nearly hurt-ing me.

"How is that possible?" Thomas asks. "I saw how beaten up it was."

"I don't know, but it doesn't hurt now. Look." I stretch my arm out fully to reveal no pain and no bruises. Everyone closely examines it. Katherine even grabs it and twists it out of nowhere to see if I flinch. After a while, they all accept, as I have, that I was only being a wimp about it and my arm is com-pletely fine.

I have been wanting to talk to Thomas one on one since we arrived here, but ever since our first conversation about leaving, he and Mark have stuck to each other like glue. Not a single conversation be-tween me and Thomas hasn't involved Mark chang-ing the subject and finding ways to distract Thomas from me. I worry he may have overheard when I said that I don't trust them, because Mark, very clearly, has a problem with me. Anytime we end up alone in a room he blatantly expresses that fact.

"I don't care for you, and I don't trust you," he said to me on my third day here.

"Funny, I feel the same way about you," I riposted.

On several occasions since then he has not been slack in reminding me how much I "irk his nerves." I'm sure the only reason he hasn't snuck into my room and put a pillow over my face while I'm sleeping is because Katherine has a fondness towards me.

Avoiding conversations about her work or her sketchy findings is life or death, but to both my luck and dismay, she loves having deep talks with me and trying to pry into the darkest parts of my mind. She irritates me to death with her constant conversations, but a part of me knows it's the only thing keeping me alive right now, because Mark definitely wants to kill me.

It concerns me how much Mark wants to keep me and Thomas apart, and how chatty Thomas is around Mark, but apparently they share a lot of the same interests.

Yesterday, I overheard them talking about their favorite cars. It took everything to hold back my sarcastic comment about how talking about cars is a waste of time since they may never run again.

Today, I'm determined to speak to Thomas alone and sort this out. After I agreed to stay, I told him I would only remain here a short time while we figure out a new plan, and that time has long since passed.

I walk downstairs, wearing the same outfit Katherine first gave me. She has given me multiple outfits and I will wear one, then wash it in a bucket, hang it out to dry, then put something else on. But most of them are either not to my taste or don't fit correctly, because Katherine severely overestimated how small I am because of how tiny I looked in my jumpsuit when she met me. So, I've been channeling my inner cartoon character and wearing the same one almost every day.

This morning Thomas is wearing an all black outfit accompanied by the same green army jacket he's worn for four days. His face is better today. The remnants of his injuries have started to fade and he looks almost himself again.

Mark starts the fire in the backyard again, to cook breakfast. This time, Thomas does not join him, but stays in the kitchen, staring out the window in a daze. He appears deep in thought and I don't want to interrupt him, but I see this as my only opportunity to speak to him. Only now, Katherine is refusing to leave my side. I think she knows that I am trying to get away to talk to Thomas, because she pulls me into the living room and starts bombarding me with a million different questions. I can't get away from the conversation until Mark announces that breakfast is ready.

Everyone heads out to the backyard, grabs a paper plate, and stacks it high with an assortment of beans. Even with all of Katherine's special trips, the food supply is getting low. I'm worried what might happen once it's too low and Mark and Katherine realize how much longer it would last without two extra mouths to feed.

I sit down on a patio chair and try not to think about what will happen if we stay here much longer, because we won't. We will leave today, and if Thomas isn't on board with that, I'll have to leave him behind.

Eating the beans takes immense effort, because it's so dry and salty that it absorbs all the saliva in my mouth. It's the equivalent of eating saltine crackers with extra salt.

I'm shoving the fourth revolting spoonful in my mouth when I hear a strange noise. I look up at the rest of the group who have all taken notice of the odd sound. It takes a moment, but the revelation dawns on all of us. The noise we heard was the revving of an engine.

We rush inside, through the house, and leap for the front windows. I don't believe what I am seeing when I look outside. Several armored cars, full of soldiers, are driving on the road. They split up and pull into several different driveways.

"How did they get them running?" I ask. I thought every single vehicle on the planet, or at least in Ohio, had stopped working.

"I don't know, but we gon' find out," Mark chuckles.

"They're coming this way," Katherine exclaims.

We all look outside and see one of the trucks pulling into the driveway. Mark starts cursing violently, then runs to a hall closet and pulls out two backpacks and sets them down by the back door.

"What are those?" I ask.

"They have all the supplies we need in case we have to leave," Mark replies.

Thanks for not telling me about this sooner, or I would have grabbed one in the middle of the night and ditched you guys.

"Only two?" I question.

"Sorry." He smiles a little as he says it.

Someone knocks at the door and the room suddenly fills with silence, then another knock comes. I look over at Thomas, but he's staring at Mark, who has just pulled Katherine's handgun out of the closet. He tosses it to her and she begins to load it. He reaches back in the closet and pulls out a shotgun I didn't know he had.

"Woah, I don't think that's necessary," Thomas says in concern.

"Better safe than sorry. Y'all two start heading out back. We'll catch up with you in a minute," Mark says. An unnerving concentration has become evident on his face. It's the same look he gives me when we're alone, only more intense.

Thomas and I both stand frozen as Mark and Katherine walk over to the door and open it where three men, fully armed and decorated, stand with menacing glares spread across their faces. Katherine hides her gun behind her back and Mark hides his behind the door.

"Hello, my name is General Kaine," the oldest, and most decorated one, says in complete monotone. "We are here to temporarily govern this town, making sure every citizen is safe, until it is back up and running. Right now, we are gathering the number of the population so we may know exactly how many people have survived and are in need of care. May we come in? How many of you are here? Are there children?"

"You may not come in," Katherine says bluntly.

I start quietly inching my way back. I do not want to be here if this goes bad, and from what I know about Mark and Katherine, I'm sure it will go bad. Thomas slowly follows my lead towards the back door.

"Then how many people are residing here? Do you have food and water?" General Kaine asks, trying to lean in to get a good look around.

"It's none of your business how many people live here," she says, much more firmly, "and I'm not telling you how much food we have here. You'll only take it."

"Please cooperate with us, ma'am."

I've reached the backdoor now, so I grab one of the backpacks Mark left here. Thomas grabs the other one as I reach slowly for the doorknob, trying to remain as still as possible. Too much movement

might catch the eye of the general and his armed soldiers.

"Don't tell me what to do!" Katherine shouts.
"Get off my property!"

"We just want to help!" one of the soldier says.

"We don't want yer help!" Mark bellows.

I quietly open the back door, but neither of us
leave. We both watch what's playing out in front of
us with fixed gazes. The two soldiers have now
joined the general who is trying to calm down Mark
and Katherine, but they are both frantically yelling.
The soldiers slowly inch their way in the front door,
so I start inching my way out of the back. Luckily,
they pay no attention to me. They're too focused on
the furious people yelling at them.

"Don't make this difficult!" the youngest of the
soldiers exclaims, then makes the devastating mistake
of putting his hand on Katherine's shoulder.

I can't see her face, but I can see the soldier's,
which has turned from rosy pink to plaster white. He
quickly moves his hand away, but it's too late. She
whips her gun out and shoots the young man in the
chest. His body drops to the floor, blood pouring out
of his wound. As soon as that happens, Mark tackles
the general to the ground, and the second soldier
shoots Katherine. She falls backwards and hits the
wood floor. Her lifeless eyes stare up at the pat-
terned ceiling.

I don't wait to see what happens next. I turn away
and run full force into the woods behind their yard

with Thomas right behind me. I keep a tight grip on my backpack and I don't look back for anything. I can only hope that amongst the chaos, no one noticed we left, or that we were ever there to begin with.

A shot fires off soon after we reach the tree line, and I wonder who it came from. Whether Mark shot the general, or the general shot him. But when I don't hear another one I get my answer. There were two soldiers remaining, only one Mark. Only one shot. Mark is dead.

SEVEN

I continue to run full speed ahead through a haze of dull brown and green, as the vivid pictures of what I just witnessed replay in my mind without ceasing. The young soldier's corpse falls on the floor in slow motion a hundred times, and the same thing happens to Katherine a hundred more. I'm shaking so terribly from the shock that I can hardly stand it. The shaking quickly becomes too much, along with the nausea suddenly rising up in me, and I'm forced to stop running so I can vomit. I run behind a sizable tree so Thomas doesn't see me, if he's even still behind me.

I keep one hand tight on the strap of my backpack that formerly belonged to the now-deceased Mark, and the other holds me steady against the tree. My stomach quickly empties and all I manage to spit up is stomach acid that burns up my entire throat.

Once that awful experience is over, I move to a different tree, very far away, and sit down. Thomas quietly asks me if I'm alright and I want to ask the same of him. His face is drained of all color and his eyes look as if they're trying their hardest to focus on any single image other than the violent ones now burned into his retinas.

"I'm fine," I say through a scratchy, vomit burned throat. "I just need a moment to breathe, and we need to be sure none of those men followed us."

"Yeah, and Mark might've gotten out of there and started heading this way," he says innocently and unknowingly, as he looks back at the path we took to see if anyone else is coming this way.

I squint at him, perplexed, and then speak without thinking, "Mark is dead."

"How do you know that?" he asks suspiciously, and I immediately regret saying anything, but it's too late to back out of it now.

"Well, after we left, I only heard one more gunshot. He would have to kill the last two soldiers to make it out of there, which would have taken two shots. One shot means, you know..."

He does know, and he slumps defeated onto the ground and sighs, "He's dead."

"I'm sorry."

"No, don't be sorry." He takes a long pause. "It's for the best we got away from them."

I'm taken aback by his suddenly positive outlook on the dreadful situation, but I do agree with his statement.

"Yeah, I'm pretty sure they were conmen and thieves, and they probably killed a few people. But I know you were close with Mark," I say, even though

I don't understand why. I never liked or trusted Mark, and the feeling was mutual.

"I couldn't stand Mark." He lets out a halfhearted chuckle.

"Then why did you spend so much time with him?" I ask in utter shock.

Thomas crumbles up withering leaves in his hands as he speaks, and avoids all eye contact with me, which is very unusual for him.

"I knew they were up to no good from the moment we met them, but I was too focused on staying safe to care. I was so sure we would get caught by the police if we stayed out in the open. I know there are more important things — the world might be ending right now — but I couldn't go back, Anna. When we found Mark and Katherine, I tried to stay on their good side so they would keep us safe, because it was obvious they had the resources to do so. Didn't you notice how different I acted around them?"

I did notice. Thomas was extra talkative and energetic, but it didn't click in my mind that behavior was all an act to make them more comfortable. Looking back, I was dumb for not realizing something so obvious.

"We could have found those resources somewhere else from people more trustworthy. I think Mark and Katherine were definitely planning something dangerous — something they thought they would need two criminals *like us* to help with." I roll my eyes when I say 'like us.' "That's why they were so willing to stitch us up and nurture us back to health. They needed us. That's the only reason they didn't kill us."

"Yeah, I bet they were, but I don't care. I know it wasn't right, but I was more concerned about keeping us safe," he says, and a twinge of happiness runs through my body, knowing that he was thinking of my safety as well, but frustration rushes in right after it.

"We can't do that anymore."

"Do what?"

"Go against what's right for the sake of our safety. If we have to sacrifice our morality to survive, then we might as well be dead."

"I guess that doesn't really matter since we'll probably die out here," Thomas says hopelessly, then scatters the crunched up leaves that have piled up in his hands.

He's right about the dying part. There's no telling what the state of the cities around us are, in the aftermath of the blackout, but chances are, unless the entire police force has fallen prey to a self-destructing society, they may not so kindly ignore us as they did before. Katherine said things had gotten out of hand back in town, but it surely can't be so chaotic everywhere. They must have regained some sort of law and order by now.

Both of us sit quietly on the forest floor for a while and the prison breakout re-enters my mind. I want to ask Thomas why he left me, but I look over at him and realize he's trying to suppress emotions that are working their hardest to surface.

"You can cry, if you want to," I tell him.

Men have this need, or programming, to contain their emotions. Whether Thomas has always been this way, or it was something he had to learn in prison, I don't care. I only want him to know he doesn't have to be that way anymore.

"Thank you, but I'm not sure I should cry over someone like them," he mumbles.

"But you can." I attempt to console him and encourage him not to suppress his pain. "There's nothing wrong with it. They may not have been good people, but they were still people. Their lives were taken from them, and you had to be a witness to it. Mourning them is okay. I'll give you some space."

I step up and walk down a nearby slope. I plant myself at the foot of yet another tree and lean back against it.

I hear the mumbled sound of what can only be Thomas trying to cry discreetly. I always assumed everyone else handled these kinds of situations better than I did, but even with the uncontrollable, horrific images flashing in my brain, I might be handling this better than him. Of course, he didn't vomit afterwards.

Maybe he's crying for Caleb. Mark was probably the first male "friend" Thomas had since his death, because most of the men at the prison never so much as spoke to him. It must be hard to lose them both, and to have one bring back memories of the other. I know seeing girls in the prison so close knit with each other reminded me of how Julie and I used to be. I never truly experienced closure over her. I never finished mourning. I shed a lot of tears, but it was always at a police station, or in a holding cell, or in front of an unsympathetic jury. None of those tears felt right. But now, I'm out here in the middle of a beautiful forest with no one but an already sobbing Thomas to stop me. No cops, no security cameras, no angry prosecutors.

So, I cry, because just like Thomas, I lost my best friend. And she deserved more than being stranded in a ditch. She deserved more than being a news story with an ugly actress re-enacting her death. She deserves more than the tears I have, but it's all I can give to her memory. So, I cry and let nature soak up my tears until it no longer seems right and I have to make myself stop.

I use my sleeve to wipe away the tears that cover my drenched face. Since we aren't moving forward and I need a distraction, I pull off my backpack and inspect the contents of it. I find food; trail mix, crackers, beef jerky, and a few MRE's that are all barbecue rib flavored. Some weapons; a knife, a handgun, and bullets. At the bottom of the bag is a bottle of water, a lighter, and a sleeping bag.

I have no knowledge of how to fire a gun, so the handgun and bullets are useless to me. The knife, lighter, and sleeping bag all seem to be useable items.

I open the water bottle, take a tiny sip, and put everything back in the bag.

My stomach is growling. I need to save the MRE's for a time when they might be more vital than they are now. I could eat some of the crackers to tide me over, but I know better than to consume such salty foods without a guarantee of more water very soon. It's common sense, and it's also the entire plot of chapter 12 of The Hunger Games.

It's been a few hours since we first took a break and Thomas hasn't come to meet me. I don't know if he's done mourning yet, but we can't stay here any longer. I pull my backpack over my shoulder and return to where I last saw Thomas. He's still in the same spot he was before. His eyes are red, but dry of tears, and his backpack is sitting in front of him. I guess he used the same distraction tactic as I did.

The crunching of leaves under my footsteps startles him and he looks up at me.

"We have to go," I say to him. "We need to find somewhere else to stay, and at the very least, we need to be farther away from here."

He nods in agreement and puts his backpack on. He taps mine and asks, "You don't happen to have an endless supply of food in yours, or a portal out of here, do you?"

"I wish. All I've got is a bunch of hundred dollar bills and a map to a secluded location," I smile.

It's now midday and the refreshing sunlight blinds my eyes, yet the cool wind still makes me shiver. Winter has reached its end, but remnants of it have endured the rest of nature's attempts to wipe it out completely.

I hold my hand above my eyes to protect them from the sun and suddenly wish I had accepted Katherine's offer to take one of her $300 pairs of sunglasses she had on display in her walk-in closet.

I peer through the blinding light to view what is seemingly an endless line of trees. There's no clear direction to walk in and there's no way to tell which way we came from. All we can do is keep walking until we find something, and hope we have not been wandering in circles the entire time.

"I think we should probably find a place to stop for the night," Thomas says right at sundown.

We've covered miles and miles of forest today, but have yet to find any way out, so as much as I don't want to spend the night out here, I have no choice.

Although I used to stay awake until midnight or later on a regular basis, these past few weeks I've been sleeping whenever the sun does and my body has already adjusted to that routine, so I'm more than ready to sleep.

We come across a small clearing and start unpacking there. Even though I'm dying of thirst, I only take a few sips of water and I urge Thomas to do the same. We only have one bottle each and there's no telling when we will have the chance to refill them.

The air is quickly getting colder as night settles in and I'm thankful our deceased accomplices thought to pack thick sleeping bags in the backpacks we stole from them.

Thomas unrolls his sleeping bag right next to mine, then walks away to hang his backpack on a tree. When he does, I push his sleeping bag farther away, then crawl into mine.

When he turns back, he doesn't seem to notice the extra distance now between us. He slips into his sleeping bag without a word and faces the other direction. I roll over so we're back to back.

The temperature continues to drop quickly. The cold, dry air, paired with the hard surface of the ground, is painful, but it's nothing compared to the overwhelming torment within myself because of the dark images of Katherine and the young soldier both slipping away from life that are constantly pushed to the forefront of my mind.

I heard the gunshots at the prison that sent chills down my spine. I saw the pictures of Julie's cold body lying on a slab when it was shown as evidence in court. I have seen the dead, but watching the exact moment someone's soul departs from their body is a completely different and newly terrifying experience. I barely knew Katherine, I had never met the soldier, but both of them will be with me forever now.

I stay awake for hours because my body may have shut down, but my brain hasn't. It must be at least midnight by now, and yet I'm still awake, staring at a worm in the moonlight. It inches its way across the ground in front of my face. Seeing the worm has made it even harder to fall asleep for fear that a worm, or something worse, may crawl into my ears while I sleep.

I roll over to look at Thomas, who I know is still awake too, because he hasn't started snoring. His snores are so loud that they used to keep me awake when we shared a cell. I could occasionally hear him at Mark and Katherine's house, snoring in the room across the hall.

"Thomas," I whisper to him.

No response. Minutes pass and he doesn't even move. *Maybe, he is asleep.* I think to myself. Silence continues to fill the air. *Definitely not asleep.*

"Thomas?" I whisper again.

"Did you say my name?" he murmurs in a tired, raspy voice, then rolls around to face me.

"Yes."

"What's up? Are you okay?" he asks.

"I'm fine. I just can't sleep," I whisper yet again, although I don't know why. There's not anyone around here I need to protect our conversation from.

"Neither can I," he whispers back to me.

"Why can't you sleep?" I ask, staring into his tired eyes.

"Very important parts of me are very, very cold," he laughs, and the echo of it returns to us, "and I don't want to fall asleep and see their faces staring at me."

He doesn't say their names, but I know exactly who he's talking about.

"My problem is I see them more when I'm awake. If I could sleep I would be okay," I mumble.

"I would much rather see their faces when I'm awake and I know none of it is real," he says, and I see a blink of fear in his eyes.

EIGHT

The sun is barely up when I open my eyes to the gradient pastel blue sky, uninterrupted by clouds. I sit up and run my fingers through my unbrushed hair. I look over at one side of the sleeping bag and spot the same worm from last night still sitting where I last saw it. At least I know it's not in my ear. I look around and notice something very wrong. Thomas isn't here and neither is his sleeping bag or his backpack. I scan the forest in every direction, but all I see is an endless collection of trees. I leave the clearing and walk past four small trees intertwined into one oversized tree, with a withered sunflower placed in the middle. Thomas is nowhere nearby.

"Thomas! Thomas!" I call out his name, but he doesn't answer, and he doesn't come. *He's not here.*

My heart starts racing and I quickly become lightheaded. I walk back over to my sleeping bag and sit down on it. I should have known. He left me once, why wouldn't he do it again? He's probably been waiting this whole time for the right opportunity to ditch me. Pretending to care about my safety was just an act, no different than the one he put on for Mark and Katherine.

A sudden, overwhelming panic rises in me at the prospect of being completely alone, something I have only ever experienced within the confines of my own mind. I find myself shaking in fear, but that fear quickly turns to resentful anger — this is the second time Thomas has abandoned me.

My blood is beginning to boil when I hear a noise. Footsteps. I bolt up out of my daze and see Thomas walking towards me. I gape at him, stunned. I thought he had left in the middle of the night and was miles away by now. He reaches the clearing and offers me a cheery good morning.

"Is something wrong?" he asks when I don't respond.

"Why did you do that?" I shout bitterly at him, which stops him dead in his tracks.

"Do what?" he asks.

"I thought you had left me again!" I jump to my feet. "Where did you even go?"

"I just went for a walk, dude, and what do you mean left you *again*?" He crosses his arms and walks towards me.

"Why did you take your backpack if you were just going for a walk?" I grill him. "Why did you roll up your sleeping bag and take everything with you?"

"I didn't really think about it, I just did it!" He raises his voice and steps closer to me. "Now tell me what you meant by that!"

I raise my voice to match his, and back up slightly to put space between us.

"Meant by what? 'Why did you *leave* me?' I thought that was a pretty good question!"

"No, what did you mean by 'again'? I never left you," he scolds me.

"I thought you left me like you did back at the prison," I mumble, but now he looks even more confused than he did when I was yelling at him.

"What are you talking about?" His tone softens, and he steps closer, yet again, until there is almost nothing between us.

"When all of the power went out. Right before we reached the exit, that guard tasered me, but you didn't stop. You ran right out of the door and never came back for me."

"I didn't mean to do that," Thomas says, turning completely apologetic. "I thought you were right behind me and I didn't notice you weren't until I was outside. I tried to go back, but that woman came out right after me and I had to get away from her. She chased me into the woods and by then I figured you had probably run away in the other direction."

"Oh... Well..."

"I'm sorry," he says quietly, and a twinge of guilt for accusing him of something he never did fills my conscience.

"Don't... don't apologize. You didn't do anything wrong. I just thought you did. *I'm* sorry."

"I'm still sorry for scaring you. I should have told you I was going for a walk, but I didn't want to wake you."

"Don't feel bad about that," I insist. With every apology I am overcome with even more guilt.

Thomas moves even closer to me, and I know he's coming in for a hug. I want to resist — hugs are unbearably awkward for me — but after these past few weeks, I could really use one. He pulls me in and wraps his gentle arms around me. His warmth surrounds me and protects me from the chilly air, until it inevitably ends.

When he lets me go, I rush over to my sleeping bag and begin rolling it up. I pretend I didn't notice what I'm certain was a quick kiss on the top of my head from Thomas, just before the hug ended.

"We should head out. I want to find real shelter before the day is over. I'm not spending another night out here," I say, stuffing my sleeping bag into my backpack.

I take another small sip of my water, then zip up my bag and head out. We walk at a steady pace in the best straight line we can manage.

I watch the sun slowly rise higher and higher into the sky, then the breeze pulls in clouds that cover it. The gray sky makes everything around us look less vibrant. Everything that bursted with color yesterday now looks bleak and sorrowful. Yesterday, I mourned. Today, nature seems to be mourning something of its own.

"Do you think we'll ever see our families again?" Thomas asks out of nowhere.

"I don't know, but I want to," I say.

My family never came to visit me in prison, and I resent them for it, but I still miss them. I would love more than anything to go back to my old house with my parents and hug them as though nothing from this past year had ever happened.

"Maybe we could, on the off chance we don't die out here. I'm sure our families wouldn't rat us out to the police if we went home."

"Mine would," I bitterly admit.

"Then you could stay with my family," Thomas suggests.

"Do you really think your family would allow a convict and total stranger into their home?" I ask, trying to get Thomas's mind off the idea.

"If I told them I trusted you they would," Thomas says, and my heart leaps a little, but I ignore it.

"So, what about when everything calms down and the power gets fixed? The police will start looking for us then, and if we're with either of our families, they could be imprisoned for harboring fugitives. It's too dangerous."

"So, we live the rest of our lives on the run?" he shouts at me, and speeds up his pace to put distance between us.

"I don't know!" I shout hopelessly. "I have no clue what I'm supposed to do right now. I didn't know any of this was going to happen. I don't have a plan!"

"Well, we can't wander around without a clue of what we're doing. We need to figure something out!" he says, refusing to look at me.

"Yeah, well, you do that. Tell me what great ideas you come up with," I scowl.

We don't talk for the next few hours and Thomas maintains the distance he's set between us. Neither of us stop to have meals, either. We eat trail mix and MRE's as we walk. I drop a few pretzel pieces on the ground and sigh in frustration. All of my food is so dry and salty, I have to drink over half the bottle of water to wash it down. It's the most water I've had in two days and every sip is unimaginably refreshing.

I keep looking back over my shoulder at every small noise, expecting to see a dozen cops or soldiers with guns aimed right at me. Although, I'm starting to doubt that anyone is on the hunt for us, or I think they would have found us already.

It's about five o'clock now, the clouds have mostly cleared, the sun is slowly lowering down below the horizon, and the sky burns a fiery orange with wisps of pink and red floating through it. After two days of aimlessly walking, I finally lay eyes on the end of the forest and I giddily rush out onto the edge of a barren and empty road.

Trees span for miles on either side of the highway and there's no clear direction to walk in. Neither of us have any clue where we might be, so we take a chance and head left. Hopefully it will lead us somewhere good.

We walk in the center of the road, since there will likely be no cars driving by to run us over, unless more military trucks come through.

Thomas seems to be over the dispute we had earlier, because he lessens the lead he was keeping on me and he begins to discuss how the military could have working vehicles when no one else does. Thomas suggests that maybe all the power went out in a specific area and not everywhere, so some places may still have working cars and electricity. I disagree.

"Maybe we could ask that guy," he says, looking behind us.

I turn around and see a rusty, red pickup truck barreling down the highway in our direction. I dart into the woods, hoping the driver doesn't see me, and Thomas rushes into the trees right after me.

Used to, I wouldn't give a second thought to a truck driving down the road, or the people inside of it, but nowadays I can't help but be wary of anyone who has access to a working vehicle. Especially considering what happened with the occupants of the last car we encountered.

At first, I think the truck will simply pass us by as if we don't exist, but as it comes closer, the brakes screech to a halt beside us. The driver rolls down his window.

"I see you two," he shouts to the bush we're hiding behind. I don't move an inch. "Come on, now. Do you need a ride?" he asks kindly.

93

I consider his question for a brief instant, then something urges me to respond and I, perhaps recklessly, leave the cover of the bush and step onto the road. I step nearer to the driver, who seems to be alone in his truck. He looks to be in his fifties with some gray hairs showing in his beard, and his dark skin is bare of wrinkles except for laugh lines under his eyes and on his cheeks when he smiles at us.

I look into the eyes of the first seemingly genuine person I've met since the prison breakout and I accept his offer without any more hesitation. Thomas jumps out of the bushes and worriedly pulls me aside.

"Why are you so eager to accept his help? I thought you were the one who wanted to be more cautious of people from now on," he whispers.

"He doesn't know we're fugitives, like they did," I whisper back. "I have a good feeling about this. Trust me."

"I do trust you, but I know even less about this guy than I knew about Mark. How can I trust him?"

"You need a ride?" the man asks again. "Don't make me waste my gas."

"Just a moment." I quickly turn back to Thomas. "Please, I trusted you and stayed with them even when I didn't want to. Can you return the favor?"

"Sure," he sighs skeptically.

I smile at the driver. "Yes, we need a ride. But how is your truck running? All the other ones have stopped."

"Only those cheap electronic ones quit working. This here's a 1967. It's all mechanical. No tech to fry. So... where ya headed?" he asks.

I look at Thomas for an answer, but he only shakes his head.

"We don't know," I answer awkwardly.

"Well, hop in the back. We'll find somewhere to go." The man chuckles. "I'm Michael, by the way."

Thomas and I introduce ourselves, then hop in the empty truck bed. Neither of us had a clue what we should do or where we should go, but I guess fate has decided for us.

Michael talks to us through his shattered rear window and asks us if we want anything to eat or drink.

"Water, please!" I say enthusiastically.

He reaches through the sharp, broken glass window and hands back two bottles of water for me and Thomas, then he starts driving. I immediately gulp down most of what was in my bottle and set the rest down on the rattling truck bed.

As the day drags on, we cover miles and miles of uninterrupted highway at the truck's top speed, and I begin to smell something burning. I assume it's from all the smoke coming out of the tailpipe.

That's definitely good for the environment, I joke to myself, then I hear Thomas say something, but I can't understand it over the sound of the winds whipping at high speed and the roaring engine.

I point to my ears to indicate that I can't hear him, and he responds by pointing behind me. I turn

95

around to see what he's gesturing towards, but it doesn't take long to figure it out. The sky in the distance is overtaken with billowing clouds of pitch-black smoke. The tree line has greatly thinned out and allows for an unobstructed view of dozens of burning buildings. I'm sure there are more buildings on fire, but everything else is engulfed by heavy layers of darkness.

The smoke I was smelling wasn't from the truck, it was from an entire city that had gone up in flames.

NINE

Tears rush down my cheeks at the sight of buildings catching fire and being reduced to ashes. The seriousness of this blackout became apparent when I first saw the stalled vehicles on the road, but even still, I kept trying to deny it. Even with everything Katherine told me about the state of the towns around us, I tried to pretend it would get better, but looking at the horror displayed in front of me right now, I accept that I was merely playing myself. Something is immensely wrong and it will not magically go away.

"First the blackout, now a whole city has been set on fire. What is happening? Who would do this?" I ask aloud, though I know my voice is drowned out by the wind.

I lay my head on my knees and don't look back up at the burning city. Thomas puts his hand on my shoulder and I shove it away. I appreciate his attempt to comfort me, but I can't accept it right now. I didn't want to admit it, but the kiss on the head, along with talking about living with his family has left me very rattled and perturbed. I genuinely care about

Thomas and I don't want any unreciprocated romantic feelings destroying the only friendship I have left in this world.

I look back up at the sky and watch the burning city shrink into the distance until the rest of the sky finally darkens into night and I can no longer tell what's cloud and what's smoke.

My mind drifts just as a leaf in this whirling wind. The events of the past few weeks replay over in my head like a cheap movie. I broke out of prison and now I'm evading the law, though they may not be searching for me. I spent two weeks living with legitimate criminals who are both dead now (and were never convicted of their crimes. Way to go, American judicial system). All of the electricity went out in homes, in machines, in everything. All but military vehicles, and apparently this one old truck, has stopped working.

The past few weeks have been completely insane. The replaying of it all is eating me up inside. There's been too much death recently. No one should have to experience it on this great of a scale. Just thinking about it makes my eyes misty and my stomach churn.

I wonder how Thomas is handling the emotional overload. I look over at him. He's laying down on the truck bed and using his sleeping bag as a pillow so all the bumps in the road don't give him a concussion. He's laying as still as he possibly can. He wants me to think he's asleep, but I know if he was snoring

I would still be able to hear it over the sound of the wind.

I lie down beside him and try to fall asleep. We know nothing about the man driving the truck or where he's taking us, so falling asleep in his presence seems reckless, but I've gotten quite used to living with, and sleeping around, sketchy characters over the past several months.

I stuff my sleeping bag under my head and stare at the chipping, red paint on the side of the truck, and try to keep my mind clear until I can't keep my eyes open any longer and manage to fall asleep. I doze off, but I'm often jolted awake by the feeling of hitting a pothole in the road and I'm forced to start the entire process over again. Stare at the old paint, don't think, feel my eyelids getting heavy, fall asleep, wake up, stare at the old paint...

This time I'm woken up by the sound of Michael yelling something at us over the sound of the wind.

"Hey, kids! We got company!" he hollers through the back window. I sit up to find that headlights of another vehicle on the road are coming our way.

"Stay down! They may not be friendly," he shouts, and I duck down, though his comment confuses me. I know why I'm skeptical of passing cars, but why is he?

Bang! The unmistakable sound of a shot being fired explodes in the air and the truck immediately swerves off the road. *Oh no, they shot Michael.*

I close my eyes, expecting the truck to hit a tree and fling me to my death. I try to grab a hold of something in hopes of not being catapulted, but we don't hit anything. The truck keeps going farther and farther in the woods, scraping against branches. The shooter missed.

More shots are fired off and I can only assume the shooter is following us.

The terrain here is obviously worse than the road. The bumps are bigger and they don't stop coming. Multiple times I think I'm about to fly out of the vehicle and land right on top of the one behind us.

Thomas, who is stricken with an immobilizing fear, tries reaching out for my hand, but he can barely move, so I reach out the rest of the way and grab his hand. He squeezes mine so tightly that my fingers have gone numb.

Although I have recently been uncomfortable with how close Thomas has become, I am too terrified of losing my grip to be concerned about that.

Suddenly, both vehicles come to a halt. Thomas and I both jump up. Headlights illuminate the scene. The car that chased us is one of the military's armored cars. Two men exit the vehicle in combat ready outfits, all camouflage with bulletproof vests and rifles in their hands.

"How did they find us?" Thomas whispers to me. I do not answer. I'm frozen in fear as they approach us.

Michael jumps out of his truck and slams the door shut. "Why did you shoot at me?" he growls.

"Sorry, sir. We only wanted you to pull over. It's just protocol," the driver of the armored car says. He's a tall, bulky man appearing to be somewhere in his 30's, same as the passenger standing next to him.

Michael stomps towards the men, "Shooting at my truck is protocol?"

Before either of the soldiers have a chance to pull their guns on him, he's already decked the driver and snatched the gun out of the passenger's hand. He uses the tail end of the rifle as a bat and swings it at the driver.

The now weaponless passenger, rather than help his friend, runs away from the conflict and directly towards me and Thomas.

He jumps right into the truck bed, and before I have time to get away, he grabs me by my hair and starts pulling me out of the truck. He drops me down onto the ground and steps on me, holding me down with the weight of his entire body.

"How did you find me?" I demand.

"I didn't know we were supposed to be looking for you." He leans down to yank me by my hair and looks me in the eye. "What have you done?"

I don't answer, then land a good punch in his shin just as Thomas comes up behind the man and wraps his arms around his throat. He steps off me as he struggles with Thomas.

He manages to break free and wallops Thomas's nose. Thomas stumbles backwards and grips onto his face.

I send a fist flying at the soldier, but he blocks it and twists my arm back. He then grabs me by the neck and slams my head into the back of the truck so hard everything turns black...

I must have momentarily lost consciousness, because when I open my eyes, the soldier who attacked me is lying on top of his own car and the windshield is smashed in from where someone must have slammed him into it. *How long did I black out for?*

"What did you just do?" the driver asks of myself and Thomas, as he stares wildly perplexed at the man crumpled on the car.

Michael is standing over the second soldier, who has been rendered unconscious, and Thomas is still pinching his bloody nose and has his eyes shut. I thought one of them must have fought off the soldier, but that doesn't seem to be the case. Could it really be that no time has passed since I blacked out?

"He's not dead," Michael says to me. He must have seen me nervously looking at the man next to his feet. "But that guy might be. So, do either of you want to tell me what happened here?"

"I didn't do anything," I answer him, and Thomas shakes his head in denial.

"So, this man just flew all the way over here and into the windshield by himself?" His eyes switch between the two of us, who are as at a loss for an explanation as he is. "Alright then... neither of you want to tell me... that's alright," he mumbles to himself as he walks over to their car and takes the keys out of the ignition.

"What on earth just happened?" I whisper to Thomas while the driver is preoccupied.

"I don't know. How could they have found us?" Thomas whispers while still leaning his head back to stop the blood flow in his nose.

"That's the thing — they weren't looking for us. That one soldier didn't even know who we were," I tell him.

"So, you think they were after *him*?" Thomas asks, and I turn my gaze towards the mysterious Michael.

Something in my gut told me he was trustworthy when we met, but in all reality, I know nothing about the man except his name, and apparently he's a very skilled fighter. Whether my gut was right about Michael, or whether he's yet another master criminal we have befriended, I do not know.

I don't have time to respond to Thomas's question before Michael returns with their keys in his hands.

"How do you kids feel about a trip to Columbus?" he asks, hopping into the driver's seat without another word.

Thomas and I both dazedly agree to the idea of a trip to Columbus. I'm too confused by what happened with the soldier, and my head is too fuzzy from being slammed into the truck, to weigh the pros and cons of entering the largest city in Ohio.

A part of me feels bad about leaving those men alone and without their keys while they're injured. However, they did just try to kill us, so I don't have *that much* sympathy for them.

We ride, much more cautiously, on the dark road towards Columbus. I refuse to lay down, out of fear that I'll fall asleep, given the likelihood that I have a concussion is very high. And I cannot seem to shake the worry that another car will shoot at us while we sleep.

I ask Thomas to talk with me to help me stay awake, although I regret it. The dark circles under his eyes look even darker in what little moonlight is not obstructed by smoke that fills the night sky. He is in desperate need of sleep.

"I don't mind," he says. His nose has stopped bleeding and Michael had some napkins in his glove compartment to wipe off the excess blood.

"Thanks," I say awkwardly.

Michael is driving much slower now, only about forty miles per hour, so the wind is significantly less brutal, and I can hear what Thomas is saying, though I don't think Michael can hear us.

"I don't think they were after him," I say to Thomas, continuing on our earlier conversation. "If

104

that was the case, they would've both gone after him, and worried about us later. But they didn't. I think they wanted all of us dead. They didn't know who we were, but they wanted us dead."

"That doesn't make any sense," Thomas says, rubbing his aching nose.

"No, it doesn't, but I think it's what happened," I admit.

I, once again, find myself having to accept that something is very wrong here. Soldiers shooting cars at random is not normal. Cities set aflame is not normal. I have no idea what is happening to society, but maybe I'll find out when we reach Columbus, though I'm not entirely sure I want to.

"We're almost there," Michael says at about noon.

Thomas and I didn't sleep a wink last night. We chatted about random, pointless things in an attempt to stay awake, though around 4ᴬᴹ I felt too guilty for asking him to stay up with me, so I begged him to get some rest, but he refused. Instead, he continued to ramble on about things we've already discussed a million times, like our favorite colors. Mine is purple, mostly pastels. His is green, not any one particular green, but all the shades that make up a luscious forest. Our greatest fears. Thomas's is heights, or more specifically, falling for a very long time from those heights to a hard surface down below. I'm indecisive about my greatest fear. I guess I have a lot of them; wasting my life. Dying some mundane death like being choked by my headphone cords while I'm sleeping. Being remembered as a vicious murderer instead of who I really am. Not being remembered at all...

Thomas stands to look over the roof of the truck at the approaching city and I do the same. The tall buildings grow ever closer as we draw nearer and my hope grows with it.

"Well, it's not on fire," Thomas says about the city. "That's a good sign."

However, the overwhelming smog from the burning city has been pushed this way by the wind and has settled into an unnerving smoke screen that turns everything into a scene right out of an eerie horror film.

My stomach growls and I remember we've only got a little bit of beef jerky and a few MRE's left in our packs.

"Do you think we'll be able to find food in the city?" I ask.

"I don't know. I think everyone might be in short supply right now. No way to cook, freeze, or transport food," Thomas says.

"Katherine and Mark did all of those things," I say, trying to give myself a little bit of hope. Realistically, not everyone in Columbus is going to have secret ways of finding giant bags of ice, packs of steaks, or a backyard to light a fire in. Even if we could find someone with all of those things, they wouldn't offer any to us. Not everyone is a generous criminal.

106

I sit back down in the truck. Standing is too exhausting. My entire body wants to collapse on the truck bed after only a few minutes. I'm running on no sleep and an empty stomach and I'm not handling it very well. I imagine Thomas isn't either, but he tries to cover it up. I don't know why he thinks he needs to suppress his pain. He's terrible at it, anyway.

I eat half a bag of beef jerky and end up worse off than when my stomach was empty. It's taking all of my effort to keep it down.

"We're here," Thomas says, interrupting my concentration on maintaining the contents of my stomach.

I come back to reality and carefully lean over the side of the truck to see what lies in front of us. The road is packed with busy jaywalkers moving along hastily, wasting no time staying in one spot. Dozens of cars are stalled and block the entrance to several of the streets. Some buildings have broken windows and unhinged doors. They've clearly been looted and abandoned, but the people here seem to ignore it. Most are going about their day, trying to cling on to what's left of their old life and ignore what's happening. Others are leaving the city in hoards, as though they are aware of some deep, dark secret about this place that I have yet to discover.

Despite living in Ohio my entire life, I have never visited Columbus before. The atmosphere of it is much different than I imagined. Although I suppose it has changed quite a bit since the blackout.

Most of the people walking in the road refuse to move out of the way for our truck. Dozens of people have gathered around it and are looking curiously at us. Some stare as though they are ready to jump on us and take the truck by force, though they would not be able to move it anywhere. We can't be going more than three miles per hour right now. Michael ignores the threatening stares and questions from by-standers about how the vehicle is running, and I try to as well.

"You kids alright back there?" Michael asks through the broken window.

"We're good," I lie.

"I have a friend who lives up here. We should check in with him. I'll bet he's willing to help us out," Michael says to both of us. He hasn't turned his eyes away from the road, or the crowd in it, the entire time.

"Okay," Thomas and I agree.

I keep looking around at all the people, some of whom have already lost interest in us, especially when an old Camaro driving in the opposite lane comes barreling through. People flock to it, and a few are almost run over by it, as whoever is driving it doesn't seem to have any care for the abundance of pedestrians in their way.

"The more I see, the less I understand," Thomas sighs. "How can I still have no clue what's going on?" He grows more frustrated with every word.

"We'll figure it out," I assure him, though I have no idea how.

"Will we?" He rests his head on his hands. "It's been weeks and we don't know any more about what's going on than we did before. It's driving me crazy, dude. I —"

"We *will* figure it out, okay? We'll make it a top priority, right below food and shelter."

Thomas nods in agreement.

Truthfully, I'm just as frustrated with the lack of answers as he is, though a part of me has been afraid to find the answers. I thought coming here might shed some light on things, but now all I seem to know is that society beyond Mark and Katherine's little town has not adjusted well to the sudden change either, but I still have no clue what caused it. An EMP seems the most likely answer, but I've been avoiding that idea since it first occurred to me, because it introduces the questions *who* caused it, and why?

I'm looking into one of the abandoned buildings through a broken window when I notice people walking around inside of it. A short girl stands next to a tall, bulky girl with a jet black bob. They scour through isles of empty shelves looking for food. After the shorter girl manages to grab what's left on the shelves, the other girl slams her onto the floor and takes what food was in her hands and runs out the door with a smushed up bag of bread and a few canned foods. The remaining girl jumps back up, screams at the girl who stole her food, then dramatically falls back onto the floor in defeat.

"Stop the truck!" Thomas yells at Michael.

No sooner than I turn around to ask why he wants to stop, Thomas jumps off the side of the truck and runs into the store, leaving his backpack (and me) behind. I climb out and follow after him, leaving my backpack behind as well.

"What are you doing?" I yell at him. Is he going to try and help that girl? It's a nice gesture, but we can hardly help ourselves right now.

"Hailee!" he shouts enthusiastically at her.

She looks up at Thomas. At first, she is completely confused, but then a smile beams across her face, and she runs straight into his arms. He picks her up and holds onto her tightly.

Hailee? Who is Hailee?

It doesn't take me long to remember.

Hailee is his girlfriend.

TEN

"What are you doing here? Shouldn't you be in prison?" Hailee begins to question once they finally break away from each other's arms, and she begins frantically combing through her tangled mess of wavy brown hair with her fingers.

"We escaped in the chaos after the blackout. Are you okay?" he asks, then kisses her before she can answer.

"Yes, I am." She pulls back. "Who is 'we'?"

"I am... Hello," I say, awkwardly chiming in on their romantic reunion. Hailee obviously hadn't noticed I was standing right next to them.

"Oh, who are you?" I sense an edge in her tone, accompanied by a scowl on her face, though moments ago she was beaming.

"I'm Annalise." I reach out my hand. "Nice to meet you."

"I'm Hailee. It's nice to meet you, too." She shakes my hand and offers me a smile so fake I could spot it from a mile away.

"Thomas talks about you all the time. He's really crazy for you, you know," I say to assure her nothing

111

is going on between me and him, which is what she's so clearly wondering about right now.

A huge smile spreads across her face and she hugs Thomas, who looks rather embarrassed that I told her that. Although, it's a lie. He has barely mentioned her since we broke out, and it was only at my provocation that he did, but I told her anyway. I want to let her know I don't intend to be a threat to their relationship. The last thing I need right now is someone viewing me as an enemy. No, I need friends. Finding friends willing to help is the only way I'm going to survive in this chaos.

"Something about you seems different," Hailee tells Thomas cheekily.

"Prison will do that to you," he laughs.

She shakes her head. "No, it's a good different."

"You can thank Anna for that." He smiles at me. "I guess some of her annoyingly hopeful attitude has begun to rub off on me."

No! Don't do that! Don't mention me! Don't look at me.

Hailee's expression turns sour, but Thomas doesn't seem to notice. He gleefully takes her by the hand and leads her over to Michael's truck. I stop to canvass the store for any food or other supplies, but it's completely bare, so I catch up to Hailee and Thomas and awkwardly walk behind them. Even in the apocalypse, I still find a way to become a third wheel.

Thomas and Hailee walk up to the window of Michael's truck. I'm surprised Michael stayed there and didn't come after us, but I suppose leaving the vehicle that so many people are coveting, unattended, wouldn't be the brightest idea.

Thomas, Hailee, and Michael are talking to each other, but I can't hear anything over the crowd, because someone in the distance began screaming and caused a great commotion.

"Ah, I understand," Michael says once I move in closer. "I'm happy to have helped you kids this far, but I know we have different places we need to go."

"I'm glad you agree," Thomas says, holding tightly onto Hailee's hand. Michael waves goodbye to all of us and starts driving off.

"Wait, what?" I grab onto the truck, as if I would somehow find the strength inside me to stop it from moving. "Why are you leaving? Why are we splitting up?"

Michael sighs and shifts into park. "I guess this is where our paths separate," Michael answers. "You should stay here with your friends and I should go find mine. You three don't need this old man's help to find your way anymore!" he says, then takes one last look at us before reluctantly driving off.

"Bye," all of us say, then I reach in the back to grab our bags before he's too far off, but they're gone. Someone must have snatched them. Michael quickly finds a gap in the crowd and maneuvers his way through the people, takes a left down an adjoining road, and disappears from view.

"What are we supposed to do now?" I ask Thomas in defeat. We have been left on the mayhem filled streets of Columbus with no food and no way to go, and it seems it was their idea to be left here, not Michael's.

"Hailee says we can stay with her at her apartment," he smiles, but Hailee looks a little shocked when Thomas says "we." Clearly her invitation only extended to him and he misunderstood, but she can't take his words back now.

"Yeah, Thomas and... you... can both stay with me," she says to me. Mid-sentence she realized she had already forgotten my name and made a very poor attempt at covering it up.

I force myself to thank her, though I'm sure she would have let me leave with Michael or left me alone on the street if Thomas had given her the chance.

We walk fifteen blocks against the flow of foot traffic before we reach an old apartment complex in the heart of the city. We go up six flights of stairs to the top floor, and by the time we reach her apartment, I am beyond lightheaded and I nearly pass out before I have a chance to walk inside. I wish whoever stole our backpacks could have been kind enough to leave the food behind.

She unlocks her door and we step into a small apartment with dark green walls. An old chandelier, that's much too fancy for this place, hangs down right as you walk in. If I wasn't too short, I would have hit my head on it. Thomas narrowly misses a collision with it.

The kitchen, which is directly to the left when I walk in, has dirty plates all over the countertops. The dark wood cabinets sit open, bare of any supplies. All of her food, which is only a jar of peanut butter, a bag of bread, and an unopened can with no label, sits on the countertops with the dirty plates.

Hailee leads us past the kitchen into a small living room with nothing but an outdated couch and matching arm chair, a TV, a coffee table that has a huge chunk taken off one of the corners, and walls painted the same dark green as the entrance.

I go against my usual manners and take a seat on the couch without it being offered to me because I can't stand up any longer. Thomas sits down right next to me.

"So, what's going on here?" I begin to interrogate Hailee. "What do you know about the blackout? What's happened since then?"

I have evaded the truth for too long. I have spent every day since the blackout trying to convince my-self nothing was as bad as it seemed. And it wasn't — it was worse. Now it's time to find the answers I've been avoiding.

She is taken aback by my questions and takes a while to gather her thoughts.

"I don't know. Everything just stopped working about two weeks ago, and people stopped caring about the rules when that went down. People began looting stores and..." Hailee gets choked up. "They started killing people, too. Nothing mattered to anyone anymore, except their own messed up lives.

"The army showed up about a week ago. They said they were doing everything they could to 'fix the situation' and then they started taking the kids..."

"What?" Thomas gawks.

"They started tearing kids away from their parents. They said it was to keep them safe until everything was back to normal. They were taking people my age too, but I hid until they left. They refused to say where they were taking everyone. None of the people they took have come back, and nothing has been fixed." Hailee stares sorrowfully at the floor and it's obvious she no longer wants to talk about the world living outside her door. "So, do either of you guys need food or anything?" she asks in order to change the subject.

"Yeah. Do you have anything to drink?" Thomas asks.

"How else would I still be alive, dummy?" she laughs, though it seems disingenuous, and then disappears into another room.

I glance over at Thomas who is in disbelief of what he just heard, as am I. I knew most people were not handling this well, but losing any sense of morality because there's no electricity seems impossible.

But so does the military kidnapping kids in broad daylight. Everything about this seems unreal.

Hailee returns with bottled water for me and Thomas and I try to push aside all that I have just learned. I make no attempt at rationing it and drink almost the entire bottle at once. Thomas, who seems to be determined to drink more than I do, finishes his entire bottle and asks for a second.

Hailee brings back three more bottles, one for each of us, then sits down in her arm chair and stares at Thomas as he opens his bottle.

"Thomas, can I speak to you privately?" she asks.

"Sure," he nervously agrees, then follows her into a room next to the kitchen.

Hailee shuts the door behind them and whispering begins in the other room. I can't make out what they're saying, but I imagine it's just Hailee telling off Thomas for being my friend and probably demanding that he stop talking to me. I could tell by the way she first looked at me that she is threatened by me, and maybe she should be. I have no romantic interest in Thomas, but I'm not too sure that the reverse would also be true.

I examine all of the torn seams on the arm of her couch and try to come up with crazy scenarios for what may have caused them to distract my mind as I wait for Thomas and Hailee to return from their mysterious conversation.

"We're just friends," Thomas says, in obvious irritation. He's trying to whisper, but they've both raised their voices.

"Do you really expect me to believe that?" Hailee hisses.

I try to visualize their angry faces and exaggerated hand gestures in my mind. I picture Hailee with her arms crossed and eyebrows furrowed.

"Yes, I do," Thomas answers, probably stepping closer to Hailee as he speaks. It's sort of a thing he does. "If we were more than friends, why would I have run after you and kissed you in front of her? I promise there's nothing between us."

The confidence with which he says it makes me wonder if I have been misreading all of his signals, or if he's lying to put her at ease.

She sighs loudly in defeat. "Fine, but how do I know that she doesn't have feelings for you? I mean, she follows you around like a lost puppy."

I roll my eyes, though neither of them can see it. I would barge into that room right now and tell her off for saying that, if she wasn't telling the truth. I followed Thomas into places I never wanted to go and stayed there because I was afraid of being alone.

"Babe, there's a better chance she hates my guts," he says.

"How do you know?" she asks, much more calmly, and I listen more intently for his answer.

"Because I —" he hesitates, before deciding to lie straight to her face. "Because she told me so, okay? Trust me."

Hailee believes it, but I don't, because I never said that. And now I know everything he just said to her was a lie. He does have feelings for me, and that terrifies me.

"Okay... just... give her some distance. Please?" she whimpers.

"I will," Thomas says.

They both re-enter the tiny living room. Thomas sits on the opposite end of the couch, to distance himself and give me the cold shoulder, per Hailee's wishes, but fails as soon as she asks which one of us will get the only available room and which one will sleep on the couch.

"Anna can take the guest bed," Thomas says immediately.

Hailee rolls her eyes.

"No, you can take it," I say right back. It would be rude taking up the only remaining bed in a home I know I'm not wanted in.

"You take it," he insists.

"I'm perfectly fine sleeping on the couch," I say, thinking back to all the nights I fell asleep on my couch at home while binge watching TV. Though this couch is much less comfortable and much more flat than mine.

"Just take the bed." He stares at me, perplexed by my persistence.

"Why don't you guys flip a coin if you can't decide?" Hailee suggests, rolling her eyes, visibly irritated by how Thomas is treating me.

She picks up a dime off her kitchen counter, twirling it around in her fingers and a strange thought enters my mind: *Is currency even valuable anymore?* It seems as though most people are just looting and stealing. The structure of society, as a whole, seems to have collapsed, and the idea of money and its value was an integral part of that.

"Take your pick," she says, adjusting the coin on her thumb.

"Tails," Thomas declares. She flips the coin but instead of going straight up and back into her hand, the dime flies across the room.

"Good job," Thomas chuckles.

Hailee searches the floor for the coin. "So, I'm not good at coin flipping. I have other redeemable qualities. Oh, it's heads!"

She finds the dime hidden in a crack on the floor.

"Yes!" Thomas says. I won the bed, but he's celebrating a victory. Hailee glares at him. She wants him to back off, and frankly, I do too. I have no interest in being involved in a love triangle.

"Would you guys like some food?" Hailee asks, doubtlessly not wanting to linger on Thomas's nice gesture towards me.

"Absolutely," I respond without hesitation.

I eat two peanut butter sandwiches faster than I've ever eaten anything. I would ask for a third, but I

120

don't want to take all of her food, because by the looks of it, peanut butter and bread is almost all she has left.

Julie was allergic to peanut butter, I think, as I take my last bite. The unexpected reminder of her takes away all the happiness that was gained from the food. I swallow the last bite and am no longer hungry enough for a third one.

I lean back on the faded floral couch and stare at a seam breaking loose on the arm of it. So much in my life has changed drastically with no warnings whatsoever. Not too long ago, I was spending the night at Julie's house, thinking failing finals was the worst thing that could ever happen to me. Then, I thought her death was the worst thing that ever happened. I wouldn't even be here, in the capital city, in an old apartment I'm not even wanted in, had Julie not died. I would be home, with my parents and Julie, sheltering this storm together, but instead I'm here.

I have seen people hurt. I have seen people die. I've slept on the ground, in a cell, in a house with rich criminals, and on the back of a truck. None of this would have happened if Julie had not died. It's a nightmare catapulted into place by another nightmare.

The sound of Hailee's voice snaps me back into reality. I look up at her, rocking back and forth in her armchair. She had asked if I was okay.

"Yeah, I'm fine," I answer, then an awkward

silence fills the air. Thomas isn't in the room anymore and I didn't notice when he left.

"Listen," I say, breaking the silence, "I'm not your competition. I have no romantic interest in your boyfriend. None, whatsoever. I only stuck with him because I don't know how to survive in the apocalypse by myself —"

"It's not the apocalypse —"

"I know that you don't like me, but I'm not a threat to you. And whether this is the apocalypse or not, something crazy is happening. Just yesterday, I saw an entire city burning to the ground, okay? This world is going mad without power and none of us are going to survive this with petty arguments."

"You saw a city burning?" she asks in awe. "What are you talking about?"

She immediately stops rocking in her chair and her mouth hangs open.

"On the drive over here. I saw a city in the distance — it was completely engulfed in flames. The entire thing was on fire. That's why you can smell so much smoke in the air today."

"I thought someone was having a bonfire," she mutters, a little embarrassed.

"Yeah, a really big one," I laugh, attempting to make this conversation less uncomfortable.

Her eyes keep scanning the room, not wanting to make contact with mine.

"Last time I saw Thomas, I was visiting him in prison. He told me — and I quote — that I 'shouldn't

122

waste my life waiting on someone who isn't getting out any time soon.' He said I should live my life and not worry about his. All this time, I thought he said it because he cared about me, but then when he ran up to me and you were right behind him, a thought popped into my head. 'Oh, I see what really happened. He met another girl in the slammer and broke up with me to be with her instead.' I was furious and I didn't even know your name yet. I still can't remember it."

"It's Annalise," I inform her.

"Thanks." She smiles a little bit. "That's why I took him off to the side. I wanted to see where you two stood."

"There's nothing going on between us," I assure her.

"I believe you," she sighs. "I'm sorry for assuming the worst."

"It's okay. With everything that's going on around us, it's starting to feel like even when you assume the worst, you're still underestimating how terrible the circumstances really are," I sigh.

"Tell me about it," Hailee says, then lets out another fake laugh.

Slow footsteps coming from the hall to my left grow louder and Thomas reappears in the living room. Hailee's face lights up when he enters. Maybe she only acted so protective over him because she is crazy about him, or perhaps, she's just crazy. It's too soon to tell.

Hailee and I get along fairly well for the rest of the day. Thomas definitely notices the drastic change in the way we act around each other, because he keeps shooting both of us strange looks every time we're nice to each other.

When Hailee's not worried about me stealing her boyfriend, she's hilarious, sarcastic, and extremely nice. Her clinginess to Thomas is admittedly annoying; the way they always hold each other's hand and cuddle all the time. It's not because of either one of them, but I don't particularly enjoy seeing couples be mushy, mostly because I'm single. The more they cling to each other, the more I think I'm still not very wanted here. Thomas likes me and Hailee doesn't hate me anymore, but I think they would both be happier if it were just the two of them, and my absence would eliminate the risk of Thomas's ridiculous feelings towards me ruining what they have.

I remember what Hailee said about me earlier, how I follow him around like a lost puppy. It was a hurtful analogy, but an honest one. I have stuck by his side even when I thought he was making the wrong decision. Even now, when it is becoming increasingly obvious I'm intruding on their lives, I still can't convince myself to leave. Maybe I'll disappear in the middle of the night when they're both asleep and can't talk me out of it. But it's still daylight, and they're still awake, so I push the idea to the back of my mind and spend most of the day laying on the couch discussing plans I may not be around to execute.

"We're almost out of food," Hailee says, holding the almost empty jar of peanut butter.

Their food would last them a lot longer if I wasn't here to eat it. I add that to my long list of reasons to leave.

"Tomorrow morning we can check a few of the abandoned stores. There has to be some food left behind," Thomas replies.

He stands beside a window next to the kitchen as the last of the evening lights shines on his face and lights up his bright green eyes. I look over at him and notice how matted his hair is. It's always been curly, but it's beginning to resemble a bird's nest now. Almost as if he can hear my thoughts, he begins to run his hands through his hair and pull out some of the knots.

"I checked almost all of them already. No more food," Hailee sighs.

"Then we'll check the rest of them," he insists.

We eat the last of the peanut butter sandwiches in the barren living room. A lavender scented candle, sitting on the small table, lights up the room ever since the sun went down. The strong aroma of the candle mixes with the flavor of the food and makes me nauseated.

When Hailee finishes her sandwich, she lights a few more candles, all of them scented. Apparently, she loves them and stockpiled them before the blackout. Every single one of them has a different, very potent scent.

"Are we going to starve to death?" she asks casually, as she lights a candle labeled 'Euphoria.'

"No," Thomas replies quickly, scarfing down the last of his food. "I told you, we'll look for more food tomorrow."

He leans back in his seat, seemingly unaware of all the bread crumbs on his shirt.

"What if we don't find any?" Hailee ask stubbornly.

She strikes a match to light yet another candle, focusing on the fresh flame instead of making eye contact.

"We will," Thomas and I say in unison.

Hailee finally stops lighting candles, places the final one in the middle of the coffee table, and collapses into her arm chair. She slumps back into the cushions with a hopeless demeanor.

"I don't..." Hailee begins to speak, but never finishes her sentence.

Hunger may not be the only thing on her mind. She is overwhelmingly certain *something* will go wrong, that we won't make it somehow. I have no idea what she has gone through the past few weeks to make her so doubtful. Thomas never spoke of her being this way, though he never spoke of her clinginess either.

She's been surviving on her own ever since the blackout, but she's managed, and now that there are two other people to help her, she's worried it won't work. Maybe she has seen people die too, and that's what has her scared. Maybe she has always been like this and Thomas willingly chose not to mention it to me.

"We're not going to starve to death. There's plenty of food around here. We just have to find it," I tell Hailee with as much false hope as I can muster. I am momentarily transported back into prison, where I'm reminding Thomas, yet again, that things are not all terrible when they most certainly are. But that memory fades, reality reappears, and the real me still sits on the sunken couch.

Thomas walks over to Hailee, all of the crumbs falling off his shirt as he stands, and gives her a hug. I sit awkwardly by myself as they embrace each other.

Tears begin to form in her eyes, but Thomas can't see them, and she whispers, "You won't find anything."

ELEVEN

Hailee blows out the dozens of candles like a kid at a birthday party, but she leaves a few of them burning to light our way. The tiny apartment has already been filled in its entirety with a mixture of multiple different scents and my head pounds harder every time I inhale.

She hands each of us one candle to light our way. I pick 'Vanilla Voyage' because it has the weakest scent, and head down a short hall to the back bedroom that I won in the coin toss. I am relieved to find no candles have been lit in here, so I quickly close the door before the perfumes have a chance to float in.

The flame in my hand, and the moonlight shining in through the uncovered window on the opposite wall, allow me to navigate the small, rectangular room.

The light illuminates an extravagant, but mostly bare dresser. It seems to be a matching set with the bed frame.

The bed, which is tucked into a corner on the wall farther away from me, looks to have a finely decorated bedspread. Of course, if I was able to turn on the light, I might find it's dingy, old, and covered in stains, but the quality of the other items tell me it's brand new.

Curiously stacked boxes in the corner of the room, next to the dresser, indicate someone had either just moved in or was about to move out.

I walk across the squeaky wooden floor and set my jacket on the dresser. Some change, a few candy wrappers, outdated gift cards, and a few long receipts are the only other things atop it. It appears someone finally emptied out their wallet and never came back to clean it up.

Dirty clothes are piled up between the dresser and the moving boxes. A silky red dress lies at the very top of the stack. I notice the price tag is still on it, and my curiosity dares me to look. I hold it up to the window and behold a $7,000 price tag. I immediately drop it back on the stack and turn my eyes away.

Does all of this stuff belong to Hailee, or did someone else live here before the blackout? If so, who was it, and why are they no longer here? Something about it reminds me too much of Mark and Katherine, so I don't linger on the thought.

I set the candle down on the dresser and blow it out. I take off my shoes, jump into bed, and pull the sheets over me. Everything on the bed smells new and fresh, and soft silk sheets invite me to sleep forever, but I can't.

The prospect of leaving this place bubbles to the surface of my mind, yet again. In just a little while, Thomas and Hailee will both be asleep and I can leave unnoticed, unable to be stopped by Thomas, who will surely beg me to stay, even though we both know it's for the best that I am not around to intrude on their lives.

They would surely be better off without me, though I would probably die on my own. I know Hailee said she believes me, but I don't want to have to constantly reassure her there's nothing going on between Thomas and me, or run the risk of something actually happening. Not to mention, the food supply is running awfully low. So, when they're asleep, and I'll definitely know Thomas is asleep by his snoring, I will sneak out. I will disappear from their lives forever and they will soon forget that I was ever a part of it.

I sit up in the bed so I don't drift off. I stare at a clock on the wall with its hand stuck, telling me it's 12:30 for the next two hours. When the lawn mower starts up — I mean, when Thomas starts snoring, I step out of the silky sheets onto the icy floor. I grab my jacket and I tiptoe across the room. I step out into the pitch black hallway and press my hand up against a wall. I let it guide me to the exit. Every single step lets out a long creak that sounds infinitely louder than it did in the daytime.

I make it into the living room where the candle Thomas was using flickers on the coffee table, lighting up his face.

I tiptoe to the front door and reach around for the doorknob. I'm slowly twisting it when a cold rush of air freezes my toes and I realize I left my shoes in the bedroom. I have to go back.

I turn around, heading back to the only fancy room in this dingy apartment. I re-enter the living room and watch Thomas exhale so strongly he puts out the flame of the candle in front of him and I'm left in total darkness. I stop in my tracks. A lightbulb goes off in my head the same time the light is extinguished. Instead of going forward down the hall, I take a left and inch my way across the living room, to the door that leads to what I believe to be Hailee's room. I brush up against the coffee table, which does not seem to wake Thomas, and eventually find my way to the door. I slowly open it, which lets out a creak that echoes so much it should have woken up the entire apartment complex.

I shut the door behind me and now I'm standing in the pitch black of Hailee's bedroom.

"Hailee?" I whisper. No response. "Hailee?"

"Wuhhh?" she mumbles from a state of total oblivion. She's awake but she doesn't know it yet.

"It's me — Annalise," I whisper. That seems to have caught her attention.

"Is Thomas okay?" she asks in concern.

"No, yeah. He's fine. Everything's good. I just have a few questions for you."

"What?" she mumbles, followed by the sound of her banging into something. I hear the strike of a match and the candle on Hailee's nightstand begins to flicker, casting waves of light on her half-awake face.

"Who lived in the room I was staying in? What happened to her?" I venture a risky question.

She looks down at her hands while she twiddles her fingers, or maybe it's only the quivering flame casting the illusion that she is. "Why do you want to know?"

"C'mon. Someone really rich had just moved in. She's not here, and you haven't mentioned who or *where* she is. Did she die? Is that why you're so concerned about the food situation?"

Hailee starts sniffling and the candle light reflects brightly off her glassy eyes.

"Clara — she was a rich, trust fund baby until her parents had cut her off. They let her keep some of what they had previously bought for her. She moved in two weeks before *it* happened. She hadn't finished unpacking yet. Then the night after it went down, people were going crazy, fighting in the streets, screaming for loved ones they couldn't find. We hid in the apartment, but some guy, he came in..." Her voice cracks and she begins to shake. "He broke in and tried to rob us. He didn't think anyone was home. Clara tried to stop him while I hid away in here because I was too scared." Hailee is bawling now, so I sit next to her on the bed and put a hand on her shoulder. "Two days ago was the first time I left the apartment since she died, and the only reason I could convince myself to do it was because I had no food left. I looked all day and found nothing. Everything had already been cleared out. She died because I hid and now we'll all starve to death because I continued to hide."

"No, no. Don't blame yourself for what happened to her! And we're not going to starve!" I insist.

"Who else is to blame?" She pushes me away.

"How about the guy who broke in here and killed her?"

"He wouldn't have killed her if I had stepped out of my room and helped her," she whimpers.

"No, he would've killed both of you," I say to her.

Her face is wet with tears, and in the reflection of them, I see myself sitting in my room crying over Julie. People blamed me endlessly for her death, to the point I began to carry the burden of responsibility. I knew I hadn't killed her, but if I had been with her when it happened, could I have stopped it? Should I have been there? I know the pain Hailee is experiencing, so I have to be strong for her. She cannot blame herself for this. She cannot linger on something irreversible.

She presses her face into her hands and whispers, "At least then she wouldn't have died alone."

"Hailee, you can't do this to yourself. What happened wasn't your fault. I'm sorry I brought it up. I knew something happened there, but I didn't realize how painful it was for you." I try to hug her, though hugs are unbearably awkward for me. She pushes me away again, to my relief and frustration.

"We won't... We won't make it," she says to me through sniffles. "We'll all die, like her. All there is here is death."

"No, we won't. We'll survive," I say, but I'm not sure if it's the truth. "I've seen death too, but there's still life. There's still hope. I'm not going to roll over and die."

Hailee ponders this for a moment. "You've seen death. Is that why you were in prison, for killing someone?"

"I was falsely imprisoned," I mumble hastily, then slowly get up and make my way to the door. This is not what I came in here to talk about, and I'm not sure how either of us are going to handle this discussion, though I feel guilty for backing away from someone who so clearly needs comfort.

"Falsely imprisoned for what?" Her voice shakes as she asks me.

"They said I murdered my best friend, but I didn't. I would never, ever do that."

I wait for some kind of response, but Hailee never gives one. She only cries into her hands. I get the sense that she now wants me to leave, so I swiftly exit the room, but instead of walking out of the front

134

door as I initially planned, I return to the guest room.

There's a chance Hailee may not want me here now, but I can't abandon them. Leaving them behind would be the same as telling Hailee they are doomed, so I hightailed it out of that situation, while simultaneously dooming myself, because I have no way to survive on my own. I have to stay. Besides, if I left, I would be doing exactly what I accused Thomas of doing twice. It would be wrong to leave, as much as I may want to.

Hailee wakes me up around midday and I could still go back to sleep for another five hours. My body is definitely trying to make up for the previous days unrest.

After she wakes me, Hailee hands me a pile of clothes to wear, but she acts suspiciously cold and distant.

"They may not fit too well, but at least they're clean," she says blankly, then rushes out of the room without another word.

Maybe she is still not over the initial shock of what I told her. I guess it can be a lot to process, but it's not like I told her I *actually* killed someone.

I sort through the clothes — a T-shirt for a band I've never heard of, that's twice my size, high waisted skinny jeans that fit surprisingly well, underwear fresh out of the package, and yellow socks that fall off my feet as soon as I put them on. No jacket, though, so I have to put on the once very nice, but now very stained and dingy bomber jacket Katherine stole for me.

I slide on my boots that Katherine also stole for me, and walk down the short, squeaky hallway into the living room to find that Thomas and Hailee are already dressed, waiting on me.

"The grocery store I used to work at over on Henderson might be worth looking over again," Hailee says, seeming to only acknowledge Thomas when she does. She starts heading for the door but topples over and crashes into the wall.

The room has begun to shake violently. Thomas dives to cover Hailee, apparently aware of what's happening, but it takes me longer to realize it. We're in the middle of an earthquake.

I'm about to dive for cover, but something right in front of my face makes me abruptly jump back. I look around and it's everywhere; some sort of pale purple, translucent field all around us, covering the room. I can see straight through it, but everything on the other side seems slightly distorted and unreal.

Part of the roof falls off and hits the amethyst formation filling the room. It falls right off the side of it and leaves no visible signs of damage, but I twinge at the impact. It was as if the broken roof had slammed straight into my back without touching me.

The unidentified substance trespassing in the room resembles a forcefield you would find in a sci-fi movie, but it's too wispy, too erratic. It's more along

136

the lines of a malfunctioning prototype of a forcefield, and its light purple flashes a darker shade when more of the roof hits it, but then returns to something almost pastel and ghostly.

Hailee and Thomas are both curled up next to the wall and Thomas is covering Hailee, protecting her from falling objects, and staring aghast at the peculiar field of color.

"What are you doing?" Hailee screams at me in horror.

The old chandelier in front of the doorway is ripped from the ceiling by the earthquake. It shatters on impact and thousands of glass shards are sent flying in every direction.

"Are you okay?" I shout back at her. "And what are you talking about?"

She looks up to reveal that her face is now red with her own blood. Thomas was burrowing his face into Hailee's jacket when it shattered, so he may have gotten out unscathed, but I can't tell.

"I'm fine," Hailee lies. "How are you doing that?"

An immense fear pours over her, one even greater than what I saw as she bawled her eyes out last night, and it baffles me.

"What the heck are you talking about?" I shout back at her, but then the realization hits me with the same violence as the earthquake.

I stare in disbelief at the wispy mass that fills the room, the one that is focused entirely around *me*.

TWELVE

The violent earthquake finally stops, but only after several more gigantic chunks of ceiling fall away and are deflected by the enigmatic forcefield. The strange mass finally dissipates into the air after the shaking dies down.

"How did you do that?" Hailee lividly demands, then marches towards me, though she is shaking with fright and her panicked eyes betray her angry scowl and harsh voice.

Several small cuts cover Hailee's right side and Thomas wipes them clean as she attempts to grimace at me. Her face is pale from blood loss and fear.

"I — I don't know. Was I even doing that? I couldn't have been..." I fumble over my words and I become lightheaded. I have no way to explain or comprehend what I have just witnessed, and I cannot bring myself to put on a persona like Hailee is.

"Then why was it —"

"I don't think we can stay here anymore," Thomas cuts in before Hailee can probe me any further, though right now he appears as terrified of me as she does.

A large part of one of the walls fell down, along with most of the roof. You can look upwards and see the mostly clear sky up above. Smoke from the fire still lingers on, but if you can ignore that, it seems as though nothing is wrong, but then you look out of the holes in the walls and people are lying dead in the street, or at least that's what Hailee said when she made the mistake of peering outside.

"That guy's head is sma —" She turned away quickly, tears in her eyes, and ran to Thomas for comfort. She may not have finished her sentence, but it's not hard to figure out she was about to say "smashed."

All the walls that didn't fall down are cracked and weak. If we stay in here any longer, there is no doubt it will cave in on us.

"Let's grab our stuff and go," I urge them, "before the whole building drops."

Hailee heads to her room to grab a few things and Thomas follows her, still trying to wipe her face clean. I stand in the living room, regaining my composure and balance instead of packing up, because it didn't hit me until now that I don't own anything to take with me. The closest I have come to owning anything since I was convicted was having the clothes on my back, and briefly, the stolen backpack of a dead man.

I notice the last of Hailee's food sitting on the kitchen counter and I walk over to grab it so we don't leave it behind.

139

Creaaaakkk! A noise comes from beneath me as soon as I take my first step. I look down to see I've been standing directly on a crack that spreads the length of the floor. Bits and pieces had already fallen off to the apartment down below. I lightly step around it, snatch up the food, turn around, leap for the door, and... fall through the floor.

I land on a pile of plywood from the room above and the impact knocks every bit of air out of my lungs. Pain surges through every inch of my body and I inhale a bucket full of plaster dust while trying to regain my breath.

As soon as I sit up and take a deep breath, the pain suddenly ceases. I look around at a room that was probably decent five minutes ago, but is now covered in large chunks of the apartment above. The walls are lined with growing, unsettling cracks. It's the same setup as Hailee's apartment, except it has significantly more furniture, decorations, and shattered picture frames, though no other living person seems to be present here.

"Are you okay?" Thomas says from above me. He's leaning over the hole in the floor. He places his hand on the edge. It breaks off and lands beside me.

"I'm fine. Back up before the floor gives in on you!" I shout at him.

"Are you sure you're okay?" he asks again without backing away.

"It's only a seven foot drop! I'm fine. I'll meet you guys right outside," I insist.

140

"Okay," Thomas sighs.

"Move, Thomas! You're going to fall through the floor," Hailee insists. I can't see her, but I see the floor above me bend and bow with every step she takes.

"I'm not that heavy!" he proclaims in defense.

"You weigh more tha —"

Thud! The floor under Hailee gives way and she comes crashing through it, landing on her feet, right beside me. As she hits, she drops to her knees and the floor we're sitting on begins to creak and rattle too.

"Are you okay?" Thomas and I ask in unison.

"Fine. Fine," she repeats as she tries to stand. I rush over and help her the rest of the way up, but she pushes me back and almost knocks me into a pile of rubble. "I'm alright!"

"Now there's holes in front of me and behind me. I can't get out!" Thomas says.

"Then climb down here, it's not that far," Hailee replies, and Thomas casts a wary look to the floor we're standing on too.

"Hey, exactly how unstable was this building before, if it's cracking so easily now?" I laugh.

"Rent was only $300 a month, so it was probably on the verge of collapse already," Hailee bellows. The laugh is frighteningly loud, fake, and unsteady.

Thomas slowly drops down to our floor, which is beginning to crack as well, so I make no effort to stick around.

The wooden staircase is splintered and sticking up in many places. It makes an unnerving crunching sound with every step we take. Other people are also walking down the broken stairs, but for the most part, it's empty.

"Every room in the building is rented out. Where is everyone?" Hailee ponders.

"They're probably not coming out because they're dead!" an old man, walking in front of us, says to his wife, as if she's the one who asked.

"Don't you say things like that, Richard!" She slaps his arm.

"I'm only telling the truth!" he chuckles.

After six flights of stairs on the verge of collapse, we're out into the open air. Everyone on the streets looks horrified — everyone still living, that is. All around are cracked roads, buildings turned to rubble, and the empty shells of the unlucky souls who did not survive. I've experienced earthquakes before, but never at this magnitude.

"Can we help them?" Thomas asks, distraught.

"We can't raise the dead," Hailee mumbles, "and whatever we could say wouldn't ease the living's pain. We need to get out of here. Which way?"

"We should head that way." I point to the right with my finger, though I'm not sure *why* we should head that way. My mind is still stuck inside apartment 623, staring at the purple mass encasing me...

"I think that's north," Thomas says. "Maybe Ashland. I know some people up there, but that might be too far."

"Anywhere is fine with me. I just want to get away from here," Hailee murmurs, and begins stomping away in the direction Thomas mentioned.

There are dead bodies all along the streets and we do our best to ignore them. There's nothing we can do to help, and if I look at them for too long, think about them for too long, I will break down, but it seems wrong to pass them by as if they aren't there.

"Yes, so that's north, which means we came up from that way." I point back the way we originally came from. "Which is south, so keep heading north. Yeah..."

I trail off. Both Thomas and Hailee stare awkwardly at me. Evidently, they expected me to say something eloquent and important, but I failed miserably. Every second is more confusing and harder to bear than the last. I want to be helping people but I don't know how and I, too, want to get away from here; far away from whatever that was in Hailee's apartment that I did *not* cause.

"Anyway, that way we go." Thomas points dramatically, mocking me.

Hailee giggles. "Who do you know in Ashla — What was that?"

That was gunfire. At the sound of it, every living person in the vicinity immediately drops to the ground. Dozens let out screams, but it's impossible to tell if it was from terror or being shot.

"I don't want to die," "What's going on?" and "Who did that?" are being muttered by several people who are huddled in all around us. These strangers are pressed in far too close for comfort.

"Everything is going straight into the toilet, isn't it?" I whisper. "Next thing you know, it's —"

"It's the military!" a random man, two feet to my left, shouts at everyone. My ears begin to ring as my heart sinks into the ground.

Hailee, Thomas, and I simultaneously look up. Armed men in uniform are coming near the crowd, with trucks moving in right behind them. One man barking out orders leads them, marching right toward us.

The crowd is growing erratic, pushing at each other. Some pushing towards the armed men, and others away from them.

Hailee's face has turned white as a sheet and I think she is about to pass out, but instead she narrows her eyes at the gunmen and says, "We have to leave. Now."

Thomas immediately grabs mine and Hailee's hands and slowly pulls us away from the crowd. Most are flocking towards the soldiers and demanding medical attention. Everyone else has risen, so I stand up too, knowing my small frame is lost within a sea of tall people, and none of the men up ahead can see me through it.

The rushing in of people like flood waters is making my heart beat a hundred times faster than it should. I'm going against the current and I'm drowning under the waves, about to be swallowed up and trampled by it.

"We're going to die," I whisper.

"I told you so," Hailee whines bitterly, which only makes my panicking worse.

"You three! Stop!" a man shouts in the distance.

My heart stops, seemingly in sync with the crowd which has come to a stand still. *Oh, no. They spotted us.*

I cannot see the man who was shouting, but more gunfire goes off and some people who were so eager to run towards the soldiers are now falling back.

The gunman must have shot down another trio, not us, but my heart is pounding so hard it has become almost impossible to breathe. I'm overwhelmed by a great discomfort, far different from anything I have ever felt before, and the entire crowd is rapidly backing away from me. Even Hailee and Thomas are retreating.

The dysfunctional lavender mass has reappeared all around me, and only me. Everyone is staring at it in awe and trepidation. A young child squirms out of her mother's arms and reaches out for it. She places her hand on the curious creation, five feet away from my face, and I *feel* it somehow. Now I know I am truly causing this. This horrifyingly real forcefield belongs to me and me alone.

"Stand down!" a voice bellows. I whip around and my eyes land on the person who shouted. It's the man who was leading the march. At first, he was too far away to recognize him, but now I do. It's General Kaine. The man who showed up at Mark and Katherine's house. He survived.

He points his hand up at me and without hesitation a dozen of his soldiers advance and surround the edge of *my* forcefield, guns aimed at me.

"Don't shoot!" I yell, and fall onto the ground.

"Kill *it!*" the general viciously urges the soldiers.

I close my eyes so I don't have to watch as they fire at me. A dozen gunshots louder than I have ever heard in my life sound off at every angle.

I'm dead. I'm sure I'm dead, but how am I still thinking if I'm dead? How am I not in pain? Do I hear myself crying?

I open my tear-filled eyes to see the disastrous place I thought I had left behind. I'm not dead. I'm not laying on the ground, bullet riddled and bleeding out. Instead, every man who shot at me is collapsed on the street.

THIRTEEN

The bullets ricocheted off the forcefield and back into the men who fired the shots. I stare at the dead soldiers in wonder. It takes a moment to process all of it, but then the realization of it strikes me down. I am now responsible for the death of a dozen absolute strangers because something I don't know how to control decided they should die instead of me.

The horrified faces of the crowd are pressed up against the broken background that used to be the bustling, lively city of Columbus. Some bystanders are shaking in fear of me and others are, somehow, more afraid of the men who shot at me. The trembling families leave out in herds. The general doesn't stop them. Almost all of his men are dead, and he's furious.

Hailee and Thomas look back and forth between me and the dead men. The forcefield morphs their faces a bit but I can tell they are just as afraid of me as everyone else is.

I want to scream for them to run away with the crowd, but I don't. I sit. Unable to move. Unable to speak. Unable to process what I've just experienced — what I've just done.

It makes no sense, but at the same time, it explains so much — the guard at the prison who was mysteriously lifted off me and slammed into a tree, the soldier who flew into the windshield of his car. That was *me.* That was my forcefield doing that — protecting me.

The purple mass dissipates into nothingness and I have no protection from the crowd or from the remaining soldiers, who surely want me dead more than ever, yet I can't move. Everything within me is urging me to run, but I'm paralyzed.

The remaining men storm at me and push me to the ground. My face smashes into the asphalt as they pull my arms behind my back and tie them up. One of the men puts a fabric bag over my head while another one pats me down. I see nothing but bits of sunlight shining through worn pieces of the bag. The men force me to stand, then I'm blindly guided where they want me to go.

We draw closer to the sound of a revving engine. I'm pushed inside the vehicle that will carry me away to a court, back to prison, where I now truly belong, or maybe to a death chamber, where I will immediately be executed for my crime.

"No, no! I haven't done anything wrong! I'm not with her! I'm not responsible!" Hailee cries from behind me.

"Don't you dare touch her! Ow! Let her go!" Thomas shouts at the men, who then gag him so he will stop yelling about Hailee.

148

General Kaine is taking both of them with me, to be punished for the unexplainable and heinous act I have unintentionally committed.

After hours of riding in the back of a vehicle in darkness and silence, we finally come to a halt, accompanied by the unmistakable screech of a giant fence being opened.

I'm back at the prison, the thought crosses my mind and sends me into yet another panic. We move forward a few hundred feet and the engine shuts off. Someone pulls the bag off my head and all my unbrushed hair falls in front of my face.

With my hands still tied, I am ordered to exit the vehicle, along with Hailee and Thomas, two innocent bystanders being punished for my abnormality.

The soldiers grab onto us and lead the way to what appears to be an old warehouse with a giant number "8" recently sprayed painted on the side of it in crimson. It doesn't look to be a prison, but something about it reminds me of one and it gives me an unnerving, creeping sensation that puts me farther on edge than I thought was possible.

We walk to the entrance, escorted by the furious general, along with a tall, bulky man with dark skin, and a pale, scrawny man that's too skinny for his uniform. He has a scar on his forehead that he's trying and failing to cover with his bleach blond hair. He wears a bitter façade and squeezes my arm much too tightly.

To my left are rows of other warehouses with the numbers 1 through 7 spray painted on in the same crimson red. In the distance I see a few unnumbered buildings and an open field behind them. I risk a glance behind us and I see a building identical to the one we're headed towards with a giant "16" painted on it. Surrounding all of this is one bleak, towering wall, more sturdy and reinforced than the one I crawled through after the blackout. What kind of place needs better security than a legitimate prison?

Muffled screams and shouts penetrate through the walls of the warehouse and grow ever louder. The sound sends shivers down my spine and crawls through my skin like a million skittish ants. I glance over at Hailee who is still ghost pale, but luckily her wounds seem to be minor and have stopped bleeding. She notices me looking at her and shoots me a death glare that makes it evident she is not happy to be dragged into my problems. I don't blame her.

The dark-haired man takes out a key ring with dozens of almost identical keys on it, unlocks the metal door, and swings it open. The general rushes in before anyone else, and the blond soldier pushes me through the door.

Once inside, the first thing I notice are lights overhead. I thought everywhere was drained of all electricity, but this place has suspiciously maintained theirs, and because of it I can see every person packed into the room. Faces are put to the screaming

150

voices, and to my surprise, the faces aren't bloody, disfigured, or being violently tortured.

Hundreds of teenagers are running rampant through a makeshift sleeping area. Old bunk beds are squeezed right next to each other all across the building. Most people are running around or jumping from one bed to another. I'm thankful to find torture isn't taking place in here, but I'm not entirely sure what *is* taking place.

My first thought is that they must all be in the military, given they're all wearing the same regulation beige T-shirts and camouflage pants. Of course, this thought only lasts for a second before a child, far too young to be enlisted, rushes by me and I come to my senses. These are the kids that went missing. These are the kids the military took to keep them "safe." They probably had bags put over their heads, were pushed into a truck, and ended up here without a way out.

Most of the teenagers look happy and cheerful. One kid, who's jumping beds, gives the general a satisfied smirk and it suddenly becomes clear why they're doing this. It's an act of rebellion. They want to make the general mad. He's torn them away from their parents and crammed them all into one place, and they want him to pay for it.

"Calm down!" the general demands of the rambunctious crowd.

No one complies, although most probably can't hear him over the people screaming as loud as they can, for no other reason than to irritate the general.

Both of the soldiers yell for everyone to sit down, and a few people obey, but most continue being wild out of bold defiance. General Kaine's frustration is obvious and his patience is worn very thin. He looks over at one of the soldiers and nods. The soldier then proceeds to slam a random girl's head into a bunk bed, knocking her out cold.

At this, several more kids submit and stand down, but everyone else seems completely determined to do exactly the opposite of whatever the general says, running by at top speed and almost pushing me into Hailee more than once.

"I will not have this!" the general fumes, then pulls a handgun out of nowhere. Without hesitation he shoots a young boy who could have been no more than twelve years old. The bullet cracks his skull and the kid falls back, landing right at my feet. I barely manage to stifle a massive scream, then glance down at his white-blond hair, now sticky with his own blood, and his face staring up at me.

I immediately pull my eyes away from him and push back the tears starting to well in them. I cannot allow myself to, once again, break down in the presence of such evil men. If I begin to cry, I won't be able to stop, and who knows what they might do to shut me up.

The general points his gun at a terrified kid standing right next to his dead friend. "Do not force it upon me to shoot you too, son. Every single one of you better sit down and shut your mouths before I have you maimed!"

This time, everyone obeys. None of them were expecting the general to kill someone over this, but I'm not surprised. I have seen it before.

One of the guards cuts off the ropes around our wrists and leads us across the room. Faces plastered with horrified expressions follow our every move as we are escorted to two empty bunks.

"You'll stay here," the blond soldier barks.

I sit down on one bunk, Hailee and Thomas take the other.

"That bed belonged to Talia," a girl with tired eyes scoffs at me as I take a seat on my newly assigned bunk. I say nothing to her, or anyone, but many continue to stare.

"Why's everyone looking at us?" Hailee whispers to Thomas.

"I don't know," he whispers back.

But I do. Though we have done nothing that they know of, the people here will forever associate our arrival here with the death of an innocent boy, and we will not be able to undo that.

I watch as the soldier who shot the kid drags away his lifeless body, showing no regard for his life or his death, and even letting his limp head hit the wall on the way out. A definite smirk shows on the man's face as it happens.

The general and his henchmen finally leave, but only after a ten minute long speech from him about how we cannot possibly think that we get to do whatever we want here. He talks about how we're in a war and we cannot play games, but I was not informed that a war had started. All I knew was that the power was gone, but it appears even that was not entirely true.

"The rules will be enforced and people who do not follow those rules will suffer the same fate as Mr. Jackson." Mr. Jackson being the kid he murdered in order to appear powerful. "We will undoubtedly come out victorious in this vicious war, but to do so, you must obey me, not rebel against me. You will obey! You will train tirelessly and ready yourselves for battle! You will fight for *me,* not against *me!*" He shouts the last part at least ten times before leaving.

People begin to talk amongst themselves as soon as he exits, but my mind stays focused on the image of the boy and this war I was unaware we were taking part in. The war we have apparently been brought here to train for. The war the general just so boldly claimed the boy died for, but no enemy soldier ambushed us and took his life. That boy is dead for no other reason than a man wanting to prove a point. The point that he doesn't care about us, the point that he is the leader here, and he will shoot us for not obeying his orders. And I will not obey his orders.

A mandatory bedtime is enforced at 9ᴾᴹ. The power this place should not even have shuts off, and most people lie down, but continue their conversations in whispers.

"Don't let the guards outside hear you," a young girl, about fourteen, whispers to us from her bunk a few feet away.

"Yeah, they hate when we talk past curfew," her friend says.

"Okay, thanks," I whisper back, and they return to quietly talking and laughing with a group of their friends.

Time ticks on as I lay staring at the bunk above my head. More and more people fall asleep. After a few hours, all the whispers die down and snoring takes its place. Once most everyone is asleep I whisper to Thomas. "What are we going to do?"

The heads of our beds touch each other. Thomas took the bottom bunk, because Hailee insisted on having the top one all to herself. She would not even allow me to take the top of this bunk because she didn't want anyone beside her.

"About what?" he asks in a groggy voice. He had nearly fallen asleep when I disturbed him.

"Um, about the giant cage we've just been locked in," I scowl, and he looks up at me and rubs his eyes. "Does this not feel wrong to you? The second things went bad they used it as an excuse to enforce this madness into place and now they're acting like the

155

ultimate authority. What's the point of forcing us all in here, and what *war* are they talking about?"

"I don't know, Anna. I'm as confused as you are," he mumbles, and lays his head back down.

"I can't hear what you guys are saying," Hailee says, leaning over the bunk to pop her head into the conversation.

"Just come down here," Thomas says.

Hailee climbs down and cuddles up next to Thomas to listen in.

"What are you two talking about?" she whispers to Thomas.

"I think they caused it," I reply.

"Who caused what?"

"I think the people here, the government, the military, whatever — I think they caused the power outage. They obviously had a plan in place. They had trucks rushing out the moment it happened and they've obviously been hoarding teenagers here ever since, maybe even sooner," I mumble, and Hailee repeatedly rolls her eyes at me, but I keep talking anyway. "Why would they do that just because the power went out? Not to mention, they have very quickly turned to using violence and fear tactics. There's something else going on here. I mean, they still have *electricity*. How is that even possible?"

"That's a little crazy, don't you think? Turning the power off to round up teenagers?" Condescension flows out of her mouth.

"Of course it is, but it's also the only thing that makes sense," I say.

"Well," she snaps, "you can't go around accusing the government of something like that, especially without a single ounce of proof."

"I haven't gone around anywhere," I snap back more fiercely. "I've only said it to you two. Our government has never been the brightest or the most honest, why should we start believing they are now, after all of this? Besides, I plan on finding proof."

I have spent far too long hiding from the truth of what happened almost three weeks ago, but after all I have seen today, I can no longer ignore it with a clean conscience. Too much death and pain has occurred in my oblivion. Maybe my intuition is wrong, but it tells me finding answers is the only way to prevent it from happening again.

"How will you find proof?" Thomas asks curiously.

"You don't actually believe her theory, do you?" Hailee glares at Thomas.

"I haven't got any better ones."

"Maybe we really are at war and they're here to help us. There's a theory!"

Hailee leaves and climbs back up on her top bunk without saying another word. Thomas has one of those Jim-from-The-Office looks on his face right now. How Hailee can bring herself to defend these monsters after watching them kill a child is beyond me. I might be jumping to conclusions, but I have a strong feeling she's only doing it because she doesn't want to agree with anything I say.

"Maybe, she's right," Thomas says halfheartedly in the interest of defending his girlfriend.

"She's not," I mouth back to him.

"So, uhh, how do you plan on finding proof of your theory?" he asks, and rests his head on his arms, now only inches away from my face.

"I have absolutely no idea. Maybe, I could snoop around, ask some of the other people here? Or I could get one of the people guarding this place to talk…"

"Talk to the blond one, if he's guarding this place," Thomas suggests.

"Why?" I inquire.

"Because he was staring at you," he informs me. "As we walked down the driveway, even when the other guy shot that kid, he was looking at you."

"The shooting didn't even faze him?" My jaw drops.

"No, it didn't phase any of the soldiers. I guess they're used to them. Do you think they happen a lot here?"

"Probably, but I don't think someone unfazed by murder is exactly the kind of person I want to talk to," I say nervously. "Maybe I could find a less violent accomplice?"

"I think he's your best shot, man," he sighs. "The odds of finding someone who doesn't want to be here and has secrets ready to be spilled could be slim

158

to none. If they are hiding something, with the scale of it all, it couldn't be something they would give up easily. I think your best chance is to seduce someone into telling you."

I gawk at him wide-eyed. "Seduce? I can't seduce someone. I can't even flirt, and how would I casually bring up what's going on in a conversation? 'Hey, cutie. You wanna tell me if the government sabotaged itself in order to round up teenagers? By the way, you look cute in that uniform.'" I offer Thomas an exaggerated wink for effect. He rolls his eyes at me.

"It won't be that hard, and at the very least, maybe you can get him to sneak us out of here —"

"Yes," Hailee says from above us and pops her head back down. Apparently, she *can* hear what we're saying from up there. "Get us out of here."

Hailee's insistence on leaving only proves to me she really does see what I'm talking about, but refuses to admit it.

"Why don't one of you seduce him?" I resentfully insist.

"Because this was your plan," says Hailee spitefully from above me. Her long hair flows down to the bunk below and Thomas plays with it.

"And he doesn't seem to like either of us." Thomas smirks, twirling Hailee's wavy hair in his fingers.

"I'll try," I sigh, "but this feels wrong."

"Anna, if you're right, *and you are*," he whispers almost inaudibly so Hailee won't hear him say it, "and they're not here to protect us, then we're in danger, and everyone in this building could be in danger, too. You know how they kill people without hesitation," he says, more fearfully now. "I don't want any of us to die. Just promise you'll try?"

"Okay," I resentfully agree.

"Good, now get some sleep."

He lays down and is out in seconds, but I can't sleep. How could I in a place like this, surrounded by caged children and armed guards?

Thomas spoke in fear of the murders our captors committed, but willfully ignored how I killed a dozen men only hours ago, though I'm sure it won't leave his mind any time soon. Is it possible he is just as afraid of me as he is of them? I know how terrified he looked when it happened, but has that terror not left him? It hasn't left me...

I struggle for hours to find rest, and I finally find my peace after a good thirty minutes of racking my brain about who the Talia girl is that previously resided on this bunk, and why she's no longer here. I don't enjoy any of the possibilities that come to my mind. Sleep finally comes somewhere between the idea that she was brutally slain, or the ignorant hope that she was simply allowed to leave peacefully.

The sleep I find disappears again. Then returns. Then leaves. On and on again until it is morning and the guards come in shouting at us to get up and be

160

ready to be escorted to the cafeteria in fifteen minutes. I notice the blond-haired man with the scar is among the guards. He strides over to us and hands us the same regulation uniforms everyone else is wearing. His eyes linger a little too long on me when he hands me my uniform. Now I know Thomas was right about him, but part of me had hoped he was wrong, so I would have to find a different approach to getting information.

"Where do we change into our clothes?" I ask Thomas. He hesitates to answer me and then I realize why: There's nowhere else to change other than right where I'm standing. Everyone else is undressing right in front of their bunks, so I rush to put the uniform on while all the people are distracted with their own clothes. Hailee kindly agrees to stand in front of me and block me from most everyone's view. I return the favor. For a moment I think her offer means she is no longer mad at me, but I know that cannot be true. I know this is not a typical argument that will blow over in a few days.

Hailee may have only met me two days ago, but she hates my guts from now until eternity, with good reason.

FOURTEEN

On our way to one of the two giant cafeterias, people emerge from multiple buildings identical to ours as we pass by them. Apparently, the buildings people reside in are referred to as "Reds," so I am a resident of Red 8. The buildings the soldiers stay in, the cafeterias, and a few buildings with secretive uses are called "Blues." Today we are eating breakfast in Blue 2. Like high school there are meal schedules here. However, the schedules are pretty loose and you usually end up eating with groups from different buildings every day. Or, at least that's what the oddly chatty girl walking next to me said, minus the comparison to high school, which I added myself, because something about this horrid place has an air of similarity. Maybe it's the prison aspect of it, which coincidentally reminds me of the time I spent in an actual prison. It's strange to think back to that time only a few weeks ago, where at only eighteen I was living out a life sentence, ineligible for parole, seemingly no future ahead of me. It's also strange to think of how far away my time there feels, but I should be used to that sensation. All of my life feels so far away from me now.

Everyone is flooding into a cafeteria at least five times the size of the one at my old school, with walls painted ugly, cracking shades of gray and beige, and high ceilings. The place is dingy and has a mixed scent of old age and cleaning products, with no smell of food to be found anywhere.

As I'm waiting in line for my meal, I have a chance to look around at everyone. People from ages six to thirty, all of various levels of health and fitness, are being held here. Most of these people would never have been allowed in here had the government not decided it needed to kidnap a bunch of people to fight in their potentially fictitious war.

I stand in line for well over half an hour before finally getting cold and unappetizing looking sausages with toast and blocks of eggs. I seat myself on a bench at a table near the middle of the room, squeezed between Hailee and the girl who has introduced herself as Kaetlynn while chatting my ear off in line. Yes, K-A-E-T-L-Y-N-N. That's her real name and that's how it's really spelled. Thomas sits opposite of us, in between a man and woman in their mid-twenties who look exactly alike.

Before I can convince myself to take a bite out of an egg block that definitely isn't made out of real eggs, General Kaine's voice echoes around the room through a megaphone, commanding us all to be quiet so he can speak. Thomas and the twins block my view of the general, not that I particularly mind not having to look at his wrinkled face shouting authoritative nonsense.

"I see we have more new recruits today, so allow me to thank all the newcomers for giving your loyalty and service to us." His shouts of false enthusiasm are warbled through the megaphone. *"Recruits," huh? That's an interesting slang term for "prisoners" that I've never heard before.*

"He gives the exact same speech every morning," one of the twins states before stuffing his face.

"We have been attacked by enemy forces," the warbled voice of the general says.

"Who threaten our very existence!" the other twins says in an irritated tone, in sync with the general's speech.

"They threatened our families, our friends, and our own lives, and they have declared war on us with an EMP strike that has knocked out all of our electricity and technology, crippling our society and putting us on the brink of total destruction," he shouts as the lights flicker. Yes, this unnamed enemy has *definitely* knocked out all of our electricity. "They wish to wipe out everything we know and we have a need, no, a moral duty to fight back against it! That is why you have all been assembled here. That is why we are going to train you into the best militia this country has ever known. We will destroy their plans. We will snuff out their fire. We are at war and we will win!"

The megaphone cuts off in the middle of the word "win" and everyone slowly returns to eating their foul food. He never mentioned the kid he killed last night. Instead, he spoke triumphantly, with an overwhelmingly delusional belief that we cannot see he is the bad guy here, even after displaying his rage right in front of our eyes.

"That idiot really expects us to buy his plot-hole filled bull, then fight a war with him, no questions asked. It's crazy," the twin brother rants to us. "I'm Chadwick, by the way, and this is my sister — Charity."

Charity, the girl sitting on the other side of Thomas, waves awkwardly to everyone at the table. The rest of us introduce ourselves to the group and Chadwick can't help but laugh at Kaetlynn's name when she announces it to him.

"Kaetlynn? How white are you, girl?" He bursts into laughter.

I chuckle a little bit too, but stop when I see Kaetlynn withdrawing herself.

"You can call me Kate," she mutters as she reaches out to shake the sibling's hands, and I notice some bruises on her left shoulder. She must have seen me staring because she pulls her sleeve down, though it does nothing to cover them.

"One of the soldiers hit me when they brought me in," she tries to whisper, but her version of whispering is normal speaking volume for most people.

"I'm sorry," I whisper back, and she hugs me gently.

"Thank you," she whimpers, treating my simple sorry like the greatest kindness she's ever received, and it makes me wonder how little of it this girl must have been shown in her life.

"How long has everyone been here?" Kate asks the group after she lets go of me.

"About four..." Chadwick contemplates with a piece of egg hanging out of his mouth. "Or five days after the power went out. We were at our auntie's house..." He looks at Charity to confirm he is correct and she nods in agreement. "We were there and they came and took all of us and all of the children, including our eight year old cousin, Kelly."

"Where is she?" I ask.

"We haven't seen her since we got here," Charity mumbles. Both of their faces turn sorrowful and become lost in thought and I can immediately tell that I asked the wrong question.

"They," Kate chimes back in, pulling their concentration away from their worrisome thoughts, "hauled me out of my bed at 8:30 yesterday morning. Said it was 'absolutely necessary' and 'for my own safety' that they take me in," she sneers.

"We've been here since yesterday evening," I tell them, but it seems so minuscule compared to the weeks Charity and Chadwick have been stuck here.

"Oh!" Kate suddenly shouts. "You were the people who walked in when Ronnie was shot."

My mind flashes back to the boy who died upon our arrival last night and shivers are sent tingling down my spine. I don't know how to respond to her outburst, so I stuff my mouth with some eggs, but I have to stop myself from gagging at the taste.

"Did you know him?" Hailee asks in a soft, nurturing tone.

"He was my friend's little brother," Kate answers. Tears well in her eyes as she speaks.

Hailee awkwardly reaches around me to put her hand on Kate's shoulder and I can't help but selfishly wonder where this nurturing side of her was when his lifeless body nearly fell on me last night.

Things go silent. Well, not really, since the entire cafeteria is alive with chatter, especially from a group of boys at a corner table. They make stupid, obnoxiously loud jokes, and they howl with laughter when one of the older boys points to a girl at the table next to them and whispers something to the rest of them.

Cliques have formed here. Groups of girls. Groups of boys. Kids. Attractive people. Then us, sitting in a bubble of silence as if we've all had an unspoken agreement to honor Ronnie in this moment.

The prison atmosphere, the cliques, the ridiculous training we are required to participate in, and the kids who are blissfully unaware of how nonsensical it is. Yep, this is just like high school.

I get the unnerving sensation I'm being watched, and not in a Big Brother sort of way, so I turn my head around and the lanky blond soldier I met last night is guarding the entrance. His wide eyes are fixed on me, and he reminds me of the man with the eye tattoo who used to hit on me during meals in prison. Only he didn't have an AR-15 strapped to his shoulder.

Blondie pushes away a kid who made the mistake of walking a little too close to him. After he knocks the kid over, then chuckles as his tray of food crashes to the ground, his eyes return to me.

I want to stare him down. I want to show him very clearly my disgust for him and what he has just done. I almost do, but then I remember what Thomas said last night. This man may be our only chance, so instead, I force a little smile onto my face, then quickly turn away. Thomas looks up at me from across the table.

"He's smiling now," he mentions curiously.

"Shut up and eat your toast," I insist.

Immediately after breakfast, everyone is told to meet out in the training field. I follow the crowd to an open space behind the rows of warehouses and cafeterias. It's an enormous field with multiple training courses scattered about it. Several flag poles around the field stand barren, stripped of the American flag, as I have suspiciously noticed all of the flagpoles around here are. Perhaps there are plans for a new flag to take its place. Maybe one with a Hydra on it that they will force us to pledge our allegiance to.

Everyone is broken up into groups to perform various training exercises, each led by their own drill sergeant. Groups are separated based on how long you've been here, so my group consists of me, Hailee, Thomas, Kate, and about two dozen others they've rounded up in the past two days.

Some groups sit down on the grass and tediously take apart their guns and put them back together. Others, who have been here the longest, like Chadwick and Charity, practice firing at a gun range at the edge of the field. Those who have already managed to upset their sergeants are doing push-ups.

Right now, my group is having to do twenty push-ups each because a bratty fourteen year old kid in our unit cursed out Sergeant Conner and we must all face the consequences.

Sergeant Conner is a short, light-haired woman whose face almost looks like that of a twenty year old's if not for the wrinkles that show her true age. The bags under her eyes and lines on her cheeks speak of how long she has spent relentlessly yelling at people who refuse to obey her.

A pair of brothers make quick work of the push-ups, but it's not so easy for the rest of us. The bratty kid who got us into this can barely even lift himself up. Conner yells at everyone in a monotone voice for going too slow, which doesn't make any of us go faster.

Thomas finishes after the brothers. Hailee is next. Then me. Then the kid. Then, after a long time, a little girl no more than eight years old completes her set. She is weeping from being repeatedly yelled at by

Conner for going too slow. I hug the little girl and she is quick to accept my embrace.

"Hugging is prohibited on the training field, you mewling babies!" yells Conner, as she grabs the young girl by her hair and drags her from me.

I jump to my feet, ready to launch myself at Sergeant Conner. She reaches to her belt for her gun, but I push her to the ground before giving her a chance to fire. Hailee grabs my arm and tackles me, leaving me utterly confused. She should be defending the child, not Conner.

"What are you doing?" I shout, trying to wrestle her off me.

"Don't hurt her!" she screams at me, then releases her hold on me.

I had only planned on pushing and maybe punching Conner, but by the looks on Hailee and Thomas's face, they were under the impression I had other plans.

I had already accepted Hailee would never forgive me for what I did, but Thomas might not either, and that terrifies me almost as greatly as all the other horrors that have unfolded. I should have seen it coming, though. They were both witnesses to what took place yesterday. They know I have unexplainable powers. To them, I am a monster to be feared, and I cannot change that.

Conner picks herself up off the ground, regains her composure, then shouts at us to head to our training course. There we spend hours climbing up and down a ladder rung wall, crawling under barbed wire and through a muddy trench, swinging from pole to pole on an adult version of monkey bars, and climbing over an inclining wall. Once you're done with that you run back to the start and do it again.

As time goes on, more people flood in from their half hour breakfast and soon the entire yard is filled with thousands upon thousands of people running through courses, taking apart their guns, shooting, getting into fights, and slacking off.

Every single prisoner in this camp is present on this field and it's overwhelming the sheer amount of people they have captured, brought here, and fed lies to.

"We are at war!" I can almost hear the general say. Yeah, a war against ourselves.

After everyone else is finished, Conner makes me run the course two extra times as punishment for attacking her. She wears an evil grin as she watches me trudge through the slimy mud.

After I finish the course, it's time for lunch, which is another half hour of inedible food, ridiculous speeches from the general, and waiting in line to use the bathroom sink to wipe off all of the mud I can.

Luckily, the blond guard isn't in the building so I can eat my meal without having his eyes burn holes in the back of my head.

After lunch, our group is convened behind the cafeteria and a man who addresses himself as Lieutenant Rand gives a long, rehearsed speech to properly inform the newcomers about what has happened these past few weeks.

According to him, Russia sent an EMP to wipe out all of our power and leave us defenseless. Our government is quickly working to regain power, which is their excuse for how they have electricity here, but I'm betting their electricity never went out for a second.

Lieutenant Rand claims that Russian soldiers have already begun invading parts of our country and many of our soldiers have been deployed to fight against them. But they need more, so they're training us up to fight with them, but we are pressed for time. Our society has very rapidly collapsed after this unexpected tragedy and must be rebuilt. This is our opportunity to rebuild it better and stronger than before, A.K.A, more to the military's liking.

We will be trained to fight against this "enemy" and we will be put in charge of this crumbling nation to restore its order and its safety.

Basically, he tells us we're going to be the leaders and we will defeat our enemies, but not really. The general will be our dictator, as I see it. He's been "temporarily" given all control of Ohio until everything is back in order, and there are other generals residing over the other states for the time being. Lieutenant Rand claims our current president is still in power, but I suspect they will get rid of him as soon as they can and then blame it on the Russians.

General Kaine is obviously the only authority they respect here and he's power hungry.

We, the new militia, will be keeping the people in check and keeping the law. An entire set of much stricter laws is already in the process of being made to maintain control over the people and "keep them safe" during this difficult time in our history.

Some of us, he tells, may even be selected governors by General Kaine (not the president he so boldly declared was still in full power. *Gasp!)* if we prove to be good soldiers. We should have legitimate political backgrounds to be considered for those positions, but I bet General Kaine only wants puppets, not leaders. That must be how he views the youth, as impressionable puppets he can sway in whichever direction he pleases. But he is sadly mistaken. I will not bow down to him, and with the scene I witnessed when we first arrived, I know there are others here that won't obey him, either.

Lieutenant Rand's speech of pure mumbo jumbo eventually comes to an end and I sigh with relief.

The Russians aren't coming after us. The Russians are probably sitting in front of their televisions with bowls of popcorn, watching us burn, like the rest of the world is.

After that speech, I'm more certain than ever this was an inside job, and I tell that to Thomas and Hailee, despite the supernatural rift formed between us by my unexplained abilities.

General Kaine wants full control, and Russia is his scapegoat — that I know for sure. My only question is how long do they expect to keep this charade up? Eventually everyone will realize there's not an enemy to fight, right?

We barely have time for another training exercise before dinner because Lieutenant Rand's speech droned on for so long, but what little time we do train is spent grumbling amongst ourselves about how ridiculous everything he said was. I've never seen a person spew so many lies, all at once, without even flinching.

Some of the people here, however, were more than willing to accept what he said as truth, including the fourteen year old who is now ready to "kill some Nazi's," because he clearly has no idea what he's talking about. Not all of us are as naïve as him. Not all of us blindly believe what the general is shoving down our throats.

Everyone hurries to the cafeteria after dinner is announced. I guess most people here enjoy eating bricks for dinner, but I'm not particularly up for that, so I take my time and end up at the back of the crowd and stare up at the sky that has become a beautiful swirl of cotton candy pink with hints of orange. Life as everyone knows it has fallen apart, but nature is still the same. Still beautiful. Still peaceful.

The remainder of today's sunshine beams down and it's as if my body is absorbing it, allowing it to refuel my energy and calm my spirit.

I've almost made my way off the training field when a hand touches my shoulder. I jump a little at the unexpected touch and turn around to see who the hand belongs to. I freeze up when my eyes land on the soldier who murdered Ronnie yesterday.

"My friend wants to see you. Eight o'clock to-night. Outside Red 8," he says in a calm, deep voice.

"Oh, okay. Sure," I mumble, then rush into the crowd of people headed for dinner.

My legs are weak and shaky and I'm sure my face is drained of any color it may have had. I knew who he meant: His blond friend who creepily stares at me from across the room and pushes kids down. He wants to see me. This is a part of my plan, but the thought of going through with it terrifies me.

I catch up with Thomas and Hailee, who are walking with Kate, Chadwick, and Charity.

"Dude, are you okay?" Thomas asks once I've joined them.

"He wants to see me at eight," I whisper to Thomas.

"That's perfect," he smiles.

"No, that's actually really terrifying," I inform him.

"But this is exactly what we wanted," he says, but it sounds more like a question.

"That doesn't change the fact that he's a violent creep who may not even give me any information. Why are you so okay with this? If he gets me alone, something really bad could happen!"

I don't give any details, but I'm sure he can figure it out for himself. We saw it all the time at the prison. Men in positions of power abusing women who couldn't speak up against them.

"I'm not okay with it. I wish you didn't have to do it, but what other options do we have right now, Anna? And yeah, normally I would be worried about you, but now I know you can protect yourself," he reassures me. "You can... *You know?*"

I do know. If my forcefield can deflect bullets, it could easily protect me from Blondie. There's no need for me to be worried, but of course, I still am.

"Hey." Kate puts her arm around me. "What are you guys whispering about?"

The rest of the group looks to us curiously after Kate's not-so-quiet inquiry.

"Oh..." I turn to Thomas, searching for confirmation that telling them what we are discussing is the right thing to do. I hadn't yet considered whether or not I could trust them. After all, I had only met them this morning.

Thomas nods to me, then I make them walk a little slower so we fall behind the starving teenagers trampling each other for inedible food.

The rushing crowd begins to form a semi-organized line that's piled up all the way out of the door, so I have ample time to explain the situation, and I tell them everything I know. They had already come to the conclusion that General Kaine and his minions were lying, but I tell them things they had not been made aware of; like when soldiers tried to kill us and our friend Michael when they passed us on the road. The chaos that has broken out in the towns, the burning city we saw in the distance, and how eager the general is to kill people — something they got a taste of when Ronnie died.

Chadwick and Charity have been trapped here since this entire thing began, so they have been completely oblivious to how quickly things outside these walls had gone downhill, and they are flabbergasted when I tell them. Kate has just as strong of a reaction, though she was well aware of how unwell society had been adjusting.

I avoid telling them about my strange power just yet. I barely know enough about it to tell, and my stomach twists in knots just at the consideration of bringing it up, so I steer the conversation towards our plan and how Blondie wants to meet with me tonight.

"I'm going to get information out of him. He might know what's really going on, and if he likes me enough, he might be willing to get us out of here."

I had initially planned to find a way to stop this madness altogether, but after seeing the thousands of people gathered together in the field today, and hearing the people who believed the general's lies, this might be too big to stop. A small, quiet escape could be our only option.

"Innit that creep a little old for you?" Chadwick asks. "He's twenty-something and you're like, fourteen."

"What? No!" Blood rushes to my cheeks and I try to cover my face. "I'm eighteen! I'm an adult!"

"Oh, my bad, girl! My bad!" Chadwick replies, and Thomas snickers at his mistake, so I shoot him a dirty look. This is not the first time in my life I have been mistaken for younger than I am; it is one of the lifelong struggles of being short, but it is never pleasant.

"So, you're really going to go through with that plan to *seduce* him? Are you capable of doing that?" Hailee sneers.

I can't tell if she's trying to insult me by suggesting I lack any flirtatious ability or inquire if I've been enticing her boyfriend when she's not around.

"No, I'm not exactly skilled at that, but this is our only plan," I sneer back, and take a small step forward in line.

"What about, oh, I don't know — just leaving?" Hailee rolls her eyes, and moves closer to the entrance of the cafeteria, along with the rest of the crowd.

"And get ourselves shot on our way out?" Chadwick derides. "I don't think so."

His comment shuts Hailee right up, so Thomas comes to her defense. "It was just a question."

178

"A stupid one," Chadwick mutters.

"It was reasonable!" Hailee insists, shuffling closer to the doors.

"Everyone stop! You're only arguing because you're hungry," Kate says, as she shoots Chadwick and Hailee disappointed looks.

Chadwick mutters to himself, "No, it's because what she said was dumb as —"

"Just drop it," Charity whispers to him, as we finally make it through the front doors of the cafeteria.

"I'm going to talk to this guy tonight and find out everything I can, and we'll find a way to leave here without getting shot, okay? But for now let's lay low and wait it out," I demand, and pick up a tray.

"Be careful," Kate says to me.

"I'll try."

The cafeteria is full of energy. Everyone is relieved to be done with training for the day, but I'm dreading each minute I come closer to a meeting with Blondie.

Since I'm at the end of the line, I have to wait quite a while before finally filling my tray with meatloaf, mashed potatoes, and a handful of garden peas. It gives me time to work up enough of an appetite to eat this food. I join the rest of my group at a table against the back wall.

This place is overflowing with people and running out of room fast. There haven't been any new "recruits" arriving today, but I know these people won't stop until they have everyone they want. My gut is telling me they have more locations they are sending the overflow to.

I brace myself and dig into my food — literally. The meatloaf is the earth's crust and my fork is the shovel that bends instead of breaking through the first layer.

"It was easier to bite into when it was warm, but now it's stone cold," Chadwick announces of his own meatloaf that he can't cut through, then he bursts into a fit of laughter along with his sister.

"What's so funny?" I ask.

"*Stone* cold," he repeats.

The joke isn't that funny, but Chadwick's snorting laugh is so hilarious that I can't hold back my own laughter, and soon the rest of the table can't either, except Thomas.

"Thomas!" Hailee waves a hand in front of his face as he stares off, unblinking, into the distance. "Are you there? Whatever."

Hailee quickly loses interest in whatever is captivating Thomas, until he jumps up out of nowhere, and sprints to the other side of the building.

"Thomas!" Hailee shouts as she runs after him.

I take off when she does, followed by the clamor of the others at the table as they race behind us.

Only a couple of people stare as we run past. Most are too absorbed in their meatloaf and personal drama to pay attention to Thomas as he takes a sharp left down a hallway that leads to the bath-rooms. The rest of us follow him. He speeds ahead of me and takes another left down an adjoining hall-way. As soon as I turn down it I come to a halt when I see him on the ground. He's holding someone down. Hailee grabs at Thomas and pulls him off the unidentified person.

"Thomas, what are you doing? Get off!" she yells in befuddlement. "Are you crazy?"

"How are you alive?" he shouts and pushes the stranger up against the wall. His voice cracks as he asks again. "How are you alive?"

I slowly move closer to get a better look at the stranger. He's a man a little bit bigger than Thomas, with black hair and dark brown eyes that are wide with fear because he doesn't have an answer for the enraged man pinning him to the wall. His face is strikingly familiar to me.

"Caleb?" Hailee whispers to the man in shock and everything clicks in my mind. He looks familiar because I recognized him from the picture Thomas had taped to the wall of our prison cell. The picture of his dead best friend, Caleb Rhodes.

FIFTEEN

"I'm sorry." Caleb says, and he says it over and over until he's too choked up to speak anymore.

I look over my shoulder to make sure no one is spying on us, but no one besides Charity, Chadwick, and Kate are there, and they all look utterly confused.

"Who is he?" Kate whispers to Hailee.

She and Thomas both ignore her question, focused only on Caleb — the ghost standing right in front of them.

I don't believe it is my place to inform the group on this very personal and bewildering matter that, frankly, has my head spinning so much I might not be able to form a coherent reply, so I stay quiet, too.

"How are you alive?" Thomas asks once again.

"I'm sorry. I didn't know what else to do..."

Thomas is blisteringly livid and evidently trying to refrain from inflicting fatal injuries upon the man who I thought had already received his fatal blow. "What did you do?" Thomas demands.

"That car crash, it wasn't an accident. I faked it. I've been pretending to be dead ever since," Caleb bluntly admits.

182

"Why would you do that?" Thomas is now on the verge of tears. He tries to stifle the pain, but a tone of betrayal lingers in his voice.

Caleb's eyes dart around to make sure no one is eavesdropping when they fall on the rest of us who are eagerly waiting on an explanation.

"Who are they?" he asks.

"Who are *you?*" Thomas asks him. "Why would you ever do something like that, man?"

"Because I —" Caleb, once again, shoots the four of us a quick, suspicious glance and refuses to speak.

"These are people you can trust, Caleb. Just tell me what happened," Thomas demands in a ferocity I have only seen from him when he was speaking to other prisoners.

"I was being threatened, blackmailed. I don't know who it was, but they were demanding things from me. They wanted money in order to keep quiet about... things. But they kept sending me letters. Threatening me, my family, and you guys," Caleb says to Hailee and Thomas. "They sent me pictures of both of you; from outside your windows at night, when you were grocery shopping, driving. I couldn't take it. I didn't want to be the reason anyone else got hurt. So, I faked my death. I wanted it to look like an accident. I didn't think you would go down for it, man. Thomas, I'm sorry. I didn't plant any evidence against you. The person who was blackmailing me must have done it. I thought once I was dead they would stop. I'm so sorry."

183

As soon as Caleb finishes speaking, Thomas does not hesitate to bring him in for a hug. Any anger he had vanished into thin air. Both of them fail to hold back their tears as they clutch onto each other like they will both disappear if they dare to let go again.

"What does he mean 'Thomas went down for it?'" Kate attempts to whisper only to Hailee, but Thomas still hears it. He pulls away from Caleb to look Kate in the eye.

"I was imprisoned for killing him," Thomas admits.

Kate and the twins gape at him in sheer stupefaction, which quickly turns to excitement when they realize they are in the presence of a legitimate convict.

"What's it like in prison?"

"How long were you in?"

"Did the military pull you out of prison?"

Thomas doesn't even have time to answer them before their questions and curiosity turn to a tense Caleb.

"How did you fake your death?"

"Where did you hide?"

"What were they blackmailing you for?"

"I'd rather not answer that last one," Caleb speaks softly, without looking anyone in the eye, "but faking it was pretty simple. I crashed my car on an empty bridge, left some of my own blood at the scene, then hid out with people who knew how to stay off the grid. Well, until I was brought here anyways."

The three of them listen intently and excitedly to everything he says, and they seem so accepting of every aspect of the situation that I decide to take this as my opportunity to drop the bomb of my imprisonment as well. Then, I'm forced to bite my tongue.

The only reason they are all okay with this is because they know Thomas is not guilty. The evidence is right in front of them, refusing to look them in the eye while having a conversation with them. None of them would believe me if I told them I was, coincidentally, also locked up for the murder of my best friend and didn't actually do it either. Just like Hailee didn't believe me. She is currently giving me a peculiar look that's telling me she is expecting me to come clean, but I keep my mouth shut.

Thomas brings Caleb in for another hug, then everyone goes around and introduces themselves to Caleb, who accidentally re-introduces himself to us.

"What are you doing back here?" a voice snaps from behind me and sends chills through my spine. Blondie stands behind us, fuming with rage.

"We —" Hailee begins.

"*You,*" Blondie interrupts, "scum aren't allowed back here! Get back in there and sit down before I tell the —" He stops mid-sentence when he suddenly realizes I'm standing amongst the scum he's yelling at. "Get back to your seats! Go!"

Kate, scared out of her wits, rushes past Blondie without any need for any extra incentive. He puts his hand on her back and pushes her forward as she runs past him. She trips but gets back up and keeps running at full speed. The rest of us quickly follow her, stepping a little farther to the right to avoid an encounter with Blondie.

"I hope you choke!" he yells after we pass him. I whip my head around to glare at him, but he shakes his head at me. I can tell it's supposed to mean "no, not you."

Aw, you hope all of my friends choke but don't want me to? How romantic! I'm falling in love as fast as Kate fell after you tripped her.

I return to our table, where Caleb now joins us. A boy at the table directly behind me chuckles as soon as I bring a forkful of cold mashed potatoes up to my mouth. My paranoia tells me the boy is laughing at me, and considering how long my food was left here unattended, I decide not to take my chances with it and advise everyone else to do the same.

"So, is this the cool kids group?" Caleb asks.

"Yeah, dude, and just like the cool kids we're going to ditch class!" Thomas chortles. The sadness he was overwhelmed with only moments ago, the sadness I have seen in him so many times, has vanished and been replaced with pure joy.

"I'm in!" Caleb teases.

"Yeah, no. We really are!" Thomas says with an enthusiasm I have never seen from him. He has always been more reserved and intimidating, but he has transformed into a peppy golden retriever.

"We're all going to bust out of here together. Anna's

going to seduce that lanky guard back there into giving us information."

"Could you quit saying *seduce*, please?" I beg Thomas, as Caleb gives me a strange glance, but immediately looks away. "I've never even spoken to the guy. He's attracted to me and everyone here thinks it's a good idea to use that to our advantage, right?"

I look to the rest of the group for confirmation, most of whom nod their heads in agreement, except Caleb who only listens curiously.

"You can convince him to get us out of here," Thomas insists, while he pokes at his inedible, possibly poisoned food.

"I hope so," I say.

I try hard to emphasize that I'm only doing this for the good of the group. I don't want anyone to think that I enjoy manipulation or that I would even be in the same room with a man like Blondie under normal circumstances, but I sense myself trying particularly hard to convince Caleb of that. I don't want him thinking negatively of me. Eventually, he will find plenty of things to hate me for: My powers, or the dozen men I killed. But I want to hold off on tainting his image of me for as long as I can.

"So, that tantrum back there was his way of showing affection?" Caleb inquires, once again looking at anything other than who he's speaking to.

"Trust me, it would have been a lot worse if I

wasn't there," I answer him. I wait for him to look up at me with any sort of expression that could indicate his opinion about all of this, but I get nothing.

"I'm glad you were there," Kate says. Her voice is softer and squeakier than normal. "Who knows what he would have done to me if he knew you weren't watching."

My gaze turns to the bruises on her arm. Suddenly, I am certain Blondie is the one who put them there.

"So, how many people know about this little ruse?" Caleb asks me.

"Just us." I gesture to everyone at the table.

"Shouldn't we tell more people, so as many of us can get out as possible?" Chadwick asks.

"Not until I'm sure he will help, and then, only people we can trust. If this plan leaks to General Kaine, it could get every one of us killed."

"Being alone with that guy might get you killed," Caleb says nonchalantly.

"Says the dead guy," Hailee retorts sardonically.

"I still can't believe you're really alive, dude," Thomas says to Caleb, and the three of them become absorbed into their own conversation. The idea of me being murdered behind a warehouse by a wide-eyed weirdo is washed away and replaced with tears of laughter and detailed inquiries of what the past year has been like for each of them. Caleb dodges most of the questions aimed at him, but Thomas and Hailee are an open book.

Thomas spills every detail of his time in prison, but intentionally excludes myself from his story for my own sake. No one other than Thomas and Hailee know of the time I spent there. Even Hailee is still not aware that Thomas and I shared a cell for over six months, and I think she just might kill me if she did.

The rest of us make awkward conversation as our stomachs rumble for something other than the cold, toxic food sitting in front of us.

Kate — who's the only one who can seem to break the awkwardness that has befallen us and get a full conversation going — is sitting awkwardly close to me. Not on purpose, of course. Since Caleb has joined us, the rows are a little tighter. Chadwick, Thomas, and Caleb are all sitting on the bench opposite me. Hailee, Charity, Kate, and I sit squished together, with myself on the edge, forced up against the wall. Hailee reaches her hand across the table to hold onto Thomas's as they chat.

"So, you're going to see that guy right after dinner?" Kate asks me.

"Yeah. I'm hoping he will give me information on the military's plans and I can work 'hey, can you break us out of here?' into the conversation somehow," I chuckle. I try to be humorous because thinking about how detrimental it could be if this goes awry might make me cry instead of laugh.

"What plan is that?" Caleb jumps in to the conversation. My comment has caught his attention.

"The military's plan for taking over the country. It's obvious they did it on purpose — the EMP — to recruit all of us here. It's all an elaborate scheme to gain greater control and I'm hoping I can get Blondie to confirm that tonight."

"Well, *Blondie,*" he mocks the nickname I hadn't meant to say out loud, "seems quite hot tempered. You might want to tread lightly around him. These people are quick to pull a trigger."

"I'm well aware of that and I can protect myself," I declare with confidence, but Caleb looks as if he's withholding a snarky remark.

The clock on the back wall tells me it's 7:30. Dinner is supposed to end now, but Chadwick says they usually let us stay here until 7:45 before they get impatient. After that, I only have time for a quick shower before I have to meet with Blondie.

Kate and Chadwick become enveloped in their own slightly flirtatious conversation about childhood memories. One of them will recall an exciting event or a beautiful place they visited and the other will casually mention how they wish they could have been there together. Charity willfully ignores them and listens to Hailee, who loudly goes on about how she spent her time without Thomas and Caleb. She mostly rambles on about playing tennis, claiming her coach said she was "the most talented and skillful person he had ever trained," though I have a feeling that story might be somewhat embellished.

All of us quickly get bored with Hailee's fictitious tennis skills and Thomas kindly tries to change the subject to something more interesting. Hailee repeatedly interrupts him, switching the topic back around to her delusional belief that she may have one day beaten Serena Williams in a match and that the *only* thing that stopped her was the "EMP that ruined all of her plans."

With time ticking down until my rendezvous, the conversation changes and everyone at the table rushes to give me tips on how to approach the situation.

"Don't say anything whatsoever about the plan; ours or the military's. Only hint to them. You don't want him coming to the realization that's the only reason you've got to talk to him."

"Smile a lot. Laugh a lot. Talk about him and his interests."

"Convince him helping us escape was his idea."

"Try not to mention your... abilities very much if that's possible," Thomas remarks. "He may not be too fond of them."

"What abilities?" Caleb interrupts. He and the rest of the group, who do not yet know about my powers, are all looking at Thomas curiously because of his slip up.

"Her ability to seduce men," Thomas quickly corrects himself, letting out a small, fake chuckle.

Everyone else shrugs it off, but I can tell by the look on Caleb's face he didn't believe Thomas's excuse. However, there's no time for him to question it. It's 7:45 and the guards are insisting we've been loitering for too long.

I step out of the double doors into the cool evening breeze and let the air fill my lungs. The smell of the grass is a relief after inhaling the mixed scent of suspect food and sweaty people for so long.

Showers are more uncomfortable than I had anticipated. There are two communal shower rooms: One for men, one for women. Each room is, basically, one big, mildewed box with shower heads sticking out of the walls and drains at random spots on the floor.

There is zero privacy involved. Everyone can see everything, but most of the girls are kind enough not to look. There is a limit to how long they keep the water running, so we wash ourselves quickly, then leave so we don't get stuck with shampoo in our hair and no way to rinse it out.

I grab a uniform that isn't muddied and wait outside the shower building, with wet hair chilling in the breeze until almost 8PM.

I walk back to Red 8 with Hailee, Charity, and Kate, who all stay at the back of the pack with me so I can slip away unnoticed.

"Good luck," Charity says to me before she walks in.

My heart races and my mind is focusing on everything that could go wrong as the guard, who informed me of the meeting, closes the warehouse door behind all the other girls, leaving only myself out in the cold.

He looks to me, then nods towards the edge of the warehouse. I walk around the corner of the building and there I find Blondie leaning against the wall with both hands in his pockets. He's doing his best to appear relaxed, tough, and composed, but his attempt fails. He looks cowardly and nervous.

"Hey," he says in a much deeper voice than I expected. His pitch was much higher when he was yelling at my friends, so I know he's intentionally affecting it. "I wasn't sure you'd meet me."

"Why wouldn't I?" I say, as I force a smile and begin to hate myself just a little bit more than I used to.

I'm not the kind of person to lie or manipulate people, but all that lies ahead of me this evening are façades, and possibly sentencing myself and all of my friends to death if I'm not convincing enough.

"So, how's life?" he asks, stepping uncomfortably close to me as he speaks, while still forcing a deep voice.

"As good as it can be, I guess," I mumble, as I lean my head and shrug. The key to getting out of here is first planting subtle seeds about how unhappy I am trapped within these walls.

He takes me for a walk around the perimeter where our path is illuminated by dozens of flood lights and it allows me to take in the massiveness of this camp. They have sixteen buildings specifically for the purpose of housing kids and teenagers. Overall, they must have around twenty-five buildings inside the walls. I'm convinced they must have been secretly building this place for months before the EMP strike happened. It is far too big to assemble overnight.

The metal fence towering high above us, encircling the camp, reminds me why I'm doing this. Thousands of kids, teenagers, and young adults are being imprisoned here and something must be done about it.

Blondie and I make lots of small talk. I give him no specific details about my life, but I make sure to ask as many questions as I can about his to fool him into thinking I'm much more interested than I am, and it works. He loves to talk about himself while using a large variety of intelligent sounding words in all the wrong ways. He seems to be quite convinced that "readily" means to thoroughly enjoy reading something. He uses it a lot, though I highly doubt he has read near as much as he claims.

Our walk halts in the shadows behind a building that Blondie says stores most of their vehicles not currently in use. I try to remember exactly where this place is located. In the event of an escape, a ride out of here will be key to a safe getaway.

"So, *Anna...*" he says. My name rolls off his tongue, despite never having told it to him. I cringe at the sound of it. I've never hated my own name so much as I do right now. "I was looking through the Triv files earlier — that's how I found your name —"

"The what?" I interrupt him.

"You know, Trivs... Trives." He grins at the revelation that I clearly *don't* know what he means. "It's a nickname for all you supernatural people. It means trivial, pointless, useless. We have separate files for all of your kind."

He folds his arms and leans in close to me, evidently believing that what he said should greatly impress me, but I'm more disgusted by the way he says "your kind," as if people with my abilities are filthy street rats. Not to mention, I'm confused by the revelation that there are more people with my abilities. I attempt to refrain from expressing that, but it leaks out.

"My *kind?*" I snap in disgust. "There are more people like me?" I add in a softer tone to hopefully reverse some of the damage from my initial outburst.

"Yeah!" he exclaims. Unable to contain his excitement on the subject, he starts pacing back and forth with energy. My tone doesn't seem to have fazed him. "That's really the big reason we've got a wild amount of people flooding in here. We want to know who all the *abnormal* people are."

"Wow. I had no idea," I feign shock, though a part of me is genuinely surprised. This isn't at all what I envisioned him telling me.

I play up my astonishment as much as possible. If he thinks I'm amazed by how much he knows, maybe he will spill out even more confidential information to impress me. Although something about his obvious distaste for *Trivs* leaves me confused about why he would want to impress me.

"Yeah," he beams, pacing back and forth ever faster. "I know a lot about what goes on around here, Anna. I'm smart. These guys I'm working with have no idea that I'm outsmarting them all."

Yeah, you're a real genius. No one can fool you.

"So, do you know who any of the other abnormal people are?" I ask as inquisitively as possible. "Who else has powers?"

"Don't worry about those people. We take care of them," he calmly assures me, but it sets off an explosion in my mind.

"You *kill* them?" I burst out in anger. I was going to keep my cool about this, but I can't hold it in any longer.

"Of course!" He stops pacing and stares right at me. "Those people are freaks. They deserve to die!"

"Then answer me this: Why are you interested in me if you hate people like me? Are you just going to kill me?" I sternly demand, as I unblinkingly stare him down.

"Because," he says, putting his hand on my arm and finally letting go of his fake voice. "I've seen you. You're nothing like them. You're cool. You've just been given the misfit," (*I'm pretty sure you mean misfortune*) "of being grouped in with those weirdos. I won't let them kill you."

I have to restrain myself from gagging at his rancid idea that's eerily similar to the trope that I'm "not like other girls." On top of that, his statement could not be more wrong. I've never met another *Triv*, but I know whoever they are, I'm surely one of them.

I'm infuriated by everything he's telling me and I impulsively want to tell him the bitter truth: I don't have any interest in him and I was only using him for information that he so willingly gave me. Because of him, I know why all of this is happening. They want to eradicate Trivs, and what better way to do that than to round them all up "for their own safety" and murder them in the background.

All of this is bubbling up inside me, ready to burst at the seams, but I shut it down. I bite my tongue. I still need him. I need him to not run in fury to the general and have myself and my friends executed for treason. I need him to help us escape, so I take a breath full of all of my rage and release it. Even with the clear repression of anger shown on my face, he seems to take this as a sigh of relief that he doesn't want me dead, not a sigh of bitterness.

"Don't worry." He steps closer to me. "I don't think of you as one of them."

Apparently, this idiot thought I was upset, not at how he views Trivs, but with the truly *wild* idea that he would consider me one of them.

"Thank you," I force myself to say, in order to confirm his delusional belief.

I realize my body has been tensed up, my teeth have been gritted, since he uttered my name, so I relax myself. He unexpectedly puts his arms around me and pulls me in for a hug, squeezing me tightly for far too long. He smells of sweat, meatloaf, and something else I can only assume is his own naturally revolting scent.

After an uncomfortably long hug, I pull away. I can tell he doesn't want to let go. His eyes long for more and it sends an unsettling chill down my spine. I almost take his look of pure infatuation as my opportunity to mention the escape plan, to convince him if he doesn't want them to kill me he needs to get me out now, but something in my gut shuts me up. It's too soon. If I say it now, he might realize I'm only using him.

"You're lucky you ended up at my camp and not somewhere that couldn't see you're not one of them," he says to me. It's frightening how whole-heartedly he believes he's saying all the right things.

The fury that had momentarily subsided rises up again. Another jab at Trivs, along with trying to subtly hint that he's the only person who thinks I have any value.

"There are more camps?" I ask him. I had suspected as much, but without being able to leave, I hadn't been able to confirm it.

"Yeah!" He gets excited again. Talking about the murder of innocent Trivs makes him horrifyingly happy. "It's happening all over the country. Soon all of America will be one big, happy army."

He's gushing about the details, getting ready to pace again, but before he can, I take this as my chance to finally bow out of the conversation. I am too angry and nauseated to continue any further without blowing the whole thing.

"Well, I'm glad I ended up here with you," I say, then nearly gag as I offer a flirtatious smile that sends any self respect I had straight down the toilet. "I appreciate you keeping me safe, but today has been really long. I think I need to rest up for training tomorrow."

His expression saddens, then he mumbles, "Oh, okay then."

He walks with me back to Red 8, where I will be glad to finally get my freezing hair out of the cold wind. His friend, guarding the door, nods approvingly when he sees us coming.

"Wanna meet here again tomorrow? Same time?" he whispers so the other soldier can't hear, as if he didn't have him wing-manning the entire operation.

"Definitely," I whisper back in false exhilaration.

I'm reaching for the door handle when Blondie grabs my right arm and pulls me into him. He leans his face close to mine and I can tell he's coming in for a kiss. He exhales and his pungent, warm breath hits me in the face. His lips are almost in contact with mine when I fake a coughing fit and he jumps back. My first kiss will *not* be with him.

"Wow!" I exclaim. Blondie's face has turned bright red. "That really came out of nowhere. I'm going to get some water and then lie down. Goodnight!"

I rush into Red 8 and shut the door behind me. Blondie's friend is on the other side howling with laughter at the obvious snub, and I imagine Blondie's face looking identical to a tomato right about now.

A small crowd of kids around the door stop what they're doing to stare at me. No one is supposed to be out past shower time. One of them looks ready to question my whereabouts, so I shake my head and walk past them, through the bunk beds, to tell Thomas and Hailee the good news that I, somehow, didn't ruin anything and they're safe (for now) and the bad news that I'm not. People like me are being hunted, and I doubt Blondie, alone, will be able to convince General Kaine to keep me around for much longer.

To my surprise, Chadwick, Charity, and Kate are all sitting at my bunk, waiting for my arrival with worried expressions. I am slightly annoyed with their fear that I would screw this up, but I'm glad they are all here. I look forward to not having to repeat this entire story to them later.

Kate eagerly moves onto the floor next to Chadwick to give me room to sit down and the whole group looks at me inquisitively. Luckily, it isn't curfew yet, so the building is alive with the sound of a hundred different conversations and I don't have to worry about anyone overhearing us.

I re-tell the entire story, from the moment the guard closed the door to Red 8, until the fake coughing fit, along with my sarcastic inner monologue. I emphasize everything Blondie said about Trivs and the government herding us like pigs for slaughter. I hadn't planned on revealing that part of myself to them, but I don't see how I could keep it to myself now.

"It's all a setup," I insist, unintentionally waving my hands around to get my point across. "All of this has been to find the people who have powers and kill us. Blondie says he won't let them kill me, but let's face it, he's not exactly the kind of person the general is going to take orders from. They definitely did this. They caused the EMP solely to force this into place, to better weed out all of the Trivs across the country."

I wait for the group to process this information. It's a lot to take in all at once, and most of it is so crazy it sounds fake.

"They set off an EMP and destroyed their own country to find superheroes?" Kate asks, desperately trying to understand everything I just said. Her innocent question suddenly makes my entire theory sound like complete rubbish.

"That's insane," Hailee says, red faced from leaning down from the top bunk this entire conversation. Her remark beats me down further.

"But it —"

"Did he say they caused the EMP?" Hailee asks skeptically.

"No, but it's the only logical explanation. I mean... because —" I attempt to find the right words to say, but the eloquence with which I lied to Blondie seems to have evaporated in truth. "Russians didn't do this! They —"

"I think it makes sense," Chadwick defends me. "How about you, Charity?"

"I dunno, Chaddy," she sighs, looking around worriedly. She is clearly too afraid to take sides.

"Chaddy?" Kate giggles. "Oh wow, that's rich. I'm not letting that one go!"

"Oh, shut up K-A-E-T-L-Y-N-N!" Chadwick retorts, and Kate shuts her mouth, then turns away so he can't see her blushing.

"Anyway," Hailee says, rolling her eyes. "Your theory makes no sense whatsoever! All of you are crazy!"

Hailee jumps down from her bunk and crosses her arms.

Chadwick tries to shrug her off. "Well, if you think abo —"

"Well, if *you* think about it, we all have no idea what's going on, and everything Blondie said might be misinformation, because the guy is obviously an idiot. We should stop coming up with theories and wait for some solid evidence," Hailee exclaims boldly, to which no one responds.

"Did you talk to Blondie about escaping? All of us?" Kate asks, trying to get the conversation headed back in a better direction, but I see the worry on her face. The more we talk, the more afraid she becomes of what this place really is.

"No, I didn't get that far," I solemnly admit. "I didn't want to rush it, but I think he may be willing after a little convincing. He wants to see me again to-morrow. I'll try to ask him then."

"Really?" Kate giggles. "After *that* conversation and a rejected kiss he still wants to see you?"

Her fear has quickly faded away, replaced by her always persistent enthusiasm.

"I guess I just have that kind of effect on men," I laugh, then dramatically flip my hair for effect, "or maybe he just enjoys bragging to someone."

"I think it's the latter," Hailee jokes and snorts at her own remark.

"So, should we start informing people that a plan to break out is being put together?" Chadwick asks.

"No," I murmur. "Blondie believes in this place and what they're doing here. My only hope for convincing him to help us out is his weird attraction towards me. It would be impossible to convince him to completely turn on General Kaine like that."

"Oh..."

The energy in the room seems to shift, yet again. Knowing that we must leave behind more people, who are in just as much danger as we are, doesn't sit right with me, but it's our only option. But frankly, I'm getting quite sick of only being left with options that seem cruel and blatantly immoral.

"What if you don't have until tomorrow?" Thomas asks out of nowhere. He hasn't spoken the entire conversation.

"I will," I say, trying to reassure him, though I have no real confidence in my own safety right now. "Blondie said he'll keep me safe, and I can defend myself, and..." I hesitate to say something that's been on my mind for a while now. "I seem to deal with injuries pretty well, anyway."

"What do you mean?" he asks, and everyone leans in a little bit closer to hear what I have to say.

"Well," I hesitate, once again. This *must* sound crazy, but what part of this conversation hasn't? "Every time I've gotten hurt, since this all started, I've healed fairly quickly. Scratches and bruises didn't last more than a few hours. I even broke my arm and it was fine by the end of the day. I thought I had just exaggerated the pain, but now I think it might have really been broken."

"You think you can heal yourself or something?" Kate continues to load me down with questions as she has done throughout the conversation. "I thought forcefields were your power? Can you have more than one power?"

"I don't know. I don't know," I say, before she can ask another question. "Maybe they're related somehow? Maybe my power is self-preservation or something, like a natural instinct to keep myself alive. I have unintentionally used both the forcefields and healing to protect myself. Both of them have kept me safe, even when I didn't mean for them to."

I speak with confidence, though I have no idea if anything I'm saying is correct. The truth is, I have absolutely no idea why my body is so ready to heal itself from injuries or how on earth I can create forcefields with my mind, because I truly don't understand how being a *Triv* works. I've only just found out I'm not the only one. Can all Trivs create forcefields, or do we all have unique abilities?

I don't know.

"Yeah, I guess that makes sense. To be honest, I don't really understand anything about this, except that you're really a superhero!" Kate exclaims much too loudly, and people take notice.

A voice in the crowd responds to Kate's outburst, but he's almost drowned out by the chatter of everyone else. I would've missed it completely, had I not known those words could only be directed at me.

" *You're* the one with powers?"

SIXTEEN

"Please show us!" begs the group of people that have gathered around me. They pile onto various bunks, but most end up on the floor, eyes fixed directly upon me.

I had thought no one knew about my powers other than the higher-ups here, but apparently word had gotten around that someone with abilities had slipped in amongst us. No one was sure who it was until Kate accidentally confirmed it for everyone here.

I had to correct them on what I could do, which was difficult, considering I'm still trying to grasp exactly what that is. However, the people here knew even less than me, because they all seemed to have been involved in one big game of telephone that has wildly distorted the details of what happened on the streets of Columbus. Some thought I could control the bullets that killed the soldiers. Others said I could control the people and that I made them shoot themselves. The most accurate thing people came up with was that I could conjure up a shield — a literal metal shield — out of thin air.

"I don't know if I can..." I say over the chaos.

"Oh, at least try!" several impatient people demand of me.

"I don't know if it's safe," I announce to the crowd. "I haven't had much practice with controlling it. It might be dangerous."

"Oh, come on! No one cares. Just do it!" a pink-haired girl, about my age, urges me in exasperation.

People here seem to think this is a cool trick and not an unexplainable, possibly deadly supernatural power, even after all the stories they heard about Columbus.

"Fine," I give in, and step off my bed and stand between two rows of bunks.

The crowd is absolutely giddy at my weak resolve and grows even more excited when I ask them all to step back as a safety precaution. The tension in the room is rising within my bones. It suddenly hits me that I have no idea how to do this. I've never managed this on purpose before.

Without thinking, I reach my hand out to the air in front of me. I shut my eyes and try to forget everyone here is staring at me, but I can't ignore the whispering voices guessing what's about to happen. My body begins to shake. My legs are weak. I'm ready to give up and tell everyone I just can't do it when something indescribable happens. It's as if energy rushes out of my body through my fingertips. I open my eyes and behold, right in front of me, a tiny little wisp of lavender. I jump in excitement, along with the few people directly in front of me, who can see the small formation.

I will myself to release more of that strange energy. I open my hand up as wide as it can be and let it flow. I sense each move of it in my bones and I wonder how I never noticed it before.

It surrounds every inch of me. Each moment my brain tells me to be more and more worried about what I'm doing, but I grow more at peace. The crowd is in silent awe as the forcefield swirls around me. I attempt to make it more solid. *Be a shield, not a cloud,* I try to tell it. It solidifies itself almost into a wall before my concentration is interrupted and all of the forcefield abruptly vanishes.

"Lights out," a soldier shouts and the room goes dark on schedule.

Groans break out in the crowd before they return to their bunks and their whispering conversations. What I just did quickly becomes old news amongst more serious matters, like if Carey thinks that guy Ben from row 12 is cuter than the guy in row 8. Priorities.

"That was a wild ride," Chadwick says. "For a while there, I was worried you were making all of this up," he admits.

"Yet you spent so much energy coming up with theories to make sense of it anyway," Hailee says from above me.

"Yeah, well, I couldn't help but rack my brain about it. It's a hard thing to ignore. Now, I've gotta find my bed in the dark," he chuckles. His voice grows quieter in the distance as he walks off, surely followed by Charity and Kate.

I change into my regulation gray pajama shirt and shorts. Hailee and I don't need to guard each other from curious eyes this time because there's no light to peek at us with.

"We'll need to fill Caleb in about all of this next time we see him," Thomas mentions, before slumping back into his springy mattress. "He should know what's really happening, and that we have a plan in motion to get out of here."

"Yeah, definitely," I agree, but with everything that just happened I had already forgotten about Caleb. So, it turns out to be a good thing that I didn't make an escape plan tonight or he would not have been included.

I slide into bed and pull the thin sheets over me while I play back today's events in my mind. I am simultaneously satisfied and filled with guilt at how well I lied and played Blondie. Only a few days ago I had given a stern lecture to Thomas about not doing the exact thing I found myself tangled up in today. I'm nauseated just thinking about it, so I try to focus, instead, on what Blondie said about there being more people with strange abilities. At no point did it occur to me that I might not be the only person this happened to. Realistically, I should have imagined that if I suddenly gained supernatural powers, a hoard of other people probably did too, but not once did it dawn on me that could be the case. My delusional mind was convinced I was the only person in the world going through this experience. Amongst a group of thousands of other teenagers, all herded into the same place, I still managed to think I was alone in something. But I'm not. I don't know how, but I can tell. Blondie says all the other people here with powers have already been taken care of, but there are still more here hiding within the shadows, I can feel it.

I awake to the slight reminiscence of soreness within my bones that grows fainter as I draw closer to the cafeteria.

This morning, one of the many groups we share breakfast with is Red 2, the building in which Caleb resides. Thomas takes this time to catch him up on everything that happened overnight, while eating stale biscuits and thick, yellowish gravy. Caleb listens to everything Thomas says and nods like a mom when her toddler is babbling gibberish. Occasionally, I notice that he seems to be forcing himself to withhold a reaction, mostly when Thomas brings up something about my powers, or says the word "Triv." I have no doubt that he knows something we don't, but he doesn't want to tell us.

Before I have a chance to call him out on his

secret keeping, however, the conversation manages to take a sharp turn down a winding road after Charity makes an offhand remark.

"I don't see how anyone can believe mankind has some sort of glorious, mystical purpose, after all of this," she sighs.

"You don't believe you have purpose?" I ask sorrowfully and without thinking.

"And you do? Even after all the disasters that have lead mankind up to this point?" She stares at me in bold anger, but quickly becomes aware of herself and recedes into her normal shell. "Chadwick, do you agree with me?"

For just a second I saw a glimmer of the fierce person living inside her, but she shrivels back into her brother's shadow.

"Oh, yeah," Chadwick says, but he wasn't really listening to anything we were saying.

"I think there is a purpose to all this. I think there's a reason we survived all these disasters. We weren't put on this earth only to suffer, then die."

"No, we weren't put on this earth for any reason at all. Nothing we do on this giant floating rock matters one bit." Her voice begins to rise and her fire returns. This is the only time I've ever seen her speak up about something, and it's to say nothing matters. "This," she gestures towards the grungy cafeteria, "isn't some divine place we've all magically found ourselves together in —"

"This building may not be anything special, but look at the people," I beg her. "How can you say we were all an accident?"

"General Kaine was definitely an accident," Hailee chimes in.

"But don't you at least think that, maybe, we were made by something greater than chance?" Thomas asks Hailee.

"Woah!" Caleb jumps in. "Since when do you believe your life meant anything?"

Thomas jumps back in shock. "You think it doesn't?"

"No, I didn't mean it like that. I thought you didn't believe anyone's life meant anything."

"I do now." Thomas glances over at me when he says it. "C'mon, dude, you don't think there's a reason we're here? I can't imagine going through all of this crap for no reason."

"I can, because that's exactly what we're doing." Hailee rolls her eyes and infantilizes Thomas with a pat on the head. Thomas looks as hurt by Hailee's remark as he did by Caleb's, but continues to argue his point to them. I jump in to defend him.

The entire table has erupted into various forms of the "divine purpose or random chance" argument, with only myself and Thomas on the side of life having any sort of meaning. Kate is on the fence about it all, and everyone else is on the side of life being a pointless waste.

"If you died today," Chadwick says, pointing at me, "you would turn to dust, and nothing else. Your 'soul' doesn't go anywhere after death. You're flesh and a brain, with tiny electrical impulses controlling the flesh. Once the brain dies, the flesh is dead, and so are you."

"You can believe in superpowers, but won't even consider that your life just *maybe* has meaning, and something is done with that life after death?" I retort.

"No, beca —"

"Thomas, you can't really believe that!" Hailee barks.

"Well, I do. You may not, but I do. And I'm done talking about it. I don't want to fight with you guys."

"I don't want to fight either."

"Then we're done here. We're *all* done here," Caleb shouts over the rest of us at the table, putting an abrupt end to all conversation.

Finally, everyone is back to eating their meals in a slightly bitter silence. I stare up at Charity who has, once again, crawled back into her shell. I now see the hopelessness in her eyes. She views herself as unimportant in the grand scheme of things. In fact, she doesn't believe in the grand scheme at all, and it hurts to look at her and see that. I wonder how I didn't notice it sooner.

"Still no sign of Madisen?" a pair of girls, who just approached the table, ask Caleb nervously.

"No," Caleb confesses with his mouth full of old biscuits.

"I'm getting really worried about her," the taller of the two girls says.

"What does she look like?" I ask her. Caleb looks angry at me for intruding on their private conversation that they so carefully made sure no one overheard.

"About my height with short, red hair, and a big zit right in the middle of her forehead," the girl answers me, pointing to the center of her head. "Ow, don't hit me!"

"Then quit saying the zit thing!" the shorter one growls. "Madisen is going to kill you if we ever find her."

"See you on the field," the taller one says to Caleb before they both run off back to their table.

"Are you okay, man? Who were those girls?" Thomas inquires of Caleb, who now has unease and paleness spread across his face.

"No, man, I'm good. I just..." He carefully contemplates his next few words. "I just think it's suspicious that Madisen is missing, especially after you said they're hunting people with powers."

"You think she was one of the superheroes?" Kate looks worriedly at Caleb, her elbow unknowingly sitting in a pile of gravy.

"She told me she had powers... when we met here a few days ago," Caleb stutters nervously. "Oh, your arm —"

He points to Kate who realizes where her elbow is sitting. Her face turns bright pink. She grabs a napkin and frantically wipes off her arm.

"You think they may have taken her for that?" Kate asks Caleb, in an attempt to get the attention off of her mishap.

"No, I think they killed her for it," Caleb states blankly.

"But then, why haven't they killed me yet?" I ask in confusion. "Everyone knows I have powers."

"I don't know," Caleb sighs. "I fail to see the logic behind it. You're dangerous. They've killed people weaker than you over less than you've done."

I sink into my seat. He's right. There's no logical reason I should be alive right now. I shouldn't have even made it to this camp. I should have been executed the instant I killed a dozen of their men, but I wasn't. Ronnie, Talia, Madisen. Why not me?

"What people you talking about?" Chadwick asks Caleb suspiciously. "Who've they killed over less than what Annalise has done?"

"I've witnessed a lot of insane things over the past few weeks," Caleb snaps back, still avoiding eye contact, as always. "I don't have time to name them all, but our government certainly isn't in the business of preserving life. Anyone who gets on their bad side dies."

"Did Madisen give you any information we could use?" Thomas asks.

Caleb ponders for a moment. "All she said was she had powers, and the government has quietly been killing off those like her for years, but ever since the EMP, they've ramped it up." His voice gets quieter. "They're killing people in the streets, claiming they were 'enemy spies.' It's how they are excusing all of their brutal murders."

"Seems like you know a lil' more bout all of this than that girl, if you asked me," Chadwick claims.

"No, Madisen told me all of this," he insists, looking down at the table as he speaks.

"Did she now?" Hailee inquires, "Oh, come on! Look at me." Suddenly, she reaches across the table and grabs Caleb's face. "Look at me! What happened to you?"

"Calm down, dude!" Thomas pulls Caleb and Hailee apart from each other. Caleb still refuses to look her in the eye, even after her uncalled for outburst.

Hailee slumps into her seat, then folds her arms. "You were never like this before, but now... You fake your own death, leave your best friend behind to take the fall, and you won't even look him in the eye when you apologize for it. How mature of you." She rolls her eyes at him, but he can't see.

"I don't have to explain myself to you," Caleb mutters, tears welling in his eyes.

While Hailee's outburst was an overreaction, Caleb's lack of eye contact is annoying, but it's his lack of answers that gets to me. There are things he

217

blatantly refuses to tell us. I'm certain that somewhere in his mind are the answers to this entire
thing. I bet he has explanations for how Trivs came
to exist and why the government wants to kill all of
us.

The answers are there and I will find them.

SEVENTEEN

Training today is running laps. All day. We must trudge around the perimeter of the camp with 30 pound backpacks on our shoulders. Everyone from all sixteen buildings is required to participate. Anyone who stops running for even a second is in for a serious punishment, Conner told us, looking at me while she said it. Whatever punishment that is, it can't be too good, because almost every single soldier in the camp is lined up around the perimeter, watching us run and waiting for someone to give up. Surprisingly, Blondie is not among them. I'm relieved he has not been given the opportunity to stare at me all day. Though if he was around, he might be willing to cut me some slack, unlike the other soldiers. Every once in a while, one of them will taunt me with a snarky comment about how tired I look and how maybe I should lay down and take a nap.

After two hours of what is mostly jogging and people trying to walk as slow as they can without getting caught, someone finally drops. A boy, no more than eleven, is unable to hold up under the weight of a backpack almost as big as him. Immediately after he collapses, soldiers flock to him and pull him away

219

from the rest of us, and push him to the ground, where they repeatedly punch and kick the kid as he lets out blood curdling screams of pain.

"Someone needs to help him!" I yell through sharp intakes of breath. I would do it, but I'm already on shaky ground here, so I don't need to draw more attention to myself.

"No!" Chadwick insists from behind me. "The kid'll be fine."

Chadwick's dismissal seems cruel, but I know he's just as worried about drawing attention to us as I am. For an unknown reason, General Kaine has spared me, but I doubt he would continue his kindness if I, or any of my friends, interfered with his plans again. Against my better judgment, I refrain from helping the kid. Someone — presumably his brother — steps up to help and ends up getting a beating along with the young boy.

Everyone else on the track is forced to ignore the soldiers violent display of power and do their best to not become another victim to it.

"Almost time for lunch!" an out of breath Kate attempts to shout to the rest of the group. "That means a break!"

"If we make it that long," Hailee gasps. She has slowed down immensely, along with everyone else here, and I can see her shaking more and more with each step.

I know military training is supposed to be tough, but running non-stop for this long doesn't seem like typical training protocol. I'm convinced these people are just looking for excuses to punish us, or maybe, this is an attempt to weed out the weak ones. Those who fall early may mysteriously disappear within the next few days, as many people here have already done.

I'm not certain why they are doing this to us, but what I do know is every time I pass the building Blondie told me about, I'm tempted to run in, grab a truck, and ram down the gates out of this place.

A loud grunt comes from a kid a few feet in front of me as he drops out from exhaustion. Once again I, and probably everyone else around me, are weighing the risks of running to his aid. As if on cue, several other people start dropping right after the first kid. A girl at the very front of the line falls, causing several people behind her to trip. Soldiers rush in at every angle, snatching up those who fell, and pulling them off to the side for a beating. Even people who haven't fallen are screaming and rushing out to help, and being met with a fist to the face.

"We're going to die," Kate wheezes.

"I can't take it anymore," Hailee sighs, as she wanders from the path and collapses in the grass.

Thomas doesn't hesitate to run to her aid. I can't look the other way anymore, so I run over right behind him, and the rest of our friends follow suit.

I look up to find a hoard of soldiers with malevolent grins coming this way. I stand in front of where Hailee lies on the ground and they continue rushing

221

this way, so I lift my hands up towards them, which causes them to pause. They have clearly been informed of what I am capable of, but then take their chances anyway. One of the soldiers — a tall, muscular man, with a buzzcut and the palest skin I've ever seen — lunges at me just as I'm readying myself to make a forcefield.

"You're not as tough as everyone says you are, freak!" he yells, as we push each other back and forth. "I'd like to see you stop this."

He pulls his arm back and swings it at me, punching me right in the jaw and nearly knocking me unconscious, but I regain my senses and knock him down. While he's down, I close my eyes and try to focus on the concentration of the energy within me and unleashing it as a solid forcefield; a sensation that first came in an instance similar to this, when I was backed into a corner and had no other choice.

The sun beams down on my skin and I soak it in. It's as though I'm being energized by the light, so that I can release that energy in a different way. The warmth burns me and I begin to feel the forcefield forming around me, and then a different burn — the sting of the soldier's fist colliding with my cheekbones again, then nothing...

I jolt awake, hitting my head on the bunk above me. My face throbs violently and aches are sent shooting through my entire body. I hold my hand to my forehead that I just rammed into the bed and the pain immediately ceases.

"Oh, good. You're up," Charity says from beside me, as if she didn't notice me almost giving myself a concussion.

"What are you guys doing here? How did I get here?" I ask in a daze. We are back in Red 8, which is empty of all of its residents except for the six of us: Myself, Thomas, Hailee, Charity, Chadwick, and Kate.

"None of us are allowed to eat lunch because we beat the crap out of those guards," Chadwick snickers.

"And Caleb carried you here. He's back at Red 2. He can't have lunch either," Kate adds. She sits directly next to Chadwick, with no space whatsoever between them.

Charity, who seems disgruntled by their closeness, pretends not to notice it, and instead looks at Hailee, who is lying unconscious on Thomas's bed. She has bruises all over her face and, most likely, everywhere else on her body.

"Dude, your bruises are... disappearing," Thomas mentions to me in shock.

"Really?" I touch my face where the guard had punched me. It hurts at first and is swollen to the touch, but the swelling goes down and the pain eases off within seconds.

"Teach me how to do that!" Chadwick says, jokingly. I laugh with him, but stop when I notice his busted lip — a small injury that will surely last longer than any of mine did.

I look over at Hailee's battered face. She has a black eye, busted lips, bruised jawbone. I wish so badly that I could do something about it, but I don't know how.

By the time lunch is almost over for everyone else, I am fine, minus the hunger. All of my injuries have completely healed. However, when Hailee woke up, she cried from the pain and wouldn't let Thomas look at her face. Then she became upset when she saw a bruise on his arm.

"With the state you're in right now, you're worried about my small bruise?" he chuckles.

"It's not like I'm dying! I can still worry about you," she cries and puts her hands over her face.

"Don't be so cheesy, you two," Chadwick butts in, while he still sits millimeters away from a starry eyed Kate. He is definitely not being hypocritical whatsoever.

A soldier walks in to announce to us that lunch is over and everyone must be present on the training field in five minutes. Hailee winces in pain when she stands and Thomas has to help her remain steady. She glares at me through black eyes when I walk past her and a twinge of guilt hits me for being in good health when she's suffering.

I hold the door open for Hailee as we all head out for more training. Injuries of any kind do not exempt you from any physical activity, or at least that's what Conner told Thomas when he was carrying

Hailee back to Red 8, begging them to let her rest today.

According to Thomas, Conner was giddy to reject his request — something I take responsibility for. If I hadn't gotten on her bad side, she might have been a little more lenient towards them.

I wonder if Conner, or anyone else, will become even more suspicious of me when they see me back on the field with no visible injuries whatsoever. I'm sure Conner was giddy to watch my unconscious body have to be carried back to Red 8, by Caleb, of all people. Why would he be willing to do that? We barely know each other, and in what little time I have spent around him, I have grown quite suspicious of him. From what I saw before getting knocked out, he had no part in the fight, so why get involved by carrying me back?

"What should I say to Blondie tonight?" The thought pops into my head, so I ask the group on our way to the track, pushing Caleb's mysterious kind act to the back of my mind.

I'm shaking with nerves over the impending meeting tonight, not because I am afraid of Blondie; it became evident very fast yesterday that any toughness he has is just a façade, and the real him is just a mean, unintelligent wimp. However, I am afraid of General Kaine and the things he is capable of, and Blondie reports directly to him.

I'm certain that last night I got out every bit of intel Blondie has, though he enjoys letting on as if he still knows more. The only thing left to do is ask him to help us break out, which doesn't seem like something you should do on the second date. Chills are sent through my spine as the word "date" enters my mind.

"Are you going to ask him to escape tonight?" Kate asks me.

"Do I really have a choice?" I gesture to Hailee. "If we stay here any longer we're all going to die. I'm not even sure we'll make it to tonight."

I immediately want to take my last words back, because fear evidently grips onto Kate when I say them. I try to fix it by assuring her I can protect all of us, but with how quickly the soldiers took me down earlier, my words do not comfort her or anyone else.

"If you want him to be unable to deny your request to leave, pathetically babble on about how much you hate it here, how you want to be free, but you just couldn't bear to leave your friends. And throw in some nonsense about not being like the other superhumans," Hailee gripes through gritted teeth.

It's simple, bitter advice (that I had already thought of myself), but it could work, and Blondie might just be dumb enough to buy it.

EIGHTEEN

The rest of the day's training goes by slowly, as most people resort to slow paced feet dragging that could barely be considered walking. Some of the stronger people begin carrying the weaker ones on their backs. However, at around 3PM, in a dangerously rebellious act, every single one of the thousands of people here have agreed to drop our 30 pound weights on the ground, because we are hopeful that they would not be able to punish every person here all at once.

We drop our backpacks in unison and a wave of relief spreads over every single one of us. The soldiers groan at our disobedience, and a few throw the weighted backpacks back at us, but most accept that there is nothing they can do. They cannot stop all of us when we stick together, and that gives me a glimmer of hope, and a sliver of guilt at the prospect of breaking out of this place and leaving them all to fend for themselves.

I spot Caleb across the yard and notice he's walking with the same girls who had stopped by the table at breakfast to ask about the redhead named Madisen. I know he's withholding information from us, so I try to read their lips, but they are too far away to make anything out, though I'm almost sure I see both girls shoot me suspicious glares after speaking with him.

Dinner is scheduled early tonight so we can continue running laps even after our work day is supposed to have ended. Our meal is Salisbury steaks and mashed potatoes with a side of regret and possible abdominal pain. Normally, I wouldn't mind Salisbury steak, but the cooks here seem to have never actually cooked anything during the entirety of their existence.

Dinner talk is nothing more than regular chatter tonight. Caleb doesn't say anything to make me more suspicious of him. There's no existential arguments, and, to my bewilderment, Thomas doesn't bring up Blondie once, despite the imminent meeting with him that will determine all of our fates here. Instead, we eat our disgusting meals in peace, and I mostly listen to the boys at the table behind us. Not by choice, they are just extremely loud. They are all from military families and they rant on about how nothing here is up to standard and the punishments they have go against protocol. They all believe they are absolute geniuses and the only ones here who realize how fishy it is.

"Do you think they'll force us into the gas chamber?" one of them at their table asks the other boys.

228

Apparently, a few weeks into standard military training, you're forced into a gas chamber where you have to take off your gas mask and try not to pass out as you recite information about yourself. Lovely.

Besides my newfound and reasonable fear of being forced into a gas chamber before I can plan an escape, dinner goes off without a hitch. Then we're back to inching around the perimeter of the camp until sweat-soaked sundown.

As the sun begins to sink behind the dark, metal walls that tower over us, Conner finally relieves the soldiers of their surely painstaking duty of standing around and watching us work. Then, we are dismissed from today's torture extravaganza.

The cool evening wind blows on my sweat drenched clothes and sends chills down my spine on my way to the showers, where I spend extra long cleaning myself. I ignore the odd amount of people who glance at me far more times than is considered normal in this specific room. A girl using the shower head next to me goes as far as trying to start a conversation about my powers, but I pretend I cannot hear her over the sound of the running water.

After showers, I watch people sprint and leap forward on their way back to Red 8 as I move my way to the back of the crowd and intentionally fall behind everyone else. A girl with a ponytail gallops past me and my bones ache watching her run.

My feet drag across the browning, uncut grass to Red 8, where Blondie's wingman stands guarding the entrance, yet again. A light above the door shines down on him while he bites his nails and spits them onto the ground. He glances over at me and points towards the far side of the building where I met Blondie last night. I thank him with a nod and walk past him.

I reach the far side of the building and Blondie is barely visible in the shadows as he sits cross-legged in the grass, leaning back on the metal wall. The light above him has busted, so only the moonlight allows me to see that he smiles at my arrival, or does he? I can't tell. He's looking down and the darkness casts a million different expressions upon his face with every slight turn of his head.

"Hey, how are you?" I ask softly as I sit down next to him, because I genuinely cannot tell.

"Oh, fine." He shrugs, then turns to look at me. His wide eyes stare into mine and I'm reminded, again, of his uncanny resemblance to the eye tattoo man from prison. "I need to ask you something."

My heart stops beating when his words hit me. He has just spoken aloud the sentence no one ever wants to hear, even when their own life and the lives of their friends are not at stake.

"Sure. What is it?" I mumble nervously. I try to hide the shakiness that has surfaced in my voice.

"Let's go somewhere else," he whispers. "Derrick is right on the other side of the building. He's proba-bly listening to us."

"I sure am," Derrick says in the distance just before I hear him spit out another fingernail onto the ground.

"Okay, B —" I reply, and bite my tongue before I have a chance to finish that sentence. *No, Anna, you cannot call him "Blondie," given the remarkably high possibility that's not what his name is.*

"Ohh..." he snickers as he stands. "You were about to say Brandon! You've been looking me up. You must really like me!"

We walk around the back of the building and the moonlight illuminates his face and his joyous grin becomes clear. My error has only further convinced him of my romantic interests.

I smile awkwardly at him, then he walks next to the wall and leads me towards the other end of the yard. Several other soldiers see us and shoot disapproving looks our way. A slight anger burns inside me, and I'm tempted to mirror their own ugly expressions back to them, but then it hits me who I'm standing with, and how vehemently I hate and disapprove of this as well. So, glare on, strangers. I understand.

I move my gaze back from the onlookers to Blondie — I mean, Brandon — and his eyes are fixated on a building in the distance. It's the biggest and nicest building here. It's made of brick, with a freshly updated green roof, that's easily twice the size of Red 8, with a giant blue "1" spray painted next to the entrance. I must have passed it over a hundred times today, yet I have absolutely no idea who or what it houses.

"Is everything okay?" I ask Brandon, who seems to have gotten lost in space somewhere between himself and the mysterious building.

"Yeah." He stops in his tracks and nervously adds, "I have a question from the general."

"The general?" I gasp. "What does the general want with me?"

Oh no, General Kaine knows. He knows I'm sneaking out and meeting Brandon. I'm dead. I'm so dead. I'm going to die a horrific, painful death because I snuck out to see a boy I don't even like!

"He wanted me to ask you if you would accept a position as a Triv agent." He laughs at the name as he says it.

I stare at him, completely bewildered, and ask, "As *what?*"

"A Triv agent — a member of a small, special section of the army comprised of a few select Trivs. I think you should be one of them. We're not stupid, Anna. We know we can't defeat all of them by ourselves, so the general is handpicking the ones he thinks are best fit to fight with us. Like you. You fight like them, but you aren't one of them." He purses his lips in anticipation of my response.

"So... You're creating an army of Trivs to fight Trivs?" I ask slowly. I want to make sure I'm understanding this right, because there's no way on earth

232

he could really be blatantly asking me to go to war against my own kind.

"Yeah, well, it's more along the lines of a team of assassins," he explains. "Anyway, you'd be perfect for it. You're strong, and we both know you're not like all the other weirdos out there. There's also another girl on the team — Madisen. I think you'll both get along. She's short, too," he smirks, and I become nauseous.

I don't know what to take in first; him asking me to lead a group of assassins, the girl Caleb knew still being alive, or Brandon thinking she and I would automatically get along because we're both short? Probably the assassin thing.

"I'm — I'm not sure. What if —" I fumble over my words and I begin to stutter so much I can barely speak at all.

"It's not really a choice, Anna." He reaches out his hand and grabs mine. "Don't worry. You'll be great. I told them you would be."

"You — you told them that I..." I trail off. I can't find a firm grasp on any sentence or thought.

I look down at the ground. My façade has faded and a part of me is convinced that if he were to look into my eyes right now, all of the truth would begin pouring out of them.

"Of course I did!" he exclaims. "If I hadn't convinced them you were right for it, they would've killed you by now. I told you I would protect you." He squeezes my hand tighter.

My stomach is tied in a hundred different knots. My legs weigh ten tons and should have me sinking into the ground. My hands shake violently, no matter how much I try to make them stop.

"Okay," I manage to mutter. The words *it's not really a choice* ring in my mind. He's right. I don't have a choice. If I say no, they would kill me on the spot, and all my friends, too.

"Great!" he says enthusiastically. "The general is waiting for you. Don't be worried." He keeps his sweaty palms locked into mine and leads me to the no longer mysterious building. I know exactly what lies inside of it: General Kaine.

We're halfway to the building when I chock up the nerve and pull my hand away from his. He immediately stops walking and turns back to look at me.

"What is it?" he asks.

"Let's run away together. We don't have to... we don't have to do this." Tears well in my eyes and blur my vision. Brandon has become a blond splotch, melting into the background.

He pulls me in for the second hug in two days. Not that I don't appreciate his foolish efforts to keep me alive, but along with my lack of romantic attraction towards him, he also reeks, so for a plethora of reasons, this has to be the worst hug I have ever had the misfortune of experiencing.

"It's okay," he reassures me. "You can do this. You've killed people before. It's not that hard." His tone is comforting, but his words pour out hatred and fill me with disgust and anger.

"I don't want to," I cry, my voice is muffled against his jacket.

He swiftly pulls me away from him, clutching my arms so tightly they ache, and looks me dead in the eye, "But you have to, so suck it up. Killing people *isn't* hard."

I nod my head frantically at Brandon after his horrifying response. His cruel statements have crossed a line and turned terrifying.

He grabs my hand again, gripping it much harder this time, and continues leading me towards the general's building, past all the miniature prisons my friends are being held in.

Two guards standing outside the door let us in without question. Once we're inside, Brandon leads me down a maze of beige hallways.

I'm briefly stricken with flashbacks of the first time I was escorted through the halls of the prison. Of course, those guards weren't holding my hand.

I know I need to find a way out of this, but I'm not sure how. I have only escaped prison once, and that was a fluke. This time the power is not going to randomly shut down, the lights will not flicker out, giving me the perfect opportunity to escape amongst a wild crowd. I will have to make my own way out.

Brandon leads me down another hall and stops at the fourth door on the left. He releases my hand and opens the door for me, then I hesitantly step into a small, dark office. A variety of guns decorate the beige walls, and the shelves are covered in medals and military themed books.

Directly in front of me, General Kaine sits, leaning on a desk table with two chairs placed in front of it. A girl sitting in the chair to my right turns to look at me as I enter the room. From what I can tell she has dark brown eyes and short, pin straight red hair.

"Thank you, Private Carter," General Kaine announces plainly.

"You're welcome, sir," Brandon proclaims, then swiftly leaves and slams the door behind him.

"Sit down, Miss Atwood," the general instructs me, gesturing to the only empty chair.

I take a seat and catch a glimpse of the redheaded girl in my peripheral vision and realize she must be Madisen.

"Miss Atwood," the general says. "I assume you have accepted the discussed position?"

The shadows cast from the dim, flickering lights find their way into all the wrinkles in his face and distort his appearance to reflect the sadistic monster he really is.

"Yes, sir. I have," I answer him.

"Perfect," he says, almost sounding displeased with my acceptance. "This is Madisen Cohen. She is the leader of your team. That means you have to report to her and follow her orders. Nevertheless, her orders never trump mine. Both of you have to do what I tell you. No questions asked. Understand?"

236

"Yes, sir," Madisen and I both reply.

"I have assembled this unit of yours from the best of the worst — Trivs. You, along with the rest of your team, will work from within the shadows to take out those who should never have seen the light of day. You will find Trivs, you will kill them, and you will dispose of them where they are never to be found. They do not exist, and neither do you, which is why your task force has not been given a name. Officially, you do not exist. You never have. You never will. Do you understand?"

"Yes, sir," I answer.

"I have seen what you can do." He narrows his eyes at me, surely recalling the time my forcefield killed so many of his men. "Now, it is time to use those abilities for us instead of against us."

"Wait... right now? We're training right now?" I ask.

"Not training," Madisen mumbles to me.

"Agent Cohen, get Miss Atwood her uniform and meet Conner at the gate in ten minutes," the general demands.

"This way," Madisen says.

She leads me out of the room, takes a left turn, and guides me through yet another empty beige hallway.

"What are we doing?" I implore, at a loss for what's happening.

"I hope you're ready for it." She doesn't turn back to look at me as she speaks.

"Ready for what?" I demand.

"Your first mission, obviously. We got word of a Triv haven up in Newport. Hundreds of them are hiding out there." She opens up a door to a small storage closet, pulls out a uniform identical to hers, along with a pair of black boots, and shoves it in my hands. "Get dressed. You can change in the room at the end of the hall while I go downstairs."

"How are you okay with this?" I ask her. "And what's downstairs?"

She slams the closet door, turns to me, and whispers, "You think I'm okay with this? I'm not, but it's what I have to do to survive. The same goes for you. Now, get dressed."

I walk to the end of the hallway, still unaware of what's downstairs, and open a door into an unused office. A desk sits askew in the middle of the room, but is bare of anything else, besides a few stacks of papers piled up in the corner.

I set the boots down on the floor and unfold the uniform. I'm pleased at the sight of something other than camouflage. The uniform consists of a plain gray T-shirt, a black jacket with the word "Triv" mockingly hand-stitched into the left bicep, black jeans, a bullet proof vest, and a large belt with a gun holster and pockets.

I change into the outfit as quickly as possible. I have a little trouble with the vest, but I manage. I slip on the boots and double knot the laces.

My eyes scan every inch of this empty room, searching desperately for an answer out of here, when I realize I've been skipping over the window right in front of me. I walk over to it. It's a completely normal window; no special locks and no screen.

I have no other choice. I wanted a safe escape route, but Brandon refused to give me one. Either I'm walking out the front door to murder hundreds of innocent people, or I'm climbing out of the window and running for my life. I choose the window.

NINETEEN

I slide up the frame, then climb out onto the lawn.
I'm on the back side of the building, right next to the
fence, with no guards around to shoot me. I turn
right and make my way to the side of the building
while I try to avoid being seen through any of the
windows. I crawl under them until I've reached the
edge of the wall. I make it around to the front of the
building and sit at the corner of the two walls. To my
right are two guards posted at the entrance. A ways
up ahead, past a large stretch of emptiness that offers
no cover, are my friends.

I stand up and lean my head over the side of the
wall to look at the guards I hoped, by some magical
chance, would no longer be there. Sadly, they are.

Conner is climbing out of an armored car and
marching into the building. It's time to leave for the
mission. I don't have any time to sit here and wait, or
they will find me.

I watch Conner walk through the doors and once
I'm sure she is inside, I run for it. I don't try to avoid
being seen, because there is no way around it. I turn
my head around to look back at the guards. I expect
them to be aiming their guns at me, but they only

stare in bewilderment. They don't seem to care enough to stop me, so I look ahead and keep on running, through the uncut grass, past training courses, waiting for someone to wise up and shoot at me, but they don't. I make it through the wide, open field without a hitch, but once I reach the warehouses, a guard from Red 1 stops me.

"What are you doing?" she asks, with her gun pointed at my face.

"I'm... headed back to... back to Red 8," I tell her, gasping for air.

"Why?" She looks me up and down. "And why are you dressed like that?"

I'm so out of shape, I think to myself, as I take a deep breath. "General's orders. It's an emergency," I pant.

She ponders my response, then shrugs me off, and waves me on.

I attempt to nonchalantly jog the rest of the way to draw less attention to myself, and it works. As I approach Red 8, Derrick says something to me that I can't hear. I ignore his unintelligible remark and storm past him into the building without a word.

I swing the front door wide open. The building is alive with casual conversation, but as I rush past people, those conversations abruptly cease. Some people stare at me, others even jump out of my way with fear in their eyes. At first, I don't understand why, but then I realize I'm marching past them dressed in the uniform of a military assassin with a scowl across my face.

I make it past all the people moving out of my way and I see Hailee, Thomas, Charity, Chadwick, and Kate all gathered together up ahead, waiting for me. Thomas is the first to notice the assassin rushing towards them. His jaw drops at the sight of me. Everyone else quickly turns to me in shock. I can see all of them are ready to ask a million different questions, but I cut them off before they can start.

"We have to leave. Now."

"What did you do?" Thomas asks in horror.

"I'll explain later. We need to *leave,*" I demand.

No one seems to want to argue with me like they normally would. Instead, they readily follow my lead.

Fearful, confused people jump out of my way again as I dart to the exit. My heart aches at the idea of leaving them all behind.

"We're escaping *now?*" Kate squeals as we reach the door.

"Yes, we have —"

"You guys are escaping?" a kid behind us asks.

We all turn around, and the same crowd that gathered to watch me use my powers last night is surrounding us yet again.

"Yes," I hurriedly admit and step closer to the door. We don't have time to chat, but curious kids have blocked the door to get closer to the conversation.

"Take us with you," they say, and my heart shatters. Why did I ever think I could leave them behind to fend for themselves in a place like this?

Without answering the begging kids, I climb on to the top of an empty bunk nearby. I stand up and from here I can see everyone inside the building. Hundreds of kids and young adults are packed into one giant, dull room, barren of anything except old bunk beds and the clear sign of the military's depraved indifference etched onto confused and sorrowful faces. Confused because they are in the dark about the harsh reality playing out around them. Sorrowful because they have been snatched away from their loved ones, never to see them again. I'm sure if I walked into any of the fifteen other warehouses all across this treacherous camp, I would find myself staring at the same bleak scene.

Many of those in the room have begun to stare at me after Chadwick let out a loud whistle to grab everyone's attention. He nods approvingly to me, as if he already knows what I'm about to say to the crowd, even though I haven't figured that out yet.

"We cannot stay here," I say so softly that most people couldn't hear me.

"Speak up," Hailee barks bitterly from below. It was a rude remark, but it was just the incentive I needed. I will not give her another reason to complain about me.

"All of us are in danger here," I yell over the commotion. "We are being imprisoned and fed lies, and we cannot put up with it any longer. Our time here has run out. With or without you, I am walking out of these doors tonight and climbing over that gate, but it would be better if all of us did this together!"

To my disbelief, a large portion of the crowd begins to clap and cheer for my little speech, egged on by Chadwick. Every single person in the vicinity, even those who believed what the general had told them, evidently want to leave this place far behind.

As I watch the crowd uniformly agree to desert this prison, I am reminded of what happened during training today. All at once, every single one of the thousands of residents dropped our bags in unison and the guards were unable to do anything about it. Together, we were unstoppable.

"On the count of three," I say, when the cheering dies down, "we head out of the doors, towards the fence, and we urge the residents of the other buildings to do the same! They can't stop all of us!" The crowd cheers once again. "One..." The crowd begins to count with me, readying themselves. "Two... Three!"

I jump down off the bunk, almost falling flat on my face, and stick with my small group of friends as an enormous crowd bursts through the doors of Red 8, pushing Derrick out of their way as some sprint towards the fence and others towards the rest of the warehouses, to fill them in on the unfolding events. I start running for the fence, along with most of the residents.

244

"Wait!" Thomas exclaims from behind me. "What about Caleb?"

Crap! I forgot about Caleb again.

"Right! Let's go get him and then we need to leave," I say, then I, and the rest of my group, follow Thomas. We all march boldly together towards Red 2, along with several other escapees, who are bursting at the seams with adrenaline, ready to inform the other residents about the breakout.

The guards we pass lift up their weapons. They fire rapidly at all of us, the blazing lights of their guns coming directly at me, but the bullets are deflected off the forcefield I subconsciously created. It surrounds me and scares the soldiers senseless. I check around to make sure all my friends are safely behind the forcefield and they are, along with dozens of others assembled excitedly around us. They observe the purple shield in wonder and flinch every time a gun is fired.

"Hurry!" I yell, and we run for Red 2.

Guards continue to pointlessly shoot at us as nothing hits us, but every time a bullet lands on the forcefield, I can sense it weaken in increments. The two guards posted outside Red 2 aim at us, but both drop their weapons and hurriedly run away when I draw closer.

The barrier around me pushes open the door to the building and everyone rushes in to take momentary shelter from the rapid gunfire.

The building is packed full of hundreds of people who spare no time in breaking into a frenzy at the sight of my forcefield and the sound of bullets hitting the outer walls.

"Run! Get out!" people begin to yell.

"Where is Caleb?" I shout over the tumult. No one answers me, so I ask again. "Where is Caleb?"

"Caleb! Caleb!" Thomas yells over the sound of bullets and terrified kids, and the rest of us join in.

"He's right here!" someone shouts back at us. I look over in the direction the voice came from. The two girls Caleb was talking to earlier are clutching onto him and dragging him over.

"He's here!" the shorter girl says, out of breath. Neither of them release their grip on him.

"What's going on?" Caleb asks, gawking at my forcefield and all of the people rushing past him for the exit.

"We're getting out of here!" I say, but he doesn't move. I grab his arm and pull him along. The two girls he's with stick close to him, hiding behind him like he is their sole protector from the chaos that has rapidly ensued.

In a flash, we're out the door, running straight for the fence, with everyone in the vicinity chasing after us with guns loaded. Most of the bullets hit nowhere near us. People are shooting frantically, and most of the shooters are probably newcomers who have never held a gun before last week. I try to expand my forcefield to cover the hundreds of people running towards the massive, dark wall that stands between us and freedom, but I can barely cover my small group.

All of us are moving faster than we ever have before, but Kate is slowing us down. She keeps falling behind, nearly leaving the protection of my forcefield, which is growing weaker every time a bullet lands a direct hit.

The fence is starting to come into view, growing bigger and bigger every second, but every bullet sends a shock through my body and I can barely keep myself steady. Out of nowhere, Kate screeches and I whip my head around expecting to see she's been fatally shot, but blood is dripping down her leg from where she had just barely been grazed.

"Are you okay?" I shout.

"I think so," she whimpers.

"Hurry up! We're almost there," Chadwick says, and reaches out for Kate's hand. He holds onto her and keeps her moving at a steady pace, though she whines more with each step.

The wall is almost in reach, illuminated by blinding, white lights that drain all color from the scene unfolding before my eyes. Caleb makes it to the fence just as a girl who already looked ghostly is shot down and falls over the side. The people next to her scream in agony and terror and rush over the wall ever faster.

Hailee, Thomas, and I reach the wall at the same time. If I had gotten here only moments sooner my forcefield could have saved the ghost girl.

Thomas helps Caleb onto the fence, then pushes me up right after. As soon as I reach the top, I see the mass of people who have already crossed over the fence and found freedom, and the still bodies of those who hadn't. I am pelted with gunshots from both sides of the fence. They clash with my forcefield, sending surges of pain shooting through my bones.

Several empty trucks are parked right at the entrance of a guard tower, just beyond the fence. The tower is manned with soldiers frantically shooting at us. I try my best to ignore them and focus only on protecting the group, who have spread out so much that it's hard to cover them all. Thomas helps Hailee to the top of the wall and I pull her up next to me. Next up are the girls who followed Caleb. Then Thomas climbs up the fence.

Chadwick starts helping Charity up, then Kate, which takes a while because every time she moves she winces and complains about her leg, which is pouring blood down on Chadwick. The longer she takes, the more aggravated and weaker I become. I can see a small group of determined guards catching up to us and I don't know if my forcefield is strong enough to keep them out.

"Hurry, before we all die!" I scream at Kate and yank her the rest of the way up the wall. She lets out a loud wail and shoots me a glare of pure betrayal that tells me she will never forgive me, but at least she made it.

Chadwick quickly rushes up the wall and we all climb down to the other side. We hit the ground running, but I intentionally stay at the back of the pack and try to herd random people under the protection of my forcefield. A young boy is running for cover under it when two bullets shoot through his chest.

Caleb is leading the group and he strides towards the trucks we spotted, not looking back for even a second. A couple of other trucks have already been loaded down with people and driven off to freedom. The men from the guard tower abandon their posts to defend the remaining vehicles.

Every part of my body is strained from the forcefield, and it's taking all of my energy not to give up every time another bullet sends a stinging sensation through my body. I'm lagging too far behind everyone except Chadwick, who is still holding onto Kate's hand for dear life as she runs right beside him.

"I'm sorry," I shout. I cannot do this any longer. The forcefield dissipates into the air, with no trace it had ever been there to begin with.

We are all left completely defenseless in an unforgiving hail of bullets that shows no partiality in its destruction. I try my best to bring it back, to let the power flow out of me, but nothing comes. I am powerless.

Dozens shriek in terror when they notice it has gone away. Our entire group splits up, going in different directions, zigzagging to confuse the soldiers and stop the bullets from hitting them. I take a sharp left, but Kate and Chadwick keep heading straight. Caleb and Charity have almost reached the truck surrounded by guards, with guns pointed right at them. One pulls the trigger and misses Caleb's head by a hair.

I look away for just a second when I hear another kid screaming after being grazed by a bullet, then look back at Caleb and Charity. They are now walking over the collapsed bodies of the guards who almost killed them.

How did they take them down? I wonder. But I don't linger on it, and I don't stop running. I risk closing my eyes to focus on making a forcefield again. I start feeling it slowly flow out, then I open my eyes and it's forming right in front of me. It's just barely left its wispy state when a scream startles me.

"Kate!" The bloodcurdling scream frightens me so much that I lose my focus and the forcefield vanishes into nothingness.

I look for Chadwick, who let out the cry, and instead I see Kate, who lies motionless in the grass, blood pooling around her head.

The group of guards right behind Kate pull her up by her hair, revealing a small bullet hole in her forehead and blood dripping down her vacant face.

One of the guards, who is holding her, smiles triumphantly and waves his gun around. He must be the one who shot her. He sees me staring directly at him, so he turns his gun towards me.

My blood is boiling with anger. It rises up in me and I release it on the guard in a fury of violet that has erupted around me before he has a chance to pull his trigger. The forcefield, that has grown bigger than I thought it could, and turned a darker shade of purple than I've ever seen, pushes against the group of guards who are sent flying back hundreds of feet. Kate's lifeless body is sent along with them. Then, the forcefield unexpectedly disappears, once again, as she hits the ground.

A few soldiers are perched atop the fence, gunning down everyone they can. They are now aiming directly at me. I try, yet again, to focus my energy back into the lavender barrier I know I am capable of creating, so I can knock out these men and protect the rest of the people desperately trying to escape from their grasp. I'm staring down the gunmen, turned ghosts by the pale lights, impatiently waiting for a forcefield that is unwilling to appear. I refuse to move, to back down. I started this jailbreak-turned-death-match, and I will finish it.

The forcefield is reluctant to appear. The soldiers are pulling their triggers, but suddenly I am not in their sights. I have been pulled away and their bullets hit the ground only centimeters away from my feet.

Chadwick has taken me by the hand and leads me towards a truck. I can barely convince myself to move an inch. Right now, I think I would have been fine if their bullets had not missed, if I had died defending the people running for their lives, defending the memory of Kate. I don't run. I let Chadwick drag me along, my feet scraping against the dead grass like a rag doll.

We reach the back of the truck, stepping over the guards Caleb and Charity managed to take out. Chadwick opens the back door and pushes me in when I don't step inside.

Thomas, Hailee, and the two girls who came with Caleb, are all packed inside the vehicle that is identical to the truck I was escorted to the prison in, and what I was brought here in; plain, metal interior, with two benches nailed against both walls, and a small, closable window between us and the front of the truck, where the driver is. It looks like the kind of vehicle you would use to transport high level criminals. Of course, every time I've ever been in one, that *is* what it was being used for.

I sit down on one of the benches and Chadwick jumps in right behind me, then shouts to a few frantic girls nearby to hop in. They rush over, but just before they reach the door, bullets are sent flying through their brains. One girl hits her head on the door before collapsing.

Chadwick leans out the door to call for others to come and a bullet barely misses his forehead. Every person he calls to are, again, shot down before they reach the safety of the truck. Chadwick sighs in exasperation after watching a couple die in each other's arms, then slams the back doors shut.

"Just leave!" Chadwick says furiously, then takes a seat on the bench.

Thomas opens up the window between us and the front of the vehicle where Caleb and Charity are sitting. "Let's go!" he orders.

Caleb steps on the gas and the jolt of speed nearly causes me to fall off the bench I'm sitting on. Everyone tries to grip onto something to stop us from slipping out of our seats and sliding across the benches into each other. There's not much to hold onto, so we awkwardly slip and slide as we make our getaway.

Hailee sits with her arms wrapped around Thomas and her face dug into his chest, trying to block out everything she has just witnessed. The two girls who followed Caleb both sit next to Thomas and Hailee, gripping onto their seats, while Chadwick and I sit opposite them.

"So, you're Annalise?" the short girl asks over the sound of gunfire.

Casual conversation does not seem the proper thing to be doing right now. Thousands of kids are being shot down as we speak, and we have just left them all behind to fend for themselves. It's taking everything in me not to scream for Caleb to turn around and fight.

"Yes, I am," I reluctantly mumble, through stifled screams of horror and overwhelming remorse. "What's your name?"

"I'm Rowena," the tall one says, "and this is Scarlett."

She points to the shorter girl, who gives an unenthusiastic wave when she says her name.

"Wait, how did you know my name?" I ask them curiously.

"Caleb told us," Scarlett answers. She has piercing green eyes, brown hair tied back into a slick ponytail, and a grimace that seems to be her natural resting face, giving her the appearance of irritation, though I know inside she must be terrified. She looks far more intimidating than Rowena, despite being significantly shorter.

Rowena looks timid. Her natural expression is one of wonder. She looks as if she's staring off into space, seeing a better world than the one we currently live in. Her dirty blonde hair is disheveled and falls into her face.

"What did he tell you about me?" I ask, intrigued. Hailee and Thomas casually turn their attention to see what the girls have to say.

"Not much. Just that it was dangerous to be associated with someone like you, so we should steer clear of you. He was looking out for us, since Madisen isn't around to anymore..." Rowena trails off. *Madisen! They don't know she's alive.* "We only met her a few weeks ago, when we arrived at the

254

camp, but she was very kind to us, and she and Caleb were inseparable."

"I guess he was right about avoiding you," Scarlett scoffs, before I have a chance to tell them that Madisen is still with the living.

"Excuse me? You —" I snap, but Caleb makes another sharp left and I'm almost sent flying out of my seat and directly onto Rowena. I grip onto the bench and keep speaking. "You're still alive, aren't you?"

"Sure, we are, but hundreds of other people aren't! And why is that, now? Because of you!" Scarlett screams, pointing her finger accusingly at me, and nearly poking my eye out when we take yet another unexpected turn.

Rowena seems slightly upset at Scarlett's outburst, but she does not looked shocked, almost as if she is used to seeing this happen. However, everyone else in the truck has become visibly uncomfortable and on edge.

"Don't say that!" I shout back at the top of my lungs.

I would tell her how wrong she is, but she isn't. Thousands of people confidently marched out of the camp upon my orders. Hundreds of them have already died, including sweet, innocent Kate, who only wanted to escape the horrors of the camp, but instead died engulfed by them. There's no telling how many more people have already lost their lives since we left, and every bit of that is my fault.

There is an odd silence suddenly filling the air, and I'm convinced all of the gunshots have been drowned out by the sound of my anger echoing back against the metal walls. But I quickly realize there are no gunshots to be heard.

"If it wasn't for —"

"Shut up!"

"No, you need —"

"No! Shut up and listen. There's no more gunshots." I lean over to the front window slot and slide it open. "Why aren't they shooting at us anymore?"

"I think I lost them. A few of them crashed around the last turn," Caleb says gleefully, while tapping his fingers cheerfully on the steering wheel.

"I'm surprised we didn't crash with them!" Charity exclaims. "You have the worst driving I've ever seen."

"I'm a little better when people aren't shooting at me," he laughs, and turns his attention away from the road, swerving a little when he does. "At least we didn't die, but it sounded like someone did back there. What's going on?"

"Nothing," I respond swiftly.

"Sure. Nothing," he says, and I slide the window shut and slump back into my seat, utterly defeated. We may have escaped, but most everyone else did not.

"Are you okay?" I ask, turning to Chadwick, who has tears running down his face. He tries to hide it and refuses to look at me.

"It is your fault," he says in a low voice; just a whisper, but it hits me like a freight train.

"W — what?" I ask.

"I told you," Scarlett boasts, as though being right about this is something of an accomplishment.

I glower at her. She smiles back smugly, and I briefly get a glimpse into how twisted this woman just might be. I am suddenly uneasy having her around.

"She wouldn't be dead right now..." Chadwick murmurs. "None of them would be dead right now if you..."

"I'm sorry," I say, and rest my hand on his shoulder.

He tilts his head toward me and places his hand over mine. He looks into my eyes, and in their reflection, I can almost see when he silenced the crowd in Red 8, unknowingly in full support of my decision that would lead to the demise of someone he loved.

"I know you didn't mean it," he says kindly.

Even when I had just allowed Kate to die, he grabbed me by the hand, dragging me away from my death, and ensured my survival. I'm sure he wanted to leave me behind to suffer the same fate as her, but he didn't. Even now, in the aftermath of my deadly mistake, he is still being kind to me.

TWENTY

"What's that smell?" Hailee sniffs.

We have been riding uncomfortably in the back of this truck for hours with no idea where we are or where we're going.

"I don't know, dude," Thomas replies. "It smells like something's on fire."

Smoke begins to fill my nostrils so much that it's hard to breathe. I was already nauseated from motion sickness, but I can barely stop myself from gagging now. I pull my jacket over my nose to keep the smoke from choking me.

"Something is definitely on fire," I say. My voice is muffled by my jacket.

"What is it? Why isn't Caleb stopping?" Rowena asks. She leaps out of her seat, nearly trips, and rushes over to the window. "Caleb, what's... why's everything *burned*?"

The pure horror in her voice makes everyone else rush over to the window. We take turns looking through the tiny slot out past the windshield into something I only caught a glimpse of before Hailee pushed ahead of me. The only thing I saw when I looked out was black, but everything can't be black, right?

After every other person looks, no matter what their expression previously was, their faces now wear looks of pure horror and sorrow.

"It's all gone," Chadwick mumbles, before returning to his seat.

"What?" I push my way over and finally see out the window into what lies beyond.

I wish I hadn't. Everything *is* black. The moonlight shining down, coupled with the beams from the headlights, reveal everything around us has been burned to a crisp and coated with a fine layer of ash. Houses are heaps on the ground, probably filled with the corpses of those who didn't make it out in time.

A hand touches my shoulder and I jerk back, momentarily convinced it belongs to one of the people who lost their lives, crawling out from among the ashes, begging for life. It's only Thomas. He has already seen what lies outside.

"It's the city," he tells me, a glimpse of terror still in his eyes. I shake my head at him. I don't understand what he's talking about. "It's the city we saw burning," he elaborates, and then it hits me. Not long ago, we saw a city in the distance lit up in flames. This is that same city.

"What happened to this place?" Charity asks Caleb through sniffles.

I lean closer to the window to hear his answer, but I don't expect him to know what's happened either.

"This city was a safe place for Disvariants," he begins to tell her. My mind is already in knots at the word *Disvariants*. "When everything shut down, everybody was in the dark. The military used that opportunity. They took them out — all of the people that were living here — without word getting out. Most people still don't know it happened."

Charity, as usual, doesn't seem to have a response. I glance back at the rest of the people in the truck. They've all started talking to each other and didn't notice what Caleb had said.

Scarlett steps up and pushes me out of the way to see the burned city. I ignore her rudeness, rather than start another argument with her. I didn't notice it while we were running away, because I was too focused on not dying, but Scarlett has this strange look in her eye. Maybe I'm imagining it, because no one else has seemed to notice, but something about her doesn't set right with me.

Scarlett shuts the window when she's done, and we all sit back down in melancholy silence with our shirts covering our noses. Everyone else's minds seem to be focused on the tragedy of this city, but *my* mind is focused on how Caleb knew about it. He seems to know a lot of things that we don't. I'm a Triv, and yet I don't even seem to know as much about Trivs as he does.

He could have gotten his information from Madisen. I know he was closer with her than he wants to admit, but she failed to even clue him in on where she had disappeared to. I have yet to tell him she's still alive.

Eventually, we leave the city limits and the smoke begins to clear. Now that I don't have to hold my jacket up to my face anymore, I get up, walk over to the window, and slide it open.

"Hey, Caleb," I say firmly.

"Yes?" He turns to me curiously.

"Look at the road!" Charity screeches, and he whips his head back around to stare at the road ahead.

"Explain to me how you knew about that city back there if hardly anyone did," I demand, and I see his expression grow worrisome in the rear view mirror. "How did you know it was a safe place for Whatever-You-Called-Them, and how do you know so much about Trivs?"

"First off, don't call yourself that. It's an insult," he insists.

I don't look back to see if anyone else is now listening in on our conversation, though I'm sure they are. I do, however, glance over and see Charity looking at Caleb in concern.

"How *do* you know all of that?" she asks him.

He doesn't answer her. Instead, he looks in his rear view mirrors, making sure no one is following us, then stops the car in the middle of the road.

"Do you really want to know?" he asks coldly, once again refusing to look at me.

"Yes," I demand.

"I'd like to know, too," Thomas says from behind me.

"Alright," Caleb sighs.

He angrily climbs out of the truck, then moments later the back doors are flung open and Caleb stands in front of us, grimacing.

"Everybody out. We need to clear things up," he says.

We all step out onto a wide dirt road surrounded by overgrown trees. Left unmanaged, their branches grew over power lines and formed an arch over the road, blocking out what little light could have been provided by the moon. The trucks tail lights, that cast a harsh red glow onto everything, is what I must rely on to see Caleb, who wears a pressing look on his face. For the first time since meeting him, I remember he's only nineteen. He's so reserved and cold, and his face looks worn several years beyond his actual age. He could easily pass for twenty-five.

Everyone stands gathered around Caleb, waiting for him to finally provide us with overdue answers.

"Should we be stopped?" Charity asks in dismay. "What if they catch up to us?"

"We're fine," Caleb says with his usual lackluster.

"So, tell us what big thing you pulled over for," Scarlett grumbles with her arms crossed. It seems as if she thinks of herself as intimidating, and is under the impression that bitter words and an angry pose demands some sort of acknowledgement.

"Okay. You want to know how I know so much about Trivs — a derogatory term for Disvariants. I thought it would be apparent by now, but it's because I am one. I have had my powers since I was about fourteen and —"

"That's why you were being blackmailed," Hailee interrupts.

"Yes, that's why. I don't know who it was or how, but someone found out. They threatened to expose me. That put myself, my family, and my friends in danger, because even back then, being a Disvariant could get you killed. That's why I faked my death." Everyone stares at Caleb, but he looks off into the distance just past me as he speaks, cringing as he utters the word *death*. "After that, I found a safe place to hide with other Disvariants. I stayed under the radar until all the electricity went off. The military came in raiding the place. I got out, but they found me wandering the roads and took me back to their camp.

"That's how I know so much about Disvariants, where they hide, and how Madisen was one of them, and why she's probably dead now."

"She's not dead," I blurt out. All of their attention turns to me. "Well, maybe she is. I have no idea after the chaos that unfolded back at camp, but she was alive when we left." Everyone stares at me, confounded. "Hasn't anyone wondered why I'm dressed like this?" I tug on my black jacket. "Or why we had to leave the camp in such a hurry? Blondie tried to recruit me for the general's special task force of Trivs — I mean *Disvariants.* The general knows they aren't strong enough to defeat us all on their own, so he tried to bring some of us in as assassins against our own. Madisen is the leader of the team, though she doesn't want to be, and this is their uniform."

I point again to the menacing, all black outfit I've been wearing since before the breakout that no one has bothered to question.

"She's alive?" The usual hardness in Caleb's voice is gone. "And you left her there?"

"I had no other choice. I had to get out of there. She was about to lead a mission into a Triv — Disvariant haven at Newport," I sigh, but with each word Caleb looks more distraught and I can no longer look at him. "They were going to kill them all. I was supposed to go with them. I couldn't do it," I explain, in an attempt to defend myself. But in all honesty, bringing her along never crossed my mind. I left her just as I almost left everyone else, even Caleb.

"How can any Dis-Triv-Thing —" Hailee attempts to say.

"Disvariant," Caleb corrects her. "It's a combination of 'disparate' and 'variant." They both mean —"

"Yeah, I don't care. How could one of *you guys* be willing to do that?" Hailee asks in disbelief.

"She doesn't have a choice. They'll kill her if she doesn't do what they say," I answer. I am trying to defend her actions, but I think I would rather die than kill innocent people. However, I have an outpouring of blood on my hands as well, so I have no right to judge.

"And you *left* her there?" Caleb repeats in distress.

"Yes, I did, and I'm sorry," I admit remorsefully, still unable to look at Caleb, who is probably fighting back tears. "Maybe we could go back. We left so many people behind. They might —"

"Anyone who hasn't escaped already is dead," Caleb says resentfully, and tears begin to well in my eyes, though I'm sure no one can tell in this harsh lighting.

I led hundreds of people to their deaths and left those who remained to fight alone. Even if I had stayed, could I have saved them? No, I couldn't. My powers failed me. I cannot control it. If I had stayed, if Chadwick hadn't dragged me away, I surely would have died...

"Does Madisen know about you?" Chadwick asks Caleb.

"Yeah. We both knew about each other," he sighs, and I can hear the discomfort growing in his voice.

I force myself to look up at him. His right hand is tapping frantically on his leg and his eyes are darting around, suspiciously glancing at everyone, as if checking to see if we realize the conversation has just become far too personal for him.

"And would you mind telling us what she knew? You said you met at the camp, but how long have you really known that girl?" Chadwick interrogates, leaning nonchalantly on the back of the truck.

Earlier, Scarlett had mentioned how tight knit Caleb and Madisen were when she met them a few weeks ago, confirming that he had been hiding their closeness from us, but I think everyone here already had their suspicions about what was going on between them.

"We knew each other for a while, okay? She knows a lot about me, but you know all of it that's relevant."

"Not all of it. What power do you have?" Chadwick cocks an eyebrow.

"Why don't we talk about that later?" Caleb dodges the question, turning to look at the road behind us. "We should keep going so they don't catch up to us."

"Just tell us," Chadwick barks bitterly. "We're not gonna judge you for it."

"Yes." Caleb's coldness has returned. "You will."

"I don't think we need to be standing around arguing about this. Let's get back on the road before we end up getting ambushed," Charity says anxiously, staring out in the distance. Nothing is there, but the longer she stares, the more fearful she becomes.

"Yeah, let's go," Caleb agrees and walks back to the truck, so the rest of us reluctantly follow him.

"I'm going to sit in the back with Chaddy. Shotgun is up for grabs," Charity announces to the group.

"I'll take it," I say before anyone else can. "Sitting in the back is giving me motion sickness."

I jump in the passenger's side and close the door. I sit down in an uncomfortable, old seat, that looks in good need of a pressure washing. Soda and beer cans are scattered about, but most lay in the floor, clanking against each other. Caleb doesn't pay me an ounce of attention, and I'm okay with that. After finding out I left Madisen behind, I imagine he's not too happy with me. I would gladly take silence over hearing the pain in his voice as he asks why I left her behind, and having to explain to a heartbroken man that I simply never considered bringing her with me.

I can hear the muffled sound of everyone in the back having what seems to be a nice conversation, now that I'm no longer present. Every once in a while someone lets out a bellowing laugh. There was no laughter going on earlier. Maybe they would be happy and full of laughter all the time if I hadn't entered their lives. Maybe if I had just slipped away that night in Columbus like I had planned...

I lean my arm against the doorframe, rest my head on my hand, and try to drift off to sleep, but every time I almost do, something jolts me awake; my head slipping off my hand, hitting a pothole in the road, the sound of someone laughing loudly, or something in my brain sparking and telling me "no, no, no. Don't go to sleep. Sleep and you'll die."

After who knows how long, I finally give up. I open my eyes, sit up straight, and stare into the darkness of night that is broken up, in part, by dim headlights. I rub my wrist that aches from the weight of my head.

We travel, still, down a long dirt road, with dust flying up and being illuminated by the lights. I've never been on a dirt road this long before.

"Where are we headed?" I ask Caleb.

He jumps a little at my question, obviously not expecting to hear my voice.

"The Plains, down in Athens," he says, but it feels more like he's speaking uncomfortably to the road in front of him. "I know some people over there. They would be willing to help us."

"Does Madisen know about them?" I ask curiously, and it catches his attention.

"No," he answers swiftly. It's clear he doesn't want to talk about it, especially with me, so I try to change the subject.

"So, what are your powers?" I ask.

"I don't think you want to know that," he says brusquely.

"And I think you're wrong. Just tell me."

His eyes dart towards me for just an instant, then flash away.

"I can kill people," he says so quietly, and so quickly, that I almost didn't catch it.

"You what?" I blurt out.

"I can kill people... without touching them. I don't have to stab them or shoot them. I look at them, they die."

So, that's why he never looks anyone in the eye. That, also, must be why one second the men guarding this truck were shooting at Caleb and Charity, and the next they were dead, unlike the guards shooting at everyone else. He didn't bother to stop any of them.

"How could you let her die?" I growl at Caleb. I don't say her name, but he knows who I mean. He may never look at anyone, but he certainly must have noticed the most talkative person in our group was not present at our roadside meeting. "How could you let all of them die?"

Kate, and a hoard of other people I never got to know, were killed by guards that Caleb could have killed first, so why didn't he?

Asking him why he refrained from committing murder is a horribly twisted question, but it's one I have to ask.

"I'm sorry those people died, but killing someone is not something I can take lightly. I only do it when I know there's no other way out," he exclaims acrimoniously, and unintentionally jerks the steering wheel. His eyes narrow on the road.

"And being surrounded by men shooting semi-automatics at us didn't feel like a situation without another way out?" I retort in exasperation, and furiously kick some of the cans on the floor.

"No! You had your forcefield. You were keeping us safe. How was I to know it would disappear like that?" he remarks defensively, and has to correct his steering, yet again.

I can feel the car speeding up as he's unintentionally pressing down harder on the gas pedal. With nothing else to hold onto, I grip the dashboard and hope we don't crash into the ditch because of this fight.

"But even after it disappeared, you did nothing," I snap back at him in rage.

"No, I took out the guards at the truck!" he ripostes. I feel the truck speed up a bit more.

"What about the ones who were shooting at everyone else and not just you?" I shout bitterly. "What about Kate?"

Tears begin to overflow in my eyes. The image of her dead body collapsing on the ground is etched into my brain. I want to be as far away from Caleb as possible right now, but that's hard in the confines of a two-seater truck. I slide myself as close to the window as I can and look away from him.

"I can't go around killing everyone! Just because they shot at us doesn't make it any easier for me!" he shouts back at me and nearly drives into a ditch. He swerves to get back on the road. "Her death isn't my fault, okay? Now, let me drive before we *all* die."

"Hey," Thomas slides the window open and butts in. "What's going on up here? What's with the shouting? Anna, are you crying? Why are you crying?"

"I'm fine," I mutter.

"Caleb, why is she crying? What did you do?"

"What did *I* do? Why is this my fault?"

"I heard *you* shouting. Why is she upset?"

"I'm fine!"

"See, she's fine! Everything's fine!" Caleb slams the window shut. Silence fills the air and his stone cold expression returns.

I know it's my fault that Kate is dead. Sure, Caleb could have saved her, but she wouldn't have been put in a situation where she needed to be saved if it wasn't for me. I'm the reason Hailee, Thomas, and I ended up at the camp where we met her. Then, I decided to make my own great escape and expected everyone to follow along, with no regard for how it would affect them.

It's my fault — all of it. I know it is, but I don't want to believe that right now. I *can't* believe that right now. The weight of all the bodies I saw fall lifelessly to the ground, because of my own reckless actions, are crushing me, and I can hardly breathe. Tears stream down my face and I try to stop them. I try to be mad at Caleb instead. I try to be furious at him for not saving those people, but I can't find it in myself to be mad that he was unable to convince himself to commit such a vicious and inhuman act.

"Hey, hey. I'm sorry," Caleb consoles me when I don't stop crying. He puts his arm around me and pats me on the shoulder. "I'm sorry."

"It's my fault," I say through sniffling.

"No, it's not." He pulls me close to him and I lean on his shoulder. I want to push him away. A part of me still wants to try to be angry with him, but I'm physically and emotionally tired. And though hugs are normally unbearable for me, something about his embrace feels natural and comfortable.

"It is my fault. Everyone is dead because of me."

"It's not your fault," he says, and continues to hold me.

TWENTY ONE

I open my eyes and the sun shining down through the windshield blinds me. We're no longer on a dirt road, but we're still surrounded by trees. A light layer of fog floats just above the ground and disappears as we draw closer to it.

I fell asleep on Caleb's shoulder last night and my neck hurts from leaning on it for hours.

"Good, you're awake. My shoulder is killing me," he laughs.

"Oh, sorry," I say, and rub my neck as I sit up.

"It's fine," he sighs.

I can see in his face that he's exhausted. His eyes look tired and they are darting around in every direction, trying to focus on something. He's been driving all night long.

"Why didn't you switch out driving with someone else so you could rest?" I ask him.

"No one else knew where I was going," he smiles.

I don't want to bother Caleb anymore. I've already asked him to reveal his darkest secret, then I yelled at him for it, and pathetically cried to him. But there's something I just have to know.

"Hey, since you know so much about Disvariants, how do we get our powers?" I inquire. It's something that has baffled me ever since I realized what I was capable of.

"You really don't know?" he laughs. He seems to have hit that golden stage of sleep deprivation where absolutely everything is unexplainably funny.

"Obviously not," I retort and roll my eyes at him.

"Our bodies absorb the energy from the sun. That's what gives us our powers," he chuckles.

"What?" I gawk.

"Yeah. All Disvariants get our abilities from the sun, but we begin to harness those abilities at different ages. Whenever that does happen, it's called the Variation, because that's when everything changes. They say you only experience it when you need it and you're ready. I didn't feel ready at fourteen."

"Is eighteen a normal age for it to occur?" I ponder the unusual timing of my power's arrival.

"There is no 'normal age.'. It happens because... Well, it *supposedly* only happens when you need it to. You could be eighty years old and in a nursing home before the Variation happens. It's different for everyone."

I think back to my life before, where I was safe. I never needed a shield then. But as soon as the EMP happened, it became a necessity, and that's when I found it.

"What happened to you at fourteen? Why did you need your powers then?" I ask, and I regret it immediately.

I didn't think about it before the words slipped out, but I just asked Caleb about the murder, or possibly multiple murders, he committed at fourteen, when his powers were new and he had no idea how to control them yet.

"Don't ask me that," he snaps, so I change the subject.

"So, how do we have the ability to *harness the sun,*" I say, snickering a little at how ridiculous it sounds out loud, "but not normal people? Do we have different DNA, like the X-Men or something?"

"When the sun —" He stops dead in his tracks, then sighs, and begins to further ponder my question as if, once again, deciding whether to tell me the whole story or not. I thought we had begun to move past the phase of keeping secrets about Disvariants. I guess he decides on sharing the truth, because he tells me everything, or most of it anyway. "There is no scientific explanation for why we are the way we are. Try as we might, no one has been able to find a reason for it. Some people have it, some people don't. That's just the way it is. It's often believed that everyone has abilities inside them; everyone has the potential to go through the Variation, but only a rare few of us ever experience it. Like I said, it comes when you're ready. Most people are never ready for it."

It seems such an outlandish theory that I want to dispute it, but at the same time, I couldn't fathom a scientific explanation for how looking someone in the eye could cause them to instantaneously drop dead.

My entire life has been built on hope and believing in things I can't see, like purpose, but this is much more extreme that any of that, but I can tell Caleb is being mostly honest with me. I get the sense there is something about the Variation that he is excluding, something that would further explain the strange thing that has happened to me. Perhaps, he doesn't believe I'm *ready* to hear it yet, and since I wouldn't know where to begin with questioning him about it, I let it go. I believe he is telling the truth, for the most part, and as much as I want to be logical and say it's impossible, I can feel within my soul that this is beyond our logic; an unexplainable, supernatural phenomenon that apparently lives inside every single person on the planet.

"What about General Kaine?" I ask. The thought of him being a Disvariant shakes me to my core. "Could he be one of us? Does he even believe that's possible?"

"People like Kaine look at the Variation as a disease. He probably spends his life living in fear that he will catch it," he states, taking a sharp right turn as he does, and almost driving into the ditch. "I don't know whether he legitimately believes that he could.

276

It's the most common belief, but even some Disvariants aren't willing to accept that the people who hate us so much could become one of us. I don't think anyone could experience the Variation while they still abhor us. Kaine will never experience it as long as he continues to harbor animosity towards our race."

He smiles again, though I don't know why. He is much more talkative today than usual. It's a mystery whether it's because of his sleep deprived state, or because he no longer needs to keep so much of his knowledge under lock and key.

"What's the truth about you and Madisen?" I ask. I've already walked the line with several touchy subjects since last night, but now appears to be the best time to get an answer out of him.

"Why do you want to know that?" he asks nervously.

"Because there's something you're not telling us and I want to know what it is," I answer.

Caleb sighs, then pulls into the driveway of an abandoned warehouse that is completely surrounded, up to the doors, with trees and bushes. Fantastic. I thought we were finally done with warehouses.

Caleb shifts the truck into park, stares up ahead, then sighs, "We were in a relationship. Not sure about that anymore since we left her behind," he says caustically. I'm sure he would be glaring at me if he would bother to look my way. "We met at one of the places where I was hiding out. We got together not long after I faked my death. I'm in love with her," he turns to look at me briefly. "There, you happy?"

He turns away, then hops out of the truck. I follow him to the back, where he opens the doors wide.

"Rise and shine!" he says cheerily to the group who hadn't woken up yet, putting our invasive conversation quickly behind him.

All of the girls are awkwardly cuddled up next to each other on the benches, and Chadwick and Thomas have taken the floor.

"Where are we?" Thomas yawns.

"Warehouse 47, The Plains," says Caleb.

Everyone slowly makes their way out of the truck, wiping the tiredness from their eyes and the drool from their faces. Rowena's hair looks identical to a bird's nest, and Hailee's hair is now done up in braids full of knots and tangles.

"Something's not right," Caleb says, squinting at the warehouse up ahead. "They usually have someone posted on lookout. Be careful when you walk in."

"Maybe Annalise should lead the way," Rowena suggest. "She's our only defense."

"No, she's not," Caleb remarks.

"Well, we would add you in the mix, but you're being so secretive about what your powers are, so we can't really count on you, now can we?" Scarlett says, with the ever present condescension in her voice.

Why Caleb, Rowena, or even Madisen ever be-friended this girl is beyond me. Even when she doesn't speak, her judgmental glares radiate negativity.

"I'll go in first," I say, before this turns into an argument.

I walk across the tall grass to the rusted front door. I pull a few weeds out of my way and I enter with caution, but as soon as I'm through the door, I'm smacked in the face. I'm not physically attacked, but a smell worse than roadkill hits me dead on. It's stronger than anything I've ever smelled before. Without even thinking, I rush back outside into the fresh air and let the door slam shut behind me. Everyone takes my overreaction the wrong way.

"What is it?"

"What's wrong?"

"Is someone in there?"

"It's the smell," I cough. "It reeks, like there's a bunch of dead animals in there."

Caleb's face turns pale and he rushes inside with-out saying anything. I take a deep breath, pull my jacket over my nose, and run in after him. I follow him as he takes a sharp left down a short hallway. The closer to the end I get, the stronger the smell is. The pungent odor brings tears to my eyes.

Caleb steps into a room where couches are placed randomly about, smashed tables are spread across the floor, and a few beds lie overturned in the cor-ners. A fight has clearly gone down in here, but I didn't gather that from the tables. I gathered that from the bodies. Dozens and dozens of dead people are sprawled out on the floor with bullets in their heads. Blood is splattered on the walls like a messy paint job.

Caleb runs into all the other rooms, checking for any signs of life, but I don't follow. I know he won't find anyone.

Everyone else has now made their way into the building as well. Complaints about the smell instantly turn to shocked gasps when they reach the end of the hall, mostly by Scarlett, who is now mumbling to herself about how she managed to get mixed up in this mess.

Caleb returns from the other rooms with a grim look on his face. He doesn't even have to speak. We all know what it means: No survivors.

We all leave Warehouse 47 in solemn defeat. Our chances of survival were dead long before we got here. We step outside again, taking in deep breaths of the fresh, life-filled air. Caleb shuts the door behind us and locks it.

"Where do we go from here?" Thomas asks solemnly.

I glance around at everyone, all looking to someone else for an answer. Plenty of places pop into my mind, but I have no idea if any of them are safe anymore. I don't want to be the one to lead us in the wrong direction, and neither does anyone else.

"We can't go to a place that any of us have lived before. Those are too obvious. That's where they'll check first," Caleb says, then walks over to a bush and starts picking off its bright yellow flowers.

It takes me a moment to realize he's plucking sunflowers, which is an unusual thing to see growing in the wild around here. I would question it, but that's not my biggest concern right now.

"Will they hurt my parents?" I ask him.

"No way," Hailee answers. "They couldn't do that."

"They're probably already dead," Caleb says as he plucks another flower off the bush. "What? Why are you looking at me like that? These are bad people, okay? They're not our protectors or our saviors. Did any of you look at what I just saw in there? Hundreds of Disvariants dead. Killed just because of who they were. Not a single person in that building was guilty of anything except existing. If you think the people who did that will spare your families, you're a blatant idiot."

Everyone is shocked by his words. We all knew our own lives were at stake, but none of us had ever considered they would kill our families over this. Charity mumbles something I barely make out to be a sobbing statement about her mom, then runs to Chadwick for comfort.

"I know a place a few towns over that we can stay," Scarlett says, unfazed by the loss of her family or Charity's wails.

"Where is it?" Caleb asks.

He bunches up the sunflowers and ties them together with a long weed he plucked from the ground and lays it at the foot of the door; a token of respect to all the innocent lives that were lost inside.

"I'll drive us there," Scarlett says.

"No way," I refuse.

"And why not?" Scarlett folds her arms as she glares at me.

"Because I don't know you well enough to blindly follow you somewhere," I say.

I don't trust Scarlett enough to let her lead me two feet forward with my eyes closed, much less to a supposed place of safety several towns away, with her in the driver's seat.

"Excuse me? Oh, excuse me? You don't know *me* well enough? Some of us don't even trust you, you know, yet we all followed you blindly into a gun show that got all your sheep killed."

"Don't call them that!" I stomp my foot. "If you don't trust me, why don't you just leave?" I sneer.

Scarlett inches menacingly towards me, so I do the same.

"She's right," Hailee says. She has stepped between Scarlett and me.

"About what part?" I ask as I stare her down.

"Some of us here *don't* trust you," she says.

"Why not?" I demand, and she slowly backs away from me.

"Because you killed your best friend," Hailee

answers, but it's clear she did not intend her words just for me. She was announcing it to the entire group.

Everyone gasps in shock and confusion. I had managed to keep this between me, Thomas, and Hailee, but I never should have made the mistake of telling Hailee in the first place. For a few fleeting hours she began to trust me, but the second she found out what I had been accused of, all trust was destroyed and we were on worse terms than before, and now she may have destroyed my trust with everyone else as well.

"I knew it! I knew there was something off about you! I just knew it!" Scarlett triumphantly exclaims. Yes, *I'm* definitely the sketchy one between us.

"Hailee!" Thomas shouts at her. "Dude, why would you say that?"

"Because it's the truth, Thomas!" she shouts back and folds her arms, in the same way as Scarlett. Standing next to each other, they look like devious, backstabbing sisters.

"No, it's not!" I sigh in frustration. "I didn't kill my best friend! I wouldn't do that!"

"Why didn't you tell us then?" Charity asks. Sheer betrayal glosses over her red eyes.

Chadwick stands next to her, staring at me intently. He's trying to figure out if he should believe me or not. He rightly blames me for Kate's death, but being heartbroken over that could cloud his

283

vision and make it much easier for him to believe that I have intentionally killed people in the past.

"Because I didn't do it. Just like Thomas! I was... I was framed," I cry and get choked up the more I speak. "I knew you guys wouldn't believe me. I knew it."

My heart is beating rapidly and I'm forcing myself to hold back a wave of tears. My worst fear is coming true: I'm back on trial, only now, Scarlett is the prosecutor and everyone else is the jury. Just like last time, my case is losing.

"We know Thomas is innocent because his proof is standing right there!" Scarlett points at Caleb, who has gone completely silent in this argument. "Where's yours? Oh, right! You don't have any!"

"I knew this would happen. I knew you wouldn't believe me."

"I believe you," Chadwick says to my astonishment. Even after I recklessly caused the death of Kate, he's still willing to side with me.

"You know what? Maybe *you* should be the one to go, not me," Scarlett smirks proudly. "You will be just fine on your own. That's right, just fine. Don't you agree, Row?"

Rowena nods her head in fearful agreement. I see now that they aren't friends. Scarlett is her boss, and Rowena is her terror filled minion.

"So do I. Who agrees?" Hailee says, and raises her hand in the air.

Rowena and Scarlett both raise their hands. After a moment of quiet consideration, Caleb raises his hand, too. He doesn't speak, he gives no explanation for his decision, he only raises his hand high and refuses to look my way. Just last night he admitted he was a killer, and now he's chosen to turn against me because he suspects I might be one as well.

Only Thomas and Chadwick disagree with the consensus that I'm guilty. Charity naturally sides with what Chadwick says, though I don't know if she truly believes in my innocence.

"Fine," I scowl at the people who raised their hands, especially Caleb. "See you later," I add sarcastically, then storm off down the rocky driveway.

At least this time three members of the jury believed me, I think to myself, while I make my way just between the road and the trash filled ditch, stomping off in a different direction than the way we came here.

"Stop!" Thomas shouts from behind me, but I don't quit walking. He runs down the driveway to catch up with me. "I'm coming with you. I can't leave you alone."

I stop dead in my tracks and turn to face him. "Really? You're going to leave behind Hailee and Caleb — the two people you care about most in the world — for me, when I'm perfectly capable of defending myself?" I say, intentionally letting bitterness flow out of me. "I don't need your help!"

285

"I care about you, too," he says softly, taken aback by my rage.

"Shut up," I snap, then turn away from him without another word.

I would love more than anything for him to come with me. The thought of traveling into unknown territory all alone, while the government is hunting me down, is terrifying. But I won't let him leave his closest friends behind for me, even if both of them did just vote me out in some twisted version of Survivor tribal council.

I walk away without looking back, ready to ignore anything else he might try to say to me, but he says nothing. However, I can feel what I'm sure is a look of pure betrayal and incomprehension remaining fixed on me as I disappear into a cloud of fog.

Eventually, there's the distant sound of all their voices saying something I can't understand, then the engine cranking up. The truck drives off in the opposite direction without me, to a place I do not know and cannot go. I have been abandoned, left entirely alone in an unfamiliar town, of my own free will.

I walk the narrow, muddy path between the road and the ditch, shoes squishing on the ground with every step. The day becomes more and more foggy the longer I walk. I've decided to follow what I can see of the road straight, for as long as it will take me, but I quickly become panicked at the realization I have no plan for when I reach the road's end. All I have are my defective powers and, most likely, a bounty on my head.

I can't believe I let them drive off without me. I want to take it back, but it's too late now. I have to deal with the consequences of my actions. I have no way of undoing them. I was given the powers of protection, not time travel. Yet still, I manage to get people killed instead of keeping them safe. Maybe it's better that I'm not around to drag anyone else into dangerous situations. It seems as though death follows me everywhere I go, so staying away from the people I care about makes sense.

I pass by a pile of beer cans stacked up in a pyramid and I kick it down and wonder who would have spent any amount of time putting that together, especially with chaos unfolding around them. The clank as the pyramid comes crashing down remind me of the beer cans in the floor of the truck that rattled while Caleb and I talked. I had begun to think there was a possibility he and I might become good friends, after we got over the initial argument. But he raised his hand with Hailee and Scarlett. Did he really think I killed my own best friend, or was it something else? Was it the argument? Was it because only I knew his dark secret? Was it leaving Madisen behind? There was no doubt he resented me for it, but even with the knowledge of what I had done, he still willingly shared his secret with me and consoled me. So, what pushed him over the edge? I don't know, and I guess I never will.

TWENTY TWO

There seems to be no end in sight for the old, pot-hole filled road when I notice a gas station not too far up ahead. It appears abandoned, but then again, most gas stations that are still in business look that way, too. I get closer to it and see no cars and no lights. Considering only military vehicles and pre-70's cars are working, and lights everywhere except in military bases are out, this isn't a shocking discovery.

I walk inside the convenience store. The little bell rings when I open the door and I almost expect a lonely employee, with no other ambition except keeping this store running, to pop up from behind the counter. But no one is here.

The light from the sun shining through the glass doors is all that is keeping this place from total darkness. The floor is grimy. A thick coating of dirt and grease covers it, almost completely blocking the outdated tile from view. It's apparent it was never mopped even when this place was up and running, and the building has an unwelcoming odor to it, likely from all the sweaty drivers that used to pass through.

I peer around at the shelves, still miraculously stocked. The freezers aren't cold anymore, but still hold dozens of drinks that haven't gone bad. I weigh my options, considering what lies ahead of me outside the doors — complete uncertainty (and also probably death) — and I decide to do something I used to be wildly against, but have come to begrudgingly accept as my only way of finding sustenance: Looting. But, I mean, in an apocalyptic land where all laws have already gone out the window for most, and the owner of this store has clearly left this place with no plans of return, is it really stealing? Probably. But I grab a couple bottles of water, a few sodas, several bags of chips, and a handful of candy bars.

I walk around behind the counter, grab some bags to stuff everything in, and try to ignore the scratching sounds of rats crawling around in the back room. I fill up the bags and rush outside before the rats break free.

Hours pass, midday hits, and the sun burns brightly on my face. Now that I know the sun is where I get my powers from, the way its light comforts me makes even more sense. I always knew the sun brought life to this planet, but now it brings it to me in a much more personal sense. The warmth that radiates from it energizes me and brings me peace, and I begin to wonder how I could have gone through my entire life not realizing something so fundamental to my survival and my purpose, was surrounding me, and filling me every day. Thinking about all of it only makes me ever more curious what details of it Caleb withheld from me. I have been in the dark about Disvariants since before the electricity shut off, and the answers to all the questions I didn't know I should be asking were sitting in the driver's seat right next to me. But they drove off without me, never to return, and now I may never get them.

I take a break from walking and sit down in a open field I find right by the road. I indulge on Doritos and Snickers: A healthy, balanced meal with all the proper nutrients and protein. I open up a bottle of soda and take a sip. The fizziness tickles my tongue and burns it just a little. This is the first soda I've had since I was arrested, and it's Julie's favorite flavor: Cherry Coke. It's all she drank. She was not one for sweet candy, she would even pass up chocolate, but she loved a sweet soda. It was one of the many strange and wonderful things about her.

I'm glad Julie isn't around to see what's become of the world, to see what's become of me. She held me to such high standards. I was one of the only friends she ever had who didn't stab her in the back, who didn't steal her boyfriends, who didn't abandon her. She would be so disappointed in me. I'm sitting here in the middle of a field, all by myself, because none of my friends could trust me. I led them into a deadly situation without thinking twice. I let a friend die, and I lied to all of them by keeping my criminal record a secret. I'm the biggest backstabber of them all.

I used to think one of her crazy ex-boyfriends probably killed Julie, but given all I know now, maybe she was a Disvariant and someone murdered her for it. Caleb did say the government had been quietly killing off Disvariants for years, so maybe I was just the cover up — the fall guy — so the real reason for her death never leaked out. It would explain all of the carefully falsified evidence against me. Though, I suppose, even if that is what happened, it doesn't really matter now. It's not as though I could bring the entire corrupted government to justice, especially now.

The combination of fog and sunshine create a beautiful swirling display in front of my eyes. If I tilt my head up to the sky, I have to squint at the brilliant display of sunlight. If I turn back to the surface, I'm transported into soft, quiet serenity. Where the two very different moments meet is magic, but even the beauty of nature cannot stop my anxious, wandering thoughts. I'm, once again, overwhelmed by the fear of being on my own. It's something I have never had to experience. I had Julie by my side through high school, and I was still living with my parents when I was arrested for her death. When I was sent to prison, and when I escaped, I had Thomas by my side. At the training camp I was surrounded by more friends than I have ever known in my entire life. But now I'm alone. I should take comfort in knowing that I can defend myself. I have powers; powers that others fear, but I fear them too, and I don't know how to control them. I don't know how to be confident that they will be there when I need them.

I should practice. I need it, and what's stopping me from doing that now? I'm in this field all by myself. There is no one around to hurt anymore.

I stand up and raise my hands, reaching them out into the distance. I'm not sure why, though. There's no legitimate reason for me to believe that this makes my powers any easier to control. I envision myself as Rey, learning to conjure the force, and I know I must look ridiculous right now. Where is Luke Skywalker to slap my hand with a leaf when I need him?

I try not to focus on how embarrassed I would be if someone caught me right now. I shut my eyes, trying to sense the energy around me, ready to be condensed and concentrated into a magical, wispy wall. Without looking, I begin to sense it moving around me, swirling into place. I open my eyes and surrounding me is a brilliant display of color. The vivid lavender dream encasing me is made even more beautiful by the distorted landscape in the background.

I have been so afraid of this ever since I first discovered it, but for the first time since that moment, I'm able to look at what I can do in beauty and awe instead of fear. This is a blessing, not a curse.

As I move my hands, the energy follows, maneuvering around in whichever direction I please. It doesn't take me very long before I've gained significant control over where and how it moves. I can make the forcefield as wispy and distorted, or as condensed and solid as I may need. I can grow the forcefield as large as I want, or shrink it down to the size of a bullet and chuck it at a tree. When I do, it goes clean through the tree and I realize this isn't only a defense mechanism, it's a weapon.

The constant use of my power is draining, but I take short breaks to let the sun beam down on me. It warms my body and puts me at ease. I am so relaxed I could easily close my eyes and slip away into a nap, but I don't. I keep them open, despite the blinding light, and allow that light to refuel me, until clouds pass over it and its energy does not fill me as strongly. Then the wind pushes away the clouds. And the cycle continues.

I continue to practice for hours until I've done all I know how to do. I conjure it up at will. I put a hundred more forcefield bullets through trees. I even risk stepping onto it and using it as a makeshift stairway to nowhere until, eventually, I lay down on the ground in exhaustion.

The sun is now shrinking into the distance. Half of the sky has become glowing orange with pink clouds as night draws ever closer. I eat two bags of chips, drink an entire bottle of soda, and stare up at the sky. *I can do more,* I tell myself. *I can feel it.* I

293

can also already feel regret for downing two bags of Fritos.

I reluctantly stand upright for another time. I reach my arms out, once again, channeling the force. It doesn't take long for the energy field to appear. I attempt to widen its range as much as I possibly can, the space between it and myself ever growing. I'm weak from all the energy it's draining from me, but I keep going, making it wider and stronger. The forcefield can't only be big, it has to withstand the strength of a million bullets. I won't make the same mistake twice. I will walk into my next battle ready, if another battle comes.

Crack! The sound of the nearby trees ripping apart under the strength of the forcefield. Another trees slams up against the forcefield and it sends a surge of pain through my body that nearly knocks me over.

The longer I try to hold it, the more unstable the energy seemingly becomes. It's no longer a strong wall, instead it's swirling around me so intensely I can no longer see through it. A lavender fog clouds my eyes and slowly turns deep purple. At a certain point, I am no longer able to contain the energy and pieces of it spiral out of control.

I allow the forcefield to dissipate and reveal the damage it has done. Dozens of trees are thrown around as if hit by a tornado. A large circle is pressed into the ground around me, and all of the grass that was inside the circle has been torn away. I think that is the extent of the damage, but then I notice I've unintentionally cracked up half of the nearby road. Jagged edges of pavement point upwards to the sky, making it completely impossible to drive on for all of the nonexistent cars traveling through.

I lie back down on the now grassless ground and stare into space. A wild force lies within me. Just yesterday I thought it was a curse, hours ago I thought it was a blessing, and now I don't know what it is. It's a truly magical, but truly dangerous thing that I cannot part with.

Perhaps I'm overthinking it and it's not a blessing or a curse. Maybe, it's neutral; a random thing I've been randomly chosen to deal with, and it's neither good nor bad. But it's hard to believe anything in the universe is simply neutral, as much as I might like to. Nothing is an accident. Nothing is of no consequence. I have this power for a reason. I just haven't figured out what that reason is, yet.

I begin to fall asleep right where I'm laying. Rational thoughts tell me I need to keep moving, or at least stay somewhere hidden, in case any soldiers come driving by, but I'm too tired to move. I stare up at the sky, myself encircled by the physical mark of my unexplained power, as the stars get brighter and my eyes get darker and I drift off.

I wake to a bright and sunny morning and the slight recollection of a dream about working at a radio station that only played a rap version of Riptide by Vance Joy, that sounded more like Elvis Presley than Vance Joy.

No one had come overnight to capture or kill me while I slept, but none of my friends came back for me, either. I've only been alone less than 24 hours, but I think I'm doing pretty well on my own. Not the best, given in those 24 hours I've only eaten junk food and managed to break a road. But for the past day, I have been exempt from human interference and I haven't died. Not a great feat, I must admit, but I have to find a bright side to this.

This night has given me the comforting confirmation that I can survive on my own, and reminded me of something I had lost sight of amongst all the fighting, death, and deception: My life has meaning. I preached it to Thomas when we were cell mates. I argued about it with Charity. Even though everything right now appears to be completely hopeless, it isn't.

I am not here by random chance. It wasn't by accident that I found myself alone. I have yet to suffer the horrible fate of the people who surround me, because there is a reason for me to be alive, and I'm determined, with a somehow both hopeful and pessimistic outlook, to find that reason. So, I get up, grab my bag of snacks, and head down a long, narrow road with an uncertain, but hopefully good end.

I wander for hours in the same direction as before, and the scenery doesn't change the entire dreary day. The same pothole filled road to my left and the same line of trees to my right. Time moves slower in this little section of the world, and a part of my brain is convinced I'm walking in circles, although I'm following the road in a straight line.

"I've seen that exact pothole before!" I exclaim to myself, and in the distance, an alternate version of myself yells the same words back.

As night is, once again, looming over me, the bumpy, pale gray road changes into a dark, smoothly paved road, and it lets me know I've crossed a city line. The scenery eventually begins to change from trees into familiar worn down buildings and road signs. I remember this town from my childhood, but I can't place it until a welcome sign planted right next to a cemetery catches my eye. I remember that sign well. It creeped me out as a child. It had me con-vinced this was a dead person's town, and since we only came here to visit my dying grandmother, well, I spent a really long time believing that.

I pass through the old shops I recall visiting as a kid. All of them are empty and their doors are left wide open. People rushed out of here, or were dragged out, like the old man lying dead in the door-way of his shop. He must have resisted arrest.

I walk a few miles down and enter into the rural territory. Rows of quaint little brick houses are all right next to each other. I walk up to each door and knock on it three times before walking in. Each house has its own defining feature; a bright roof, a big fence, an unkempt yard, or furniture from the 1960's.

I walk up to one of the houses where children's toys are scattered all across the lawn. I knock three times. No answer. I walk in. Empty, same as all the rest. The government must be taking all the food and hoarding it for themselves, because they certainly are not serving real food at their camps.

I finish checking all the houses and decide to head back to the first house on this row and stay in it, since it was the biggest, cleanest, and has three intact locks on the door.

On my way back, I pass by the lawn with toys scattered about it, and an anger burns inside me. I can clearly picture the scene of soldiers pulling up into the neighborhood and dragging innocent children away from parents who are begging to keep their kids safe — kids the government will train for war, program them to believe Disvariants are the enemy, and possibly murder those same children if they prove to be one of us.

After what I've seen recently, and what Hailee told me about their invasions, even if those events didn't take place here, I know it happened somewhere else to other unsuspecting families.

The sky is almost completely dark by the time I reach the big house at the end of the row. It has brick walls, a dark green roof, with a pastel green front door. It's not to my taste, but as long as there's a bed, I'll be fine.

I walk inside and find the stairs right next to the entrance and I stumble up into the hallway above. I take the first room I find. It's pitch black when I walk in, so I carefully feel around until I find a window and open up the curtains. The moonlight shines down into a room with posters covering every inch of the walls. Dead plants are placed next to a desk filled with unfinished homework. A twin sized bed sits right next to the desk, pushed up against the wall. I check to make sure no one is in the bed before I climb in. The likelihood of anyone being here at all is extremely slim, but I'm not taking any chances. I don't want to climb into bed with a lone survivor or their corpse.

I find that the bed is empty, so I lie down and pull the sheets over me. They have the faint smell of detergent and Axe cologne.

I stare at what little I can see of a Captain America poster on the wall and I plot out my next move, only to realize I still don't have one. I have nowhere to go, no one to go with, and no way to get there. I am completely and utterly doomed to die in the town my childhood self deemed the Town of the Dead.

Wait. What's that sound?

As soon as the noise registers in my mind, I'm bolt upright in bed and running down the stairs towards the distant sound of a revving engine. I'm out of the door, standing on the sidewalk, before I even have a chance to think about what I'm doing.

My first thought was that a military vehicle was patrolling the area, but that's not what I see barreling down the road. A rusty, old pickup truck zooms past me, then halts to a stop. The driver shifts the truck into reverse and backs up to me. It's Michael.

"What are you doing all the way out here, kid?" he concernedly asks me. "I thought you were safely in Columbus. Where's your friends?"

"Umm... A lot has happened since I last saw you," I say awkwardly, not knowing where to start with my explanation.

"Well," he chuckles. "Do you need a ride? Hop in!"

I climb in the passengers side and buckle myself in.

"Nice getup," he snickers, eyeing the odd word stitched into my sleeve.

"Thanks. You won't believe how I ended up in it."

TWENTY THREE

I spend the long ride to an undetermined location explaining to Michael, in great detail, everything that had happened since we last saw each other. I reveal more than I think I should, but once I start talking, I can't seem to make myself stop. Thankfully, he is more than willing to listen to whatever nonsense comes out of my mouth.

With great trepidation, I tell Michael about my powers. He gives the impression of a nice, accepting person, but you never really know where someone's heart lies. To my surprise, he seemed completely unfazed by it.

"So, there's people out there trying to start a war, huh?" he asks, once I'm finally finished rambling. No questions about being a superhuman, or a fugitive, or a terrible friend.

"Yes," I answer, still nervously waiting for a question I may not be prepared to answer.

"What do you want to do about it?" he asks, mindlessly rubbing the gray stubble on his face.

"I want to put an end to it. I just haven't figured out how to do that, yet. At least, not without an unholy amount of casualties," I answer sorrowfully.

General Kaine wants to kill every Disvariant, and he's made it clear he will go to great lengths to do so, and I have not even begun to put together a coherent way to go about stopping him. The closest I have come is forcing him to kill off a large number of people he could have used in his army, but that was the farthest thing from a victory.

"We'll figure it out," Michael says confidently, and it gives me hope. With absolutely no solid plans or any idea where the training camps are located, we will take them down. We will take down General Kaine, too.

"So, how did you end up all the way out here, Michael? I've been talking about myself this entire time."

"Turns out my old friend wasn't quite as happy to see me as I'd hoped. So, I've been driving around, stopping here and there, speeding here and there, if you know what I mean."

"How has your truck not run out of gas?" I inquire, leaning over to peek at the gas hand that points much closer to F than E.

"I have my ways, kid," he smirks. "Maybe you should get some sleep."

The paranoia in me wants to reject it. I need to be awake. To know where we're going. To be alert if something bad happens, but it has to be around four in the morning by now, and my eyes can barely stay open. I prop my arm up on the door's arm rest and lay my head down on my hand.

"Wake me up in 30 minutes," I mumble quietly, while in a state somewhere between asleep and awake. I'm not entirely sure if I actually said it out loud or only dreamt I had.

"Wake up, kid!" Michael yells about thirty seconds later, or at least I think it's only thirty seconds. However, when I open my eyes, the sun is peeking out from behind the trees and my forearm is completely numb. Michael's hand is on my shoulder, shaking me viciously.

"I'm awake!" I exclaim, but my mind is still too fuzzy to process why I need to be.

I rub my eyes, my mind clears, and I see why Michael woke me up. There's a vehicle in the distance going in the same direction we are. That's something very suspicious in this day and time. Michael shuts off his truck and waits for the tiny dot of a vehicle to fade into the skyline. It's almost gone when it turns left instead of straight, then the dot starts getting bigger. The vehicle up ahead is no longer driving away. It's made a U-turn and it's coming right for us.

Michael notices it as soon as I do and he cranks up his truck and begins speeding around, making a half donut, and driving full speed away. He slams on the gas and I get déjà vu. It seems I'm prone to being involved in car chases.

The truck is barreling down the highway, but what I make out to be a military vehicle is catching up to us fast. *How will we get out of this one?* I think, my heart racing, then a lightbulb goes off in my brain,

"Stop the car!" I scream.

"It's a truck!" Michael shouts while slamming on the brakes. "Now, what did you make me do that for?"

Without hesitation, I unbuckle my seatbelt and jump out. I run straight at the truck speeding right towards me, a forcefield forming in front of me as I move. Before we have a chance to collide, the truck slams on brakes and comes only a few inches away from crashing into the wall of energy before me.

I wait patiently for the driver to exit the vehicle. A sudden burst of confidence has me ready to force whoever it is to take me to General Kaine, himself. I'm going to put an end to all of this.

While waiting for the driver to reveal themselves, a million thoughts rush through my mind, but only one sticks with me. In this moment, I am more sure of this than anything in my entire life: My purpose is to put an end to the deception and the heartless murder, no matter what it takes.

"Kid, what are you doing?" Michael asks, slamming his door behind me.

"Get back in the car, Michael. Just drive away. Don't come back."

"No," Michael barks.

"I said —"

"And I said no."

Blondie's unmistakable bleached hair makes its way out of the driver's side of the armored car and my forcefield vanishes. He slams the door shut and reveals a twisted grimace on his face and a uniform identical to mine on his body. *No! There's no way he's a Disvariant!*

A girl in the same uniform steps out of the passenger's side. She's as tall as me, with silky black hair tied into a slick ponytail, and a stone cold poker face on her perfect olive skin.

"It's nice to finally see you again," Blondie glowers at me. I continue to stare at him in disbelief. He glances down at his uniform, then smirks at me. "Oh, this thing? Yeah, the general promoted me to your position after you abandoned ship. Don't be fooled, though. I'm not a Triv. I only joined so I could play a part in stomping all of them out."

The girl accompanying him momentarily breaks her poker face to reveal a thin layer of disgust when Blondie uses the word "Triv."

"To stomp *me* out?" I say, reminding him that I am one of the Disvariants he loathes so much. "I'm flattered, but do you really think you can take me all by yourself? You don't even have a gun." I raise my hands threateningly towards him.

"That may be true, but we do have your friends," the woman says calmly.

"I don't think so," I snap back.

"Then why are they not with you?" The woman asks, her arms crossed and face still expressionless.

"They took a different route, but I know exactly where they are," I say confidently, though it's a blatant lie. All of my real confidence has vanished into thin air with my forcefield.

"You know that isn't true. They left you. They despised you so they cut you loose. At least, that's what the boy — Caleb — told me; that he hated you, because you're a murderer," the woman informs me.

I lower my arms and the weight of a thousand pounds fall onto my shoulders, and my legs turn to lead at her words.

It's true. They have my friends. And they're not my friends anymore. They all hate me. Those who were kind enough to side with me, the last time I saw them, have surely turned against me as well.

"Take me to them," I demand.

Blondie grins at me.

"No! Don't be stupid, kid," Michael insists, and I shake my head at him.

"Why do you think we would let you back into the same training camp you just broke out of?" Blondie inquires.

"Because you guys either need me dead or on your side, and you know you can't kill me, so take me to my friends," I demand again.

"I've met toddler Trivs stronger than you," Blondie rebuffs. "We could have you killed in a minute. You only survived your first time around because I vouched for you."

Michael chuckles mockingly at Blondie's statement from the sidelines of the conversation.

"Then you guys must *really* want me on your side, because I'm not dead yet," I smile triumphantly, taking a measure of pride at my quick comeback.

At this, the woman turns to Blondie and nods.

"Alright," he says. "I think the general would be happy to see you back on our team."

I see a definite smile show on his face and I know he's happy about it, too. It makes me sick to my stomach — a feeling I can't seem to escape when I'm around him.

"Only if you keep my friends safe," I demand of them.

"Of course," the woman says, opening the back door of the truck and gesturing for me to enter.

I walk towards the truck, but Michael grabs a hold of my shoulder. "Don't do this. Don't be stupid."

"They need me," I whisper to him. "They may hate me, but I can't leave them alone to be tortured, killed, or enslaved into a mindless army."

"Then I'm going with her," Michael announces. I want to stop him from coming along, but I know it's no use.

"Sure thing," Blondie says giddily. "Is this your dad?"

I examine Michael's dark skin, the exact opposite of my pale, untanned self. "Yes. Biological." I mutter sarcastically.

Blondie seems to take what I say seriously, but the woman rolls her eyes at his blatant stupidity. I hesitantly walk over to her with my biological father right beside me. Blondie handcuffs both of us before letting us into the back seat. The woman pulls a walkie-talkie off the dashboard and talks into it. I try to understand what she says, but she speaks in code the entire time.

"Take that thing with you next time," the woman says, pointing to the gun Blondie left sitting on the dashboard.

He frowns at her. "I knew we wouldn't need it for her."

We arrive back at the camp. I tried to pay close attention to the route Blondie took to get here. Every house, every tree, every car on the side of the road, just in case I ever need to get back here again, though I hope I never do.

My plan is to find my friends, ensure they are out of harm's way, then take out the general and whoever else has pledged their allegiance to him.

A guard opens the gate to let us in and I shudder as we pass through it. I can't believe I've let myself come back here after all the pain I caused to escape.

Blondie drives the truck straight through the yard, past the warehouses and the training field. My heart breaks even more — which I didn't know was still possible at this point — when I see the field is filled up with well over a thousand unfamiliar faces. They

308

have already replaced every one of the people that died in the escape with new prisoners.

Blondie almost runs over several people while driving through the field, then he pulls up to the building where General Kaine sets up command.

"Alright," Blondie says, opening the back door to let us out. "Time to meet the general."

"We've already met," I sneer at Blondie on my way out of the truck.

"What about you, Mr. Atwood?" he asks Michael.

"No, but I sure am looking forward to it!" Michael says, with overwhelming fake enthusiasm, as he shakes the chains of his handcuffs.

"Your friends are with the general. They are waiting on you," the woman states.

Blondie and the woman escort us into the main building and down the halls. It's exactly the same as the last time I was here, only with a little extra hostility. The girl leads us, and Blondie towers behind us, burning a hole through the back of my head with his wide-eyed stare. He puts his hand on my back and pushes me forward several times, insisting that I'm going too slow, but eventually rests his hand in the small of my back. If I weren't handcuffed and in a building filled with armed individuals, I would've knocked him out by now, because he has an obvious hatred for me while also still pining for me. It's pathetic, and if I knew it wouldn't get me shot on sight I would say that to his face, then punch him in it.

As I get closer to the general's office, the entire situation sits right with me less and less until I am left with nothing but doubts. *How did they find my friends? Why would the general welcome me back after all I have done?* My stomach is tying itself up in intricate knots when the woman opens the door to the general's office.

Blondie pushes me into the room and my heart drops into my knotted stomach. It's the same exact scene as the last time I was here: The general in his chair behind his desk, and Madisen sitting in front of him. None of my friends are here.

"It is nice to see you again, Miss Atwood," the general says, blandly.

"Where are my friends?" I ask.

"Agent Carter, would you take this man to Red 17?" the general ignores me and gestures to Michael.

"Yes, General," Blondie responds and grabs ahold of Michael's arm.

"What are you going to do with him?" I ask Blondie.

"Red 17. That's where we take people for... observation," he says quickly, as he drags an uncooperative Michael out of the room and slams the door behind him. The woman swiftly moves in front of the door and blocks my chance for a surprise exit. I wanted to run after Michael. I don't trust that anyone here will keep him safe, but I have no other choice.

"Sit down, Miss Atwood," the general speaks calmly.

"Where are my friends?" I ask again, without moving.

"Your friends are not here," he answers. "But you are, and you will not be running away this time."

"Why would I stay if my friends aren't here as leverage, and how could they possibly not be?" I turn to the ponytailed woman blocking my escape. "You knew their names! You knew they hated me!"

"She is a telepath," the general says, still ever calm, "and a mind manipulator. That is why you will stay: Because she is going to make you. Agent Bennet, would you?"

She looks hesitantly at me. "Yes, sir."

"No!" I scream. I run for the door, though I know it's hopeless.

I thought Agent Bennet or General Kaine would be the ones to stop me, but Madisen tackles me and I slam into the floor. She sits on top of me. I try to push her off, but I'm only frantically wiggling around with my face pressed to the dirty, old fashioned floor tiles, my hands still tied behind my back.

"You're not getting away this time," Madisen whispers in my ear, along with a few choice profanities. "Bennet, do it already!"

"*Be still*," I hear Agent Bennet say, but she isn't speaking. Her voice is resonating within my mind. "*I will not alter your mind, but you have to pretend I have or we will both face the consequences.*"

Her gentle voice echoes in my mind, so I stop fighting back and let my body lay limp on the floor, and Madisen climbs off me. I slowly stand to my feet.

"Are you ready to listen now?" the general asks.

"Yes," I answer calmly.

"Are you going to run away this time?"

"Why would I? My purpose is here," Bennet's voice whispers in my mind.

"Why would I? My purpose is here," I repeat aloud.

"Well done, Agent Bennet," the general gleams.

TWENTY FOUR

I'm escorted by Bennet and Madisen down into the basement Madisen had mentioned, minutes before I climbed out of the window and ran for it. She never answered me about what was down here, but I'm about to find out.

As we reach the bottom of the stairs, I am met with a dark, open room, barely lit by the dim overhead lights. The place is grimy with a strong mildew smell, and the room is bare except for a few lamps and one solitary table in the middle of the room.

Bennet is excused and Madisen guides me down a small, eerie hallway to a door at the very end. I enter in and it's a communal shower room, identical to the one used by those imprisoned in the warehouses, but with a little extra mold on the ceiling.

"Take a shower," Madisen orders.

She hands me a small pile of clothes which includes unopened packages of bras and underwear (probably stolen from the houses they raided), and a uniform identical to the one I'm wearing now, minus the kevlar.

She leaves without saying another word to me and her actions have me more confused than ever. She is livid at me for escaping, but why? I thought she didn't want to be here, either. Perhaps she is only mad I left her behind. But what about Bennet, who, for no logical reason, has decided to leave my brain intact? She has already helped me out considerably more than Madisen has.

I'm the only person in the shower area right now and the water doesn't seem to be on a timer, so I take a long, cold shower and wash the filth from the past two days off of me.

I dry off, put on my fresh clothes, minus the jacket, and I feel like an entirely new person. A new person in the same exact situation as the old person.

I dump my filthy, old clothes in a giant hamper next to the door. It's full of other uniforms identical to mine, but they're stained with mud and what I can only assume is blood from the slaughter of past missions.

I walk through the dingy basement, back into the common room. Bennet stands there waiting for me.

"I'll show you to your room," she says.

I follow her down a hallway, past rooms with fingerprints scanners that must belong to other Disvariants. We reach the last door on the right and Bennet opens the heavy, steel door that is only accessible by fingerprint analysis, and I step inside. The place is nicer than my prison cell ever was. A twin bed all to myself. A small dresser just for me, with a few uniforms already folded inside of it, and two pairs of identical shoes right next to it. Two lamps rest on two nightstands on opposite sides of my bed.

Agent Bennet steps into my room and closes the door behind her. "I think I should explain what happened earlier."

"That would be really nice," I say, and take a seat on my new bed.

"I didn't alter your mind because I need your help to escape." She sits down next to me.

"You wanted to escape so you brought me back here? We could have escaped on the road where we met. It would've been three to one against an unarmed idiot!" I exclaim, but Bennet shushes me.

"I need to help my friends *here* escape. I hadn't originally planned on including you, but when Brandon and I ran into you, I knew the only choice was to blow my cover right then and save you, or bring you back with me.

"My friends — Sara, Taylor, Jonathan, Stephen — are all members of this team. There are four others here, but they are all aligned with Madisen, that witch who created this."

"She *created* it?" I gasp and jump out of my seat. "Then why did she pretend she didn't want to be here when I met her?"

"That was a facade. She wants everyone to believe she is sweet and innocent, but she doesn't have to convince you of that now, since you're supposedly under mind control. I would have bought her act too, but when we met I peered into her mind. I saw the deal she made with the general. She willfully promised to hunt all of us down, called us monsters, and proclaimed she was never one of us."

"Why would she do that?" I ask, dejected and perplexed.

"She had spent so long in hiding, having to barely scrape by, because she was a Disvariant. She lived in safe houses, not homes, but instead of hating the people who forced her to live that way, she began to hate herself, and consequently everyone like her. She blamed her foul circumstances on other Disvariants, and that hate has been quietly burning within her for years. When she met General Kaine, she was given a way to act on that pain.

"I know all of that because I read her mind. I've read the minds of everyone here and found the ones who stand with us. That's how I know you will help me."

"That's kind of an invasion of privacy, you know," I mutter, pacing around the room.

"Trust me, I do. Before everything went downhill, I kept to my own mind. I can't do that now. Now, knowing who I can trust is a matter of life or death." Her tone sharpens, and she does not break eye contact. "I need to know that when I tell someone about our escape they won't report it back to Madisen and have us all executed."

"So, how do you plan to escape?" I sigh. I want to leave, but it seems all I have been doing for weeks now is escaping everything instead of facing it. I'm tired of running away. Only hours ago I was running towards something — General Kaine and the end of his violent reign. But now that I am here, now that I know I could march out of this room, burst into his office, and execute him, I'm not sure I have it in me to do so. I may be cursed with death, but I am not a killer.

"We plan to ambush Madisen and her minions on our next mission. We don't know when that is, it's always a surprise. Madisen doesn't leak it until the last minute. But it's our best bet. There's eleven on the team, six of us want to leave, including you. They will be outnumbered."

"Wait. Wait." I stop the plan dead in its tracks. "I can't do that. I have to take Michael with me. I can't leave him here. Where is Red 17, anyway?"

"Annalise." She looks at me wide-eyed. "I thought you would figure it out on your own. There is no Red 17. That's a code. Michael is dead."

Her words hit my chest like a knockout punch in a boxing match. All of the air has vanished from my lungs.

"No, no! That's not possible." My voice shakes, and I try to contain myself as I crumble onto the bed. "Maybe they haven't killed him yet. I can still save him. Where —"

"He's dead, Annalise. I looked into Brandon's mind. I saw him kill your friend," she whispers re-morsefully.

Tears well in my eyes. He saved myself and Thomas with no questions asked, and when he and I met again, he didn't hesitate to help me. But now he's dead. Dead because he was kind enough to offer me a ride, and I was cruel enough to take it. Dead because I didn't take the chance to kill General Kaine the second I stepped into his office like I should have.

"It isn't your fault," Bennet says, resting her hand on my shoulder. "You couldn't have known this would happen. I couldn't have stopped it, or I would have blown my cover and gotten every one of my friends killed."

I stare at her. I suppose I understand her predicament. I, too, have done unholy things to save my friends. I have also caused mass bloodshed, but that was unintentional. She watched Blondie drag him away. She watched him die...

"It was in no way easy for me to watch your friend die," she adds, obviously reading into my grieving thoughts, uninvited. "I almost put a stop to it, but far too many people would have paid the price for that action."

"I can't... I can't believe he's dead," I manage to say. "He didn't deserve that. He didn't deserve to die because of me." I choke back tears that persist with each word I say.

"He died because Brandon murdered him on General Kaine's orders." Bennet narrows her eyes at me and speaks boldly. "These monsters killed him —

318

the ones who call *us* monsters — not you. Now, I have to leave because I've been in here too long, but remember our next mission. Be prepared. Train hard. Get to know the strengths and weaknesses of the ones we're going to fight. I'll let you know the details of the plan as soon as we get word."

"Can't you read Madisen's mind to figure out when the next mission is?"

"I tried, and I could at first, but she started resisting." She shakes her head. "Her mind is strong. I don't know how she does it, and it scares me that someone as powerful as her could be pitted against us." She steps closer to the door and rests her hand on the handle. "If you want the deaths to cease, and I know you do, this is how it must be done.

"By the way, my name is Talia."

She flashes me a quick smile, then quietly leaves, closing the door behind her.

I wipe my eyes of the few tears that ran down my face, despite my best efforts to hold it in, and stare at the dark, dusty room I've been assigned to. Yet another prison cell. I guess I'm destined to always end up trapped somewhere, because even when I'm not confined by four walls, I am still not free. I'm trapped in a revolving door of dangerous situations and terrible decisions that always lead to death, though never my own.

The walls of my own mind are seconds away from collapsing in on me when the door to my room swings wide open. Madisen stands at the entrance as the handle hits the walls so hard it puts a dent in the concrete. She doesn't flinch at the damage she so casually caused.

I stare aghast at her violence and strength. I see the flicker of darkness in her eyes that I also saw in Scarlett. Now I'm sure Talia was telling the truth about her, and it's become overwhelmingly clear why she and Scarlett were friends. I shudder at the thought of my former friends being alone with her now.

"You need to train," Madisen demands, with arms crossed. "Sitting on your bed all day isn't an option around here, Triv." She releases a hand from her intimidating pose and gestures for me to follow her.

I don't hesitate to obey Madisen's order, although I have a newfound fear of her. I don't want to give her a reason to treat me the way she treated my door.

Talia has given me no instructions on how to act as though I'm under the influence of mind control, so I stay silent, in hopes of avoiding saying the wrong thing, as I follow Madisen through yet another steel door into a room surprisingly much larger and much lighter than all the rest.

Large, overhead lights illuminate the room filled with a strong stench of sweat and a hint of hopelessness. Soft mats cover most of the floor, and punching bags hang from the ceiling in the left corner of the room. A plethora of workout equipment fills most of the room, and there's an area in the far back of the room where people are throwing knives. All of it seems to be quickly thrown together and disorganized.

The people I can only assume are my new teammates, most of whom are covered in sweat, all stare when I walk in.

"Is she the runaway?" asks a short man with a bowl cut and a crooked nose.

He stands not much taller than me, with his chest puffed out, clearly meaning to be intimidating, but somehow it only makes him appear more fragile. I think if I poked him he would collapse on the floor like a cardboard cutout of himself.

"This time she's here to stay," Madisen smiles menacingly.

"Why do we need to train with weapons if we all have powers?" I ask Madisen, but I worry I may have said something that the zombified version of me shouldn't have uttered.

"You have to be prepared for every possible situation and know how to use everything you can to your advantage, and only use your trivial abilities when absolutely necessary. If you can take someone down with a gun instead, use the gun. Got it?" she asks. I nod my head, then she turns to someone across the room. "Charlie! Why don't you show Annalise here the ropes."

At Madisen's command, the biggest man in the building, who was previously engaged in terrifyingly accurate knife throwing, marches towards us.

"What do you want me to do?" asks the brick wall standing in front of us. His voice is just as deep and gravelly as you would expect from someone like him.

"Whatever you want," she chortles, then gives me a not-so-encouraging pat on the back, and leaves me alone with the skyscraper.

"Let's start with hand to hand combat." He gestures to a red mat in the middle of the room.

I nervously follow him over to it, distressed at the thought of letting a man with cinderblock fists take a swing at me, but I'm given no other choice. Madisen said I had to, and rejecting orders could blow my cover and get both me and Talia killed. I will not allow any more people to die because of me.

I step onto the mat and Charlie swings at me out of nowhere. I throw my hands in front of my face before he has a chance to make contact, but he doesn't hit me. He lets out a bellowing laugh that sounds more like something from a wild animal than a human. I lower my arms and he continues to laugh. He only wanted to watch me flinch.

I try to brush off his cruel humor as he teaches me the proper fight stance and arm movements. After a few minutes of practice, and him letting me punch him a few times, I am significantly less nervous. Maybe he isn't going to break my nose.

"I've shown you the ropes," he says, putting up his fists. "Fair fight."

"Wai —" I don't finish a syllable before he's coming at me and I barely dodge a fist aimed at my jaw.

He comes at me again, but this time I'm not fast enough. I fall back onto the mat and it knocks the air out of me. I get back up before he has a chance to literally kick me while I'm down. Charlie's expression is raving mad and he has suddenly turned completely demented. He's become an entirely different person than he was only a minute ago.

I attempt one punch at his face, but that was a disastrous mistake. He grabs my wrist and twists it around. He lets out a maniacal laugh at the sight of my pain, then pushes me into the ground. This time I can't get up quick enough. He's on top of me and his weight is crushing. I think I might die under the pressure placed on top of me, but then he grabs my neck and cuts off my air flow. His giant hands are wrapped all the way around my neck, squeezing so tightly my bones just might snap. I try to beg him to stop, but my airways have been cut off and I cannot form words.

Use your powers! I tell myself, but I can already sense the darkness pulling me in. Everything, including Charlie's rabid stare and popping veins, begin to bleed together and become fuzzy.

"Charlie! Stop it right now!" a warbled voice screeches. A bleary Talia swoops into my vision and puts a chokehold on Charlie.

Immediately, the intense pressure is relieved from my throat and his weight lifts off me. I gasp for air as

323

Charlie pulls Talia off himself and slams her down on a mat.

"It was a fair fight!" Charlie declares, and storms off back to the knife throwing station.

Talia quickly regains her composure and walks over to me. She reaches out her hand and pulls me up off the mat, then guides me to the nearest wall. She releases me and I fall onto the floor, leaning back on the cold concrete wall. She slides down next to me, sitting crisscrossed. Everyone else in the room is going about their training as if a murder attempt didn't just take place in the middle of the floor, and there isn't a girl gasping for air in the corner.

"He's not... one of... one of your friends, is he?" I gasp through the sharp pains sent shooting down my throat with every exhale.

"No." She crosses her arms and glares at the sky-scraper throwing knives across the room. "Charlie is a deranged murderer. When the military barged into his home to procure all the children, they walked in on him covered in the blood of the family members he had slaughtered."

"Thanks for... the warning," I mumble in a scratchy voice and rub my throat.

"Sorry," she says, patting my shoulder.

I can sense myself already healing from the en-counter. I take a breath of air without an invisible knife scraping down my throat. I close my eyes and my heart rate finally begins to slow down.

Talia moves my hands, trying to examine my neck. "Maybe we could get you a turtleneck. You're going to be bruised for quite a while."

I push her hand away. "No, I won't," I whisper, the scratchiness in my voice disappearing further with each word. "I can heal myself."

"What?" Bennet gawks. Her eyes dart around the room to make sure no one else heard us. "Does Madisen know?"

I keep rubbing my neck so I appear to still be injured to any onlookers. "Not to my knowledge, but how did you not know? I thought you saw everything about me when you looked into my mind."

"It doesn't work like that. I can't take in everything about a person all at once," Talia pauses, once again looking around to make sure no one is paying attention to us. "I can see what someone is thinking at that moment I enter their mind, and I can look back through their memories, but I choose what I see.

"A person's mind is a library I scan through, searching for the right book to open up. I don't step into the library and know the contents of all the books straightaway." Talia rocks back and forth as she speaks.

"So, what parts of my mind did you look into?" I ask nervously.

Talia's movement is subtly contagious and I find myself unintentionally swaying side to side in sync with her rocking.

"Only the ones I thought were necessary," she assures me, though it gives me no comfort.

I think back to when she and I first met. "You saw when my friends —"

"Yes, I did," she interrupts. "I am genuinely sorry for using that against you, but I knew how vulnerable that made you. It was my best bet of bringing you back with me without a fight. Alright, now let's start training." Bennet grabs me by the hand and pulls me up. "Do you want to learn how to shoot a gun?"

"Yes!" I say. My powers are famously defective and unreliable, but as long as a gun is loaded you can count on it to fire.

TWENTY FIVE

I follow Bennet out of the room and into a gun range next door, where I wait alone while she retrieves guns from the armory.

The gun range is the same size as the training room next door. The difference is, it's much darker in here, and it has ten rows of targets to shoot at, instead of workout equipment and a giant in the corner throwing knives.

Bennet walks back in, decked out in rifles and machine guns, along with a few smaller handguns. She fits one of the smaller ones into my hand, shows me how to load it, and lends me a set of noise canceling earmuffs.

I spend the next half hour barely hitting the target. Talia frustratedly watches my stupendous failure. Shooting doesn't come naturally to me. In a perfect world, I wouldn't consider that a bad thing, but in this world, my inaccuracy might get me killed.

I fire again and hit the center of the target on nothing more than dumb luck. I turn to Bennet with a grin. She scowls at me. *Oh, right. She can read my mind. She knows it was a fluke.*

"Listen," she bitterly instructs me. "When we are out there fighting against these monsters, I don't need a fighter that's going to miss their target and get themselves killed." She puts her hand on my shoulder as her scowl weakens and her tone softens. "I know your powers are strong, but a gun is a lot more lethal, subtle, and reliable, so being able to fire one of these is critical. So, we're not leaving here until I'm sure you could shoot Charlie in the back of the head on your first try."

"Okay," I mumble back, but it seems almost improper. She speaks with such authority that I'm partially convinced I should be saluting her and saying "yes, ma'am," instead.

I spend several hours and countless bullets trying to perfect my aim. Eventually, I start hitting the target, but my aim is still not reliable enough to count on, instead of my powers, in the heat of battle.

I take a short break, but just as I put my gun down, the lights above me flicker yet again.

"How does this place have power?" I ask Talia. It's something I've been wondering about for a while, though I have come up with a few of my own ideas.

"They found a Disvariant — Rosita — who could control electricity. They forced her to get this place up and running again, then shipped her off to the next facility to do the same thing."

"Did they have her locked up before the EMP, just waiting to use her?" I ask.

"That is the only part I haven't figured out yet," she sighs, and begins taking out her ponytail to re-tie it.

"What do you mean?"

"No one around here tells me anything," Talia glumly responds, then she effortlessly re-ties her high ponytail and runs her fingers through it. "I have been getting my information from reading other people's minds, but most here don't know the half of it, so I have been piecing together bits of an annoyingly distorted puzzle," she says indignantly, in exasperated reminiscence of the process. "From what I've gathered, it was not a pre-planned attack strategy. To the best of my knowledge, it wasn't foreign invaders either. It's still a mystery to me, but General Kaine is of the suspicion that Disvariants may have caused it."

I stare at her in disbelief. "That's impossible," I refute. "If the government didn't do this, then why does it all seem so well planned? And what about this place and all the other ones out there? Brandon said it was happening all over the country! It wouldn't make any sense for this to not be intentional."

"These camps were very intentional. They had been secretly building them for months, but not for military recruits — solely for Disvariants. They had plans to take us here in hoards to keep tabs on us, but in a very hush, hush manner. They intended to hide it all from regular citizens. This place down here," Talia says, gazing around the dark, hopeless room, "was originally meant for the worst of the worst. This is where they were going to keep those of us headed for execution. That's why this camp doesn't have an infirmary. Duplicates were never meant to be housed here, but after whatever it was that happened, they took a new, cruder approach."

I can't believe what I'm hearing. I was so sure my theory was right, but I can see it now. All of the training equipment around this place was clearly a last minute rush. The military's false claims of a foreign enemy were so pathetically falsified they must not have been given much time to think it through.

"So, they think Disvariants may have done this?" I ask, still in shock. "Why would anyone do that?"

Talia twirls the end of her ponytail on the tip of her finger as she answers. "I don't know. It could have been an accident. A lot of bad things can happen to someone who has only just undergone the Variation and cannot yet contain their abilities. I'm sure if it was a Disvariant, they meant no harm."

"Yeah... I'm sure...What was that word you said earlier — Duplicate? What did you mean by that?"

"It's a term for people who aren't Disvariants. They're duplicates because they're all the same, not different, like us."

"Oh..." I look around at the dim, dingy room, trying to find a way to change the conversation to lighter subject matter. "So, when are we going to leave this place and see the light of day again?"

"We never leave unless we're on a mission. We're their prisoners, Annalise. The sooner you learn that, the better," she says, and I roll my eyes when she isn't looking. "But we're getting out of here."

Talia leaves me alone to practice. I use up the remaining bullets in my gun and head back over to the other training room. The rank smell of sweat slaps me in the face once again, but I push my way through the stench to the punching bags, trying not to make eye contact with anyone as I do.

We're their prisoners, Annalise. Talia's words echo through my mind as I take a swing at a red punching bag. I'm well aware we are their prisoners. I know what it's like to be in a real prison, and this is much worse.

After a full day of training and a small lunch, we all head for the communal shower to wash off our sweat. I wait outside until everyone else leaves, to take my shower alone, as I'm not particularly fond of the experience of showering with several strangers.

Madisen has to open the door to my room because my fingerprint is not in their system. Apparently, only Madisen, and her second in command, Talia, have access to any of the doors. We cannot enter or leave our rooms without their approval.

I step into the room and the sound of the door locking shut behind me sends chills down my spine. I walk to my bed and I see a tray of food sitting on my nightstand. It's the same gruel from the cafeteria I was forced to eat before, only now I don't have to wait in line for it.

I eat it quickly to avoid lingering on the flavor.

My self-destructive mind wishes to wander to all the horrible things happening around me, but I force myself to sleep instead. I know if I think about any of it for too long, I'll break down. If I think about how our government has a long, hidden hatred for Disvariants that has driven them to murder, or how they're now forcing other Disvariants to do the killing for them, I won't be able to take it. If I think about where my friends, who are no longer my friends are, my chest will ache. If I think of all the teenagers I lead to their deaths, or about Michael dying, I just might cry.

Okay, I guess I'm not doing a very good job at not thinking about it, I think, as tears quickly well in my eyes. My throat hurts like it's closing up, but I want to scream. I want to break the door down and run out of here without any regard for all the other people I would be leaving behind, but instead, I stay still. I don't scream, I let out faint whimpers. I weep until my tears run dry and I have lost the energy to let out another empty, soundless wail.

The door to my lonely cell creaks open and the silhouette of Madisen stands in the doorway, illuminated by the harsh yellow lights in the hall.

"Wake up! It's time to go!" she shouts at me.

With no natural light in the room, I have no indicator of what time it could possibly be, but my tired bones say it's still 2ᴬᴹ and I should return to a dreamless sleep.

"Go where?" I ask.

"Nunya business. Get dressed," she barks. *Oh, no. It's time for a mission. I'm not ready.*

It takes me several minutes to convince myself to even sit up, despite Madisen's urgency. I don't want to face what lies ahead of me. I want to remain in this dark room and shrivel up into nothingness, but I can't. I begrudgingly get up, put on my uniform, and try not to spiral into panic as I pass through the halls. I still have no clue what the escape plan is, other than to, well, escape. But that never works out like it's supposed to.

I enter the common room and everyone is gathered around the table in the center of the room. I'm the last to arrive. All turn to look at me as I walk in, giving me yet another high school flashback. I wonder when those will finally quit happening.

A timid, frail looking girl, along with a tall girl who has bright purple streaks in her hair, move apart to make room for me at the table. I squeeze in between them and notice Brandon is amongst the group today. He can't help but stare at me as I focus on a map laid on the table.

"We've gotten word of another Triv haven that has been taking in massive amounts of people fleeing from all over the state," Madisen says, pointing to a place on the map only a few cities below where I last saw my friends as they drove away in a stolen truck.

Madisen picks up the map and reveals a blueprint underneath. "This is the layout of the building. These are all the entrances and rooms. Bennet, Wiser, Johnson, Atwood, Rowell, and I will all be posted out front." *Great, I never learned anyone's last names so I have no idea who most of those people are.* "The building is two stories, with the first floor set a little below ground level. It has a concrete wall that rises above the ground, blocking the rest of the first floor from view. We'll have to be on the wall. Atwood," Madisen glares at me, surely reminiscing of when I escaped over the walls of this place, "and Wiser, you'll fire downwards into the first floor window. The rest of us will fire at the second floor. Bennet, be prepared to jump off the wall and guard the stairs *here.*" She points to a break between the concrete walls where a staircase sinks down to the entrance. "Some idiotic Trivs are bound to run out that way. Got it?

"Barnes, Rogers, Holder, Carter, and Collins, you'll sneak around back when everyone is focusing their attention on the entrance team. This is the only other exit, so people are bound to be escaping in hoards that way. Your job is simple: Make sure no one succeeds.

"Now, every one of you need to memorize these rooms. This one," Madisen's finger slides to a room at the far left of the building, "is hidden by a false wall. Remember that. There *will* be Trivs hiding in there. Once you make your way inside, you will check every single room. Twice. Leave no one standing. Is that simple enough?"

"Yes, ma'am," everyone says in unison, except me. Apparently, I didn't get the memo, although I don't think anyone noticed. Except maybe Brandon, who I can catch staring at me in my peripheral.

"Alright. Mission 8 will take place right at midnight," Madisen says, dismissing us.

Everyone goes about their own business the rest of the day. We're not allowed to train during mission days, as to not wear ourselves out beforehand, so we spend our time passing around the blueprints to the building, and gathering around the table to play an old board game they probably stole from unwitting children. We have been permitted to have it solely for days like these.

Between the role of the dice the team explodes with pointless chatter. A beady-eyed boy drones on and on to the girl with the purple streaks in her hair, who could clearly not care less about a single word coming out of his mouth. Brandon has mysteriously disappeared to an unknown location. Good thing too, or he just might have murdered the boisterous ponytail boy sitting awkwardly close to me, glancing my way every five seconds. He leads a rowdy discussion about the quality of our workout equipment, as if that is the most important thing to be concerned about right now.

"It's all old and rusty!" he exclaims, rolling an eight, and moving his shoe game piece forward.

"Shut up, would you, Holder?" the purple-haired girl insists, then grabs the dice from the board. She rolls a three and sighs in frustration.

"I can't believe I'm winning," a timid girl whispers, staring curiously at the board. She is far ahead of everyone else, but several people assure her they will beat her; their only meaningful goal in life seeming to be taking the victory from the clutches of a girl who looks like she has never won anything a day in her life.

A mission to murder innocent men, women, and children lies not too far in our future. A secret plan to escape has also been set in motion, but everyone acts as though nothing is taking place. Nothing matters except who reaches the final space on the board first. It makes me so nauseated that halfway through the second round, I bow out to sit alone in my room until time to leave. Talia doesn't come to visit me, to avoid suspicion, she tells me via a mind conversation we have from two separate rooms. She also tells me, upon my asking, that it is called "Mission 8," for the fairly simple reason of it being the eighth mission this team will embark on. The last seven went off without a hitch. Seven mass slaughters that were dealt with seamlessly. It sends shivers down my spine to have so much as a passing thought about, but a relentless army of chills marches through my whole body at the realization that I will soon be taking part in the next massacre.

At 8PM, to my displeasure, Brandon visits my room. He tells me it's time to head out. I walk to my door to leave, but he blocks the exit.

"I'm glad you came back around," he smiles. Yes, willingly coming back around is exactly what I did. My belief that the people I care about were imprisoned here was not at all a factor in my return.

I almost tell him off, but I've come too far to blow my cover now, so I smile back and say, "Me too."

"I know you only ran because everyone was running and you were scared, but you don't need to be afraid. I'll keep you safe," he grins, then caresses my arm.

I have to stifle the urge to laugh at how foolish he is being. I guess, in the chaos of things, it may not have been clear who orchestrated the breakout, but I thought he would at least have enough brain cells to connect the dots and realize I genuinely didn't want to be here.

"Thank you," I tell him, instead of all the cruelly honest thoughts swirling around in my head. It takes everything in me to refrain from expressing them.

Everyone gathers in the armory — a room filled with the biggest stash of weapons that I've ever seen stacked up on the walls. Brandon begins passing out guns. I end up with a fully automatic sniper rifle, or at least, that's what the boy next to me said it was. He seemed jealous that I was the one who got it, instead of him. I notice everyone has the same type of gun, except for myself and Brandon. We both seem to be holding souped-up versions of what everyone else has.

We all load our weapons. I have to get the jealous boy beside me to load mine, because I have already forgotten what Bennet showed me. The boy condescendingly glowers at me for not knowing how to do it, but he eagerly accepts the chance to hold my gun. He quickly shows me how to load it, hands it back to me, and reminds me to pack some bullets in my belt for reloading.

We finish up packing, and in half an hour we're up the stairs, being led by Madisen past rows of guards looking at us in a combination of reverence and contempt. I step outside in the darkness of the evening where two trucks are already waiting on us outside the entrance of the general's building. Madisen stops at the first truck and turns to the team. She smiles with malicious contentment at the group she has assembled.

"Alright. Entrance team, in this one with me." She points to the armored car behind her. "Exit team, over there with Carter. Do you little Trivvies remember the plan?"

"Yes, ma'am," everyone says, and this time I remember to say it, too.

All of us are piled into two separate vehicles. Madisen is driving our car. Talia is in the front seat.

I'm in the back left corner, with two boys squeezed in beside me. The one directly next to me is the boy with a crooked nose who called me a runaway upon my arrival. The one farther to my right is a freckled brunette that I remember all too well from his board game outburst earlier today.

"That is not what I meant! Don't take things out of context!" he boldly proclaimed.

"I literally just repeated your exact words back to you," said the girl, who had been forced to listen to all of the nonsense coming out of his mouth. He had been spewing sexist filth since the game began, along with his constant insistence that he is a nice guy — a gentleman — who would treat a woman right, as long as she doesn't give him a reason to treat her otherwise.

His face had turned a bright red in his fury, claiming the girl is twisting his words. In his rage, he flipped over the board game.

"Aw man, are you serious?" Holder said, then started putting the pieces back on the board. "Now we have to start over."

The entire group let out a low grumble, and the timid girl looked utterly defeated in her loss of first place. The sexist boy bitterly apologized, but smiled as all of the pieces were being put back at the starting line. He had previously been in dead last.

"Okay, guys," Talia says, bringing me back to the present. Her voice echoes into my mind, and also, I assume, the minds of the four other people on our

side. Although, I have no idea if any of them are sitting next to me. *"The plan in practice is straightforward, though it may not be easy to execute. When we are all in place, perched up on the wall, or aiming at the back door, we turn our weapons on Madisen and her minions. I'll give you a signal, and when I do: Shoot them. Shoot without hesitation. Don't give them the chance to hurt you or any of the people inside the haven."*

"Talia, I have a bit of an issue with that," I speak in my mind, hoping only she can hear me, and not everyone else on this weird six-way brain call.

"What is it, Annalise?"

"I have no clue which of these people are on our side."

"Oh, my bad. The one sitting to the right of you is Stephen," Talia says, and I glance at him. He smiles a little when I do. Now I know he can hear our mental conversation. *"The guy beside him is Mack Johnson. You can shoot him. The rest are in the other car. Taylor is the short blonde. Sara is the tallest girl here, and she has purple streaks in her hair. Impossible to miss. Jonathan is the snarky guy with the ponytail. As long as you don't shoot any of them, you'll be fine."*

"What if we can't fend them off?" another mental voice chimes in on our conversation and startles me. I'm almost sure it's Stephen who asked the question.

"We will," Talia assures him.

340

"Why don't you just warn the people that we're coming?" I ask.

"How am I supposed to do that?" Talia scoffs.

"The same way you're allowing me to talk without moving my mouth. Speak into their minds."

"I can't. There's a range on it. I can barely reach the minds of the group in the car behind us."

I can see Talia shifting nervously in the passengers seat.

"Well, can't you try? If they could fight with us, it would greatly increase the chances that none of us die today."

"We have about three hours until we arrive. Couldn't hurt to try while we wait," says the voice I still assume to be Stephen's.

My mind goes silent of all voices except my own. I glance at Talia in the front seat and see her expression harden as she tries to focus on the minds of people miles off. Her lips begin to subtly mouth something.

"You've all been extremely quiet," Madisen points out.

"Apologies. I'm processing the plan over and over in my head so I don't forget it," Stephen says softly.

"The plan is point and shoot, idiot. It's not that hard. You remember the plan, right Atwood?" Madisen glares at me through the rear view mirror.

"Oh, yes. Point and shoot. Downward windows. False wall. All that stuff," I say, and avoid making eye contact with her reflection.

341

"Bennet, how are you doing?" Madisen asks Ta-lia.

I watch her focus break. "Fine," she says plainly.

"I can't do it," Talia says to me, or everyone, I'm not sure.

"Can't you —"

"No. It's not working. I can't do it," Talia says in frustration, and the connection between our minds is abruptly broken. I am left to my own thoughts.

The next three hours are the most quiet and sus-penseful hours of my life. My nerves get increasingly less calm as we inch closer to our destination where bloodshed surely awaits us, but whose blood will be shed, I have yet to find out. With each turn of the tire my heart beats ever faster, but then the tires come to a halt.

TWENTY SIX

Madisen stops short of the long driveway that belongs to the safe haven and shuts off the car. The other group stops just behind us and walks through the woods to the back of the building.

"Are you ready?" Madisen asks our group. Brazen excitement fills her voice.

"Yes!" I say with fabricated enthusiasm, as do both Talia and Stephen.

"It's about time!" says the boy who I managed to forget was with us.

We stand idly by for several minutes, ensuring the exit team has enough time to get into place. Talia is keeping tabs on everyone via telepathy.

"Let's go," Madisen whispers to all of us, and we make our way through the bushes to the haven.

I grip even harder on the gun I've been holding tightly for the past several hours. We are all gathered in a line behind Madisen. I'm directly behind her and in the perfect position to shoot her in the head. But Mack Johnson, who is right behind me, is in the perfect position to shoot me if I went through with it.

As we approach the front of the building, we notice flood lights shine down all around the wall and out into the yard, of which we stand on the edge, hiding in the shadows.

"How do they have lights?" Stephen whispers from behind me.

"I don't know... Very interesting," Madisen mumbles. "I'm sure we can make one of them squeal before we take them out."

And with that, Madisen pulls a handgun out of her pocket. Courtesy of her silencer, she soundlessly takes down three guards posted on the roof. My heart drops when their bodies do. I look over at Talia, unperturbed by her actions. It hadn't yet occurred to me that to make it onto the wall, we would first have to kill the guards.

Talia can surely hear my thoughts, because she says, *"A few casualties are unavoidable. Make sure one of them isn't you."*

This is the second time I have witnessed her allow innocent people to die to further her goal of saving lives. By now, with seven missions under her belt, she has taken part in the murder of thousands of people. One kind stranger lost. One quick, silent shooting. Those things might not faze her anymore, but they still faze me.

We swiftly move into an orderly line on the wall: Talia, Stephen, Madisen, me, then Mack. The wall isn't hard to climb onto, since it's shorter than I am, but once I'm on it, I see the drop on the other side is much farther down. I squat awkwardly on the edge of

the gray barrier, a symbol for the line we are cross-
ing. There is no turning back. There is no way out. I
aim my gun into the window far below me.

"Get ready to fire," Madisen whispers to us.

"On my signal," Talia says.

I ready myself to swing my gun around and point
it at Madisen's head. Talia counts down. Five...
Four... Three...

"Wait for it," she urges us, but how much longer
could we wait?

Bang! Bang! Bang! The sound of guns rapidly firing, along with the shattering of windows. At first, I
think one of us has fired early, but then I realize the
bullets are coming at us, not from us. And it's coming from every direction.

With no time left, I swing my gun around at
Madisen while she's hopefully as disoriented as I am.
Stephen and I both have our weapons directed at
her, prepared to fire.

She looks between the two of us. "Don't even try
it," she snarls.

Suddenly I'm falling over the deep end of the
wall. I see Stephen falling, too. He hits the concrete
headfirst and I hear a crack that sends shivers down
my spine, and watch the blood pour out of his skull
onto the bleak ground. I instinctively grab my own
head to make sure everything is still inside it.

I get up as quickly as I can and reach for my gun,
but it's not there. I dropped it whenever I went flying
over the edge.

"I've wanted to do this for quite a few long, inglorious days now," Madisen declares in outrage.

I look up and she's standing perched on the edge of the wall. A rifle in her hand is pointed down at me and the wall beside her protrudes upward like jagged spikes. I guess now I know what her powers are.

My forcefield appears from nowhere and encases me as she fires down at me. I run for the double door entrance only a few feet away, the rapid fire of bullets ricocheting off my shield as I reach the door.

Suddenly, dozens of people above me come jumping down from the windows and right into the fight. One girl gently floats down and lands right next to me. The ethereal stranger and I lock eyes for a brief moment, before I twist the doorknob, sigh with relief when it's unlocked, and leap inside. I shut the door behind me and I am met by three furious adults standing at the entrance, towering above me, and staring me down. If there was not a mystical lavender wall floating between us, I'm certain they would have tackled me by now or thrown me back outside to die.

"I'm with you!" I announce with what little air is still in my lungs.

"Give us one reason to believe you," the woman on the right orders.

Before I can answer, the floor underneath me begins to give way. I think, briefly, that I am sinking, but I glimpse at the floor, and it isn't moving — I am. My body is ascending and my feet are no longer in contact with the ground. I float upwards until my head hits the ceiling. The woman who first spoke, stares at me intently. Her face resembles that of the one I had just locked eyes with, but much more hardened. It's clear she is the one causing this to happen.

"Because I am! Please, they'll kill us all," I beg, craning my neck to look down at them.

"Are you with Madisen or Talia?" the only man in the trio asks, with his bushy eyebrows furrowed into one big unibrow.

"Talia! Talia!" I answer him. They must have gotten her message. That's how they knew to shoot first.

The man calmly nods to the woman, who then lowers me back to the ground. My feet touch the floor and I sigh with fleeting relief.

"Get ready to fight," the woman commands of me.

The unibrow man walks past me and reaches for the door.

"Wait, where are your guns?" I ask them, before realizing what a stupid question it is.

"Honey, I don't need a gun," he answers boldly, swinging the doors wide open.

He marches outside and I instinctively follow him, walking up the staircase into the yard. Residents of the haven flood out of the doors behind us, trying both to run to the fight and from it.

I reach the top step to find a scene I had not at all anticipated. I have been in the dark about the abilities possessed by the other members of our team. I am still unaware of most, but I have just learned Madisen's, and now I know of Mack Johnson's as well. A hundred of his doppelgängers cover the yard, guns in hand. A few lie dead on the ground, next to deceased strangers who fought against them. Half of the remaining doppelgängers immediately lose gravity, courtesy of the woman who caused me to levitate. The rest shoot at us and I block as much of it as I can with my forcefield.

Madisen and Talia are having a fist fight in the midst of everyone else. They both seem to have lost their weapons. Talia manages to flawlessly block every move from Madisen and it drives her mad. Madisen dramatically lifts up her hands to the sky, and below her, several pieces of the ground begin to rise. They float in between the two of them and Madisen sends them flying through the air at Talia. She shrinks back and covers her face, but the projectiles never hit her. They break apart, crumbling back into the surface of the land, as they come into contact with the forcefield protecting Talia.

Madisen now turns to me with eyes wild like a rabid dog. I can almost picture her foaming at the mouth as she charges at me. She conjures up several more pieces of the ground and chucks them at me, but none of them can puncture the shield in front of me. She stops dead in her tracks at the sight of her weapons disintegrating, then does something that terrifies me more than I could have ever thought possible. She smiles. A crooked smile that says "I've got you now." She cannot touch me but it sends shivers down my spine.

She lifts her hands up towards me and I watch her green eyes turn pure black as the ground beneath me begins to shake and crack apart. I lose my balance and fall backwards onto a piece of the ground separating itself from the rest.

I stand back up and attempt to regain the forcefield that vanished when I fell. Madisen marches victoriously towards me. A sharp, jagged rock as big as Charlie, floats beside her. The wicked smile on her face grows wider. I try to create a forcefield again, but my mind and body are too frozen in fear. My lungs tighten and I can hardly breathe. *No, not again. This wasn't supposed to happen again,* I reflect. When it counts most, I have failed. Now, even more people will die because of my shortcoming, including myself.

Madisen, now consumed with blinding rage, launches the giant dagger at me. The tip of it comes about two inches from my stomach, blood dripping from its edge.

An older woman stands in front of me. The sharp end of the boulder pierced her abdomen and stopped before it ever came into contact with me. She had teleported in front of me in a flash and was dead before I had time to process it. I know she did not appear just to save my life. She was here by accident, probably trying to escape one of the many Johnsons running around here.

The stranger collapses onto the ground under the weight of the rock embedded in her flesh, and I run for it before Madisen has a chance to throw another one at me.

Without thinking, I dart back inside into a crowd of terrified people running about. Blood curdling screams echo throughout the building, bouncing off every wall. I stop myself for a split second, just to put my hand over my mouth and confirm the screams were not emanating from my vocal cords.

Parents are holding onto their children for dear life. Some children are holding onto their dead parents. Blood is splattered erratically across the walls and on faces.

Several Johnsons have somehow managed to make their way inside and are gunning down everyone in sight. I strain to create another forcefield and compact it down to the size of a bullet — something I've only practiced in the absence of another person — and send it shooting through the head of the first Johnson I see.

I send a second forcefield bullet through another Johnson's head, just as he's about to shoot a five year old boy, who screams in terror and runs away when Johnson is dead.

I follow the next duplicate down the hallway that I know leads to the false wall, where many Disvariants are sure to be taking shelter. A teenage girl stands in front of the wall, guarding it from intruders. Johnson raises his gun at the girl, so I send an energy bullet at Johnson, but it hits him too late. His gun has already fired and his bullet hits the girl. However, she is unfazed by impact. Her body morphed entirely into metal, turning her into something of a statue before the bullet hit, and it failed to make a dent on her.

Johnson's clone collapses, and the metal girl nods thankfully at me and remains at her post.

"I need to find a window!" I yell at the girl, as I run in the other direction. As if that information helps either of us accomplish anything.

I sprint down the hallway I just came through. A steady flow of scared people run past me to the "secret" room everyone knows about.

I speed through the common room and up a flight of stairs. I need to find a window. If I do, I can view the fight taking place outside without Madisen throwing giant rocks at me.

As soon as I reach the top of the stairs, I lunge for the first door I see. I reach out for the doorknob and my entire body is slammed into the wall instead. I push off whoever attacked me and flip around to see Charlie, towering over me with another person on his back, arms wrapped around Charlie's neck. The two are fighting each other and must have rammed into me by accident. The person on his back abruptly snaps Charlie's neck and pushes him to the ground, then stands to look at me.

"Annalise?" Chadwick asks in complete shock.

My jaw hangs wide open. I was not prepared to see him, and he undoubtedly wants answers for how I came to be here. I have a million questions to ask him as well. Are the rest of our friends here? Are they safe? But I don't have time for that. I frantically reach behind me for the doorknob and as soon as I grab it, I swing the door open and rush inside, running to the window on the other side of the room.

Dozens of people in the room are hiding behind knocked over tables, while one person stands at the shattered window, shooting out into the battlefield.

"Mind if I join you?" I ask the shooter. He gives me one quick glance, then moves over just enough to give me space to see outside.

I peek through the shattered glass and it's a horror show out there. More people are dead than I could have even imagined, given I was only out there moments ago. Hundreds of corpses are spread out across the lawn. The yard is lit by a brilliant display of flashes and bangs, as a hail of bullets continues to reign down on the remaining Disvariants. Talia is nowhere to be seen amongst the living or the dead. Johnson has more active doppelgängers than he did before, along with dozens of dead ones. Someone has to find the original Johnson and stop him, otherwise he will only keep creating more.

I send forcefield bullets through as many of him as I can, but none are the original, and there's no possible way to differentiate between them.

All of the Disvariants fighting display their unique powers in the midst of battle. One man grows to twenty feet tall and rams through a line of Johnsons before Madisen takes him out with a boulder to the head.

"Do you know which one of these guys is the original?" I shout to the man beside me, over the sound of gunfire.

No answer. Instead, he falls over on me and I stare down the bullet hole in his neck. I push him off and turn around and see Brandon, grinning, with a gun pointed at me. Without a second thought I break through the remainder of the glass and climb out of the window.

My forcefield appears below me at regular intervals, acting as a staircase that leads me down below. Suddenly, I'm thankful I practiced this seemingly useless technique in the field that day.

"Oh, no. You're not running away again!" Brandon shouts from behind me, climbing out onto a forcefield that disappears from under him.

"You're right," I say as he crashes to the ground. I'm not going to run away from him. It's my running that has gotten far too many people killed.

I ran from the prison. I ran from Mark and Katherine as they were being murdered. I ran from the military camp and thousands paid for that mistake. I ran to General Kaine when I was not prepared to face him, and it cost Michael his life. Running is not an option anymore.

I climb on top of Brandon before he has a chance to regain his footing, and I hold him down. I snatch the gun from his hand without much effort and point it back at his head.

"Isn't this something?" Blood drips from his mouth as he speaks. "You go from crushin' on me to killing me."

"I *never* had a crush on you," I snap at him, pushing the gun closer to his face. This is the first time since we've met I've spoken a single word of truth to him.

"Oh, I see." He rolls his eyes. "You only wanted something from me. You were using me this whole time!" He curses at me.

My finger is pressed on the trigger, but I don't pull it. He's right, but I want to put a bullet through his head just to shut him up. But I know I could never forgive myself for killing someone out of anger. He takes my hesitation as an opportunity and pushes me off of him. We both stand to our feet at the same time.

"You're so pathetic...meaningless Triv... corrupt by design. You can't even convince yourself to kill someone when you need to! You're a coward!" he snarls, spitting his blood onto the ground.

"Yes, I can," I mutter and lift up the gun. I have to go through with this.

Brandon opens his mouth to speak again, but says nothing. His mouth remains open, his eyes roll into the back of his head, and he falls limp on the ground. The sight startles me, because I hadn't shot him yet, and there are no visible signs of any fatal wounds on him.

I look around nervously for the answer to Brandon's mysterious death, and behind me I find, less than twenty feet away, stands Caleb, wearing tattered mismatched clothes, a gash across his cheek, and an exasperated countenance.

TWENTY SEVEN

"I understand your dilemma of valuing human life and all," Caleb says breathlessly, with a hint of vexation seared into his tone, "but we're kinda in the middle of a war-zone. I don't think either of us want a repeat of last time, so grow up and shoot someone."

Caleb turns away from me without another word and makes his way up the steps into the battlefield. I stand frozen. It's hard to even process that I just saw him standing in front of me, much less the cruel words he just uttered.

The last time that he is talking about is when thousands of innocent people died on account of my inability to use my powers correctly, and Caleb's refusal to use his. He's right. We can't have a repeat of that. Taking the high road and refusing to kill isn't an option right now, but it's hard. To look someone in the eyes as the light leaves them. To watch who they were disappear as a shell of them remains, whether I liked them or not, is a difficult thing. Hearing his backstabbing self tell me to do that same thing, which he was also unwilling to do, has my blood boiling.

If we both make it out of here alive, he won't avoid hearing what I have to say about that. However, at the moment, just standing here in rage is only costing more lives. I stand up straight and follow Caleb's footsteps into the fight. I pass by a group of Johnsons laying at my feet at the top of the stairs, perfectly intact, but not breathing. They are doubtless victims of Caleb.

There's a strap attached to Brandon's gun. I pull it over me and swing the gun behind me. This gun is not my weapon of choice. It is only my backup, so I push it aside and encase myself in a forcefield and tread through the army of clones shooting at me, sending energy bullets at each and every one of them as I march on.

I reach what seems to be the center of the yard and I close my eyes. Bullets hit and ricochet off the forcefield. I sense every hit graze my skin and burn my bones and I have to remind myself the sensation is not real. The bullets are not touching me. I take in a deep breath, exhale slowly, and try to recall that day in the open field.

I picture it. The brilliant display of power and color that I created. No, I didn't create it. I simply harnessed it. It is its own separate creation, but it's connected to me somehow — the ghost of another being residing inside me, protecting me. I open my eyes. I am, once again, surrounded by swirling purple, but it's no longer a soft, inviting lavender. It's a deep purple. I reach my hand out and touch it, even though I should be wary of its swirling fury. The energy that fills my body glides smoothly across my fingertips. I soak it in. I take another deep breath, then I refocus on the fight surrounding me. I can barely see anything through the energy tornado I am at the center of, but I can make out enough to realize that everyone from both sides of the fight have backed away from me. I send floods of my forcefield flying at every Johnson I get a visual on.

I move through the crowd of people, all of whom step, jump, and run out of my way. Their distorted faces stare at the barrier in wonder and fear as I approach another group of Johnsons who are ganging up on a girl. I stretch out my hand towards them, but then my forcefield encounters a tree at the edge of the yard.

Crack! The tree splits apart, splinters flying everywhere, and an all too familiar looking man falls out and stumbles as he attempts to run away. Johnson. Of course. The original was hiding in a tree. He sent all his doppelgängers to fight, while he stood back and ensured he wouldn't be hit in the crossfire.

"Hey!" I yell at him, though I don't know if he heard me through the storm encompassing me. Either way, he risks looking back at the vibrant, dizzying wall of energy while he runs.

With no one daring to get near me or him, I have a clear shot, so I send an energy bullet straight through his forehead. He stumbles onto the ground and all of his doppelgängers cease fighting, dying with him.

A sickness rises up in me when I watch him die. Though my hands are doused in the blood of strangers, Johnson is the first person I have ever intentionally killed, and every part of me is rejecting it. I suppress the shaking that wants to overcome my entire body and I must, once again, ignore the guilt I am burdened with for having ended a life.

I release all of the energy around me and it disperses into the air until only parts of it remain. I push through my exhaustion — creating a forcefield that big has drained me — and run over to the girl stuck under a pile of Johnson's bodies. It turns out to be Talia. With a flick of my hand, what's left of my forcefield pushes all of the Johnsons away from her, and another surge of energy leaves my body. The rest of the sheer barrier dissipates into the air.

"I'm so... so glad... you're alive," I pant.

"I think I might be the only one left," she says, examining a giant gash on her left arm. She's torn off a part of her sleeve and wrapped it around to stop the bleeding, but that won't work for long. "Courtesy of Madisen," she answers my silent question, when she notices me looking worriedly at her arm. "You want to share some of your super healing with me?"

"I wish.. I don't think... I don't know how."

"I was joking, Annalise," she grunts, as I help her up off the ground. She's dripping in sweat. She had been fighting hand to hand with Madisen and the

Johnsons this entire time and managed to survive, while I hid behind walls and forcefields. I wanted to be a fighter, but she's a fighter. I'm a runner.

She gains her own footing and I let her go. I turn to the rest of the battlefield. All the people who were outside fighting with us are still on guard, but seem to be looking around, wondering what to do now. I don't see Caleb or Chadwick among them and that makes me uneasy.

Out of nowhere the ground begins to shake like an earthquake, and booming sounds burst from the building. On the other side of the yard, Madisen appears, standing on top of the roof of the haven. Each step she takes makes the ground shake violently once again.

A dozen pillars of various heights spring from the ground. Madisen uses them as a stairway, each one receding into the ground after she's stepped off it.

"Goodbye, Trivs!" she screeches. She stretches out her hand and earthly daggers are pulled up out of the ground and sent flying at dozens of people. Most manage to dodge or block it with their own abilities, but an unlucky few are impaled.

"She plans to break the ground apart and crush us all, then do the same with the building and everyone inside," Talia informs me from over my shoulder.

I turn to look at Talia, who is focusing intently on Madisen from across the yard. "I thought you couldn't read her mind."

"Only when she won't allow me, but," Talia gleams at me, with a surprising amount of enthusiasm for someone as banged up as she is, "she has lost her focus."

"How do I stop her?"

"As soon as the ground begins to shake again, take your shot. She'll be too focused on the earthquake to stop you. Don't hesitate."

Before I can respond, the ground rumbles and cracks beneath me. I take my opportunity and send an energy bullet speeding right at the malevolent, venomous girl, who laughs as the earth breaks apart. But it misses the target. One of Madisen's assassins materializes out of nowhere and the bullet hits him instead.

The same boy who was so eager to hold my gun earlier, now holds that very weapon I lost at the beginning of the fight in his own hands. He absorbs the energy from my bullet into his own body. Light surges through his veins as the shot hits him and he remains miraculously unharmed.

I take Brandon's gun off my shoulder and ready myself to shoot a real bullet through this boy's head. I'm looking through the scope, trying to aim it, when vines and branches begin to block my view of the boy. They begin to wrap all around him. One massive vine curls around the rifle in his hand and crushes it to pieces.

I trace the origins of the vines back to a woman near the edge of the yard. She has long, golden-blonde hair that complements her sunflower spotted dress. She blends perfectly into the nature surrounding her. The vines wrap all the way around her arms and flow out to the man who is now invisible under a cocoon of thorny roots.

Everyone stands still, even Madisen, waiting to see what has become of the boy. The woman releases him, the vines retract back to her, and the boy is dead; suffocated by nature.

"You've killed all my little soldiers," Madisen deadpans, rolling over her dead minion with her foot, giving him a once over, and returning her gaze to the woman responsible. At this, most of the multitude steps out of the way, unwilling to get caught between the two of them.

Madisen summons a few more of her signature rock daggers from the earth below and chucks them at the woman, but she deflects them all with vines and roots, stemming from her body, that obey her every movement. The woman struggles to maintain her balance on the quaking earth, but she no longer has to when she loses gravity.

Along with the rest of us, the woman rises up into the air like a helium balloon, high up above Madisen, who is livid at the sight. One of the women I encountered when I first ran inside, hovers steadily above the entrance to the haven, keeping us all afloat and out of Madisen's territory — the land.

Queen of the Dirt lets out a bitter wail at the sight of all of us.

"Strike now, while she's distracted," Talia says, and she must be having a conversation with the floating woman too, because at her words, I return to the surface.

My legs are weak and unsteady, but I hit the ground running as fast as I can manage. This time, however, I am not a cowardly runner. This time, I am the fighter.

I jump over broken parts of the yard that have a strange resemblance to giant shards of shattered glass. Madisen's supercilious gaze turns away from the vine woman to narrow on me.

She directs a rock dagger towards me just as I'm jumping over a spike that has sprung up from the surface. My feet do not return to the ground. I am, once again, captured in mid air. The dagger passes under me and barely misses my ankle. My running momentum sends me speeding through the air towards Madisen, until I'm almost directly above her. Madisen cranes her neck to look up at me.

"You cowardice Triv," she spits at me, then commands the ground she's standing on to raise up until we're face to face. "You keep betraying us."

"I can't betray someone I was never with," I proudly admit. It's overwhelmingly refreshing to speak the truth instead of another bilious lie.

I begin channeling my energy again to form a forcefield, but I am drained. If I wasn't floating weightlessly, I might not be able to stand on my own.

"Oh, that's right," she snaps, and I notice the blood on her teeth for the first time. I shudder thinking of whether it's hers or someone else's. "Because someone like you doesn't know how to be loyal, or honest, or decent. You're a monster... scum of the earth... verminous rodent..."

"I'm a Disvariant," I proclaim boldly, then Madisen rolls her eyes at me.

"You're a Triv! Your existence is a crime," she roars, blood dribbling down her chin. "Your kind are the physical embodiment of sin, blemishes on the soul! My life was destroyed, ripped apart by your impurities!"

Pain briefly flickers in her eyes. The pain that those with hatred and prejudice inflicted upon her. The pain her warped mind has twisted back around to point towards us. But surely, somewhere in there, she must also see herself. Deep down she has admitted the truth to herself, and in that vanishing flicker of pain, I see that she had far more in mind than just our deaths.

The flicker vanishes. Her indignant scowl has returned, but before she has a chance to spew another insult at me, which I can tell she is so eager to do, I find the momentary strength to send an energy bullet straight through her brain.

Her body's descent to the ground looks as if it's happening in slow motion; her soul, so reluctant to leave, that it takes its time on the way down.

All the pillars, platforms, and cracked places on the ground, slowly return to their original positions, and in less than a minute, the entire yard has become level again.

The floating woman descends to ground level, as do the rest of us.

"She was the last of them, wasn't she?" the woman asks cautiously, scanning the yard for more assassins to pop out from behind the bushes.

"I think so," I say, glancing back at Talia from across the yard for confirmation.

"*Yes, she was the last one,*" her mental voice says, almost sorrowfully.

"I must check on everyone inside. Martin, Kelley, Strand, stay out here and keep watch," the floating woman orders of three fear stricken residents, who are apprehensive to obey her.

When she strides inside, all of the other remaining fighters outside don't hesitate to follow her lead, and neither do I. Talia catches up with me and I help her walk in the rest of the way. A random man directs us to the infirmary once inside, but I still remember it from the blueprint I mulled over for hours on end. Second floor, third door on the left.

I look down and try to ignore the sight of the death and misery filled common room on my way in, but I can't help but catch a glimpse. What little furniture they had in here is stained with fresh blood. Families hold tightly onto their loved ones that still remain, and mourn for the ones who didn't make it through the night.

I climb one grueling flight of stairs and my heart stops when I reach the top. Lying exactly where I last saw him is Chadwick. His body rests just outside the door I ran through when I encountered him. There's no doubt Brandon killed him, which means I was one of the last people to see Chadwick alive. The last friendly face he ever saw, and I ran away from him because I was at a loss for words.

Talia must not be reading my mind right now, because she doesn't comment on him. I keep walking, and pretend he's another one of the hundreds of bodies around here that I have no recognition of, not a friend I abandoned in his last seconds of life.

I drop Talia off in a packed infirmary. Most of the patients have already succumbed to their injuries, and have been covered with sheets and pulled behind curtains.

I have no way of assisting the doctor on duty to help Talia, and the dead people are creeping me out, so I start back downstairs. I decide I should go outside and volunteer to be a lookout, since we took out all of theirs, rather than stay in this awkwardly crammed together place of mourning.

I walk downstairs, past Chadwick again. I don't allow myself to look back or linger on it. If I do, the weight of everything that has happened over the past two days will come flooding over me, and I will be crushed under that weight. I have done too much damage, lost too many people, lied too many times. Maybe I deserve to be crushed by all of it.

I reach the last step. I prepare myself to re-enter the hectic common room. *Get it over with,* I think, then rush through the room, maneuvering through teary-eyed strangers I have no idea how to console. Then something catches my eye. I stop in my tracks and turn back around to confirm for myself that my eyes weren't playing tricks. They were not.

Caleb sits on the floor in the corner of the room. His eyes gaze somewhere up above me. I know he is not registering what he is staring at. His mind is in space, completely unaware of myself, standing within his peripheral.

I contemplate just leaving. If I did, he would not notice my absence since, despite his staring, he clearly does not notice my presence either. I'm sure if I walked out that door he would forget I had ever been here. I was merely an illusion of his nightmare induced panic that faded when the fight ended.

So, why am I not leaving? Why am I walking towards him? I think, as I draw closer to him. As I get nearer, I notice Charity is sitting beside him. Her face is buried in her hands and she refuses to look up. She is not sitting next to Chadwick, taking comfort in his shadow that she so desperately needs right now. She is mourning him instead.

An old lady is helped up by a young boy and moves to reveal that Thomas is sitting with them as well. He's looking down, his face covered by his hair, but I can tell he's upset. And with the move of another person in the crowd, I can see why.

It's Hailee.

TWENTY EIGHT

Hailee is lying down on the floor. Her head is in Thomas's lap. Her face is pale, and the chest of her T-shirt is soaked in crimson red that has already begun to dry a bitter, dark brown.

I press my way through the pack to Thomas and find a space next to him. I sit down only inches away from Hailee's cold corpse.

"I'm so sorry," I say to Thomas and Charity, then put a hand on Thomas's shoulder. He flinches a little at my touch.

I only manage a glance at Charity before she begins to bawl, and not wanting anyone to see her cry, she runs off to who-knows-where for privacy. It's a hard sight to watch. She is a timid soul who has just had the person she is closest to in the world stripped away from her.

My heart aches for Charity and I almost chase after her, but I can't leave Thomas. Tears well in my eyes at the sight of his pain. He tries to speak to me, but never manages so much as a full syllable. It hurts to see him so heartbroken over someone, especially someone like Hailee. Forgive me for speaking ill of the dead, but she was negative, bitter, and controlling. Still, for some reason, unknown to me, he was head over heels for her. Maybe I'm only biased because she clearly had it out for me. She thought I was a murderer with eyes for her boyfriend, and she wanted nothing to do with me for any of it.

Thomas takes a moment away from Hailee to peer at Caleb through tear-blurred eyes, but he is still staring blankly into space. I know Thomas wants him to snap back into reality and say something, or cry with him, or do anything. But he looks as dead as Hailee does. Seeing his chest move up and down with his breathing is the only thing convincing me he hasn't died where he's sitting.

"Caleb, may I speak to you outside?" I say firmly, making it clear that it was not so much a question as an order.

"Oh...yeah... Sure," he murmurs, blinking rapidly as he comes back to reality.

I stand up and stare him down until he eventually stands up as well, then follows me through the common room, down a hallway littered with bodies (I make sure to be extra careful not to step on anyone's hands, even though I know they can't feel it), and out of the backdoor.

We both step out into the open air. The darkness of early morning collides with the flood lights illuminating the battle field. I look away from the devastation and turn to Caleb. He still appears to be in a daze, not all here.

I worry he may not hear anything I say, but I speak anyway. "Your best friend is in there mourning the girl he loved, and the least you could do is show a little emotion over it," I demand, and he shows no response. "You know, even a little bit of emotion will do. Just a single tear would suffice. C'mon man!"

"I'm actively avoiding a breakdown," Caleb mumbles, staring at the ground.

"So, quit avoiding it. It's okay to be upset, and right now, Thomas is in there having his own breakdown, and you're staring into space like he isn't even there. He's your best friend and he needs you, so grow up and cry if you have to," I say, mirroring the harsh words he spoke to me during our first encounter here.

"I can't control it."

"It's okay if you —"

"No, it isn't," he cuts me off. He almost looks at me, but instead shuts his eyes tightly as he speaks. "I can't control my powers. I can kill a person by glancing at them. If I... I lose control, I end up killing people I never meant to. That's terrifying. Today, I have been executioner to more people than I ever wanted to. I don't need to hurt anyone else."

"Oh... I'm sorry. I didn't think about that," I say.

My mind again flashes back to our earlier conversation. *Neither of us want a repeat of last time.* Now, I think he was speaking more to himself than anyone else, and his words do not seem so cruel. They only acted as a vivid reminder to himself. He is not a killer at heart, but he could not bear to witness a repeat of that devastation. The weight of the lives lost weighs just as heavily on him as it does on me, maybe even more. He has been living with them a lot longer than I have...

"Don't be sorry," Caleb says, finally opening his eyes, but staring out into the distance instead of looking at me. "You're right. I should be there for Thomas. Charity, too. But I can't be. I can't risk hurting either of them." Caleb begins squinting really hard at something just beyond me. "Oh no. I told them to hide upstairs."

He walks over to where Scarlett and Rowena are both lying on the ground. I walk over with him. As I look closer I see sharp, tiny rocks embedded in both of their necks, barely visible, but big enough to cause lethal damage.

"Is this who I think it is?" he asks oddly, squinting at their faces. How can he not recognize them?

"Yes, it is. Scarlett and Rowena. Madisen killed them," I answer him.

"What? Why would she have done this? They were her best friends," he says, baffled.

It hits me that he doesn't know who the real Madisen is. I thought for sure he must have seen her rabid and foaming at the mouth during the fight, but I guess not. He still only knows her to be the victim she played so well.

"Madisen didn't have friends, Caleb," I remorse-fully inform him. "She had accomplices and employ-ees."

He is taken completely aback and nearly stumbles on Scarlett's body. "What are you talking about?"

I hesitate to elaborate. He loved her, or he loved who he thought she was. I know the truth will crush him.

"You didn't see the version of her that I did... I'm sorry, but she was a ruthless liar and manipulator. She pretended to be sweet and innocent, but she was vicious, with an overwhelming hate for other Disvari-ants. The team of assassins I was forced to join — it was her idea."

I decided not to sugarcoat anything. He needs to know she wasn't just kind of a bad person — she was a monster. Pretending she was only confused or manipulated would not be doing him any kindness.

"That can't be true," he mumbles. I can almost hear the sound of his heart dropping into his stom-ach as he speaks. "Madisen wouldn't do that. They must have threatened her, messed with her mind, or —"

"I wish that were true, but she did all of this of her own accord."

Tears start forming in his powerful, but horrified eyes. "She couldn't have... Wait. You said 'was.' Is she... is she dead?"

"Yes. I'm sorry," I say again, and put my hand on his shoulder. Yet another thing I thought he already knew, and I hate to be the one to inform him.

He pushes me away, mutters something at me that I don't understand, and storms back inside. The door slams shut behind him.

Okay, maybe I should have sugarcoated it just a little, I think, as I turn again to look at Scarlett and Rowena. If I could guess, I would say that Rowena probably wanted to take Caleb's suggestion and run and hide upstairs, but Scarlett wanted to escape, and fearfully obedient Rowena went along with it.

I look across the yard. So many people lie around Scarlett and Rowena. They all ran out this way trying to escape the fight, but *my* team killed them. I know I was not personally responsible for this, but I am inadvertently the one to blame. It was my job to stop them before this happened, and I failed miserably. Their deaths rest on my conscience.

I can no longer look at the devastation, so I trudge back inside and spend half an hour sitting with a dazed Caleb and a teary-eyed Thomas, who refuses to let go of Hailee's unnerving corpse.

I finally give up on comforting him and decide to check on Talia, once again, walking past Chadwick. His body still has not been picked up. Most of them haven't, and it is a rather morbid sight.

Talia is doing shockingly well for someone who has just gotten seventeen stitches with no anesthetics or pain medication. The doctor said they have a very limited supply of medicine, so it's only used when absolutely necessary, and even though Talia is dealing with significant pain, it won't kill her.

"You, me, and Sara are the only ones left," she tells me. "Stephen, Jonathan, and Taylor are all dead, along with Madisen's minions. I glimpsed into their minds while it was all happening. I wanted to find them to see if they were alright. I ended up witnessing their murders through their own eyes."

She runs her fingers over the bandage covering her stitches and tries to hide her emotional pain under the physical, but I know how much it must hurt. She devised this plan solely to save her friends, but most of them didn't make it out.

"I'm so sorry," I say. I genuinely mean it, but it seems false and shallow. The look of horror in her eyes deserves more than the millionth sorry I've given out today. Just as with everyone else, I find no way to comfort Talia.

"Let me know if you need me," I offer. "I'll help with anything. Anything at all. If you need to talk or... anything. Just let me know," I sigh. I'm turning to leave when someone speaks to me.

"You fought beautifully today," the woman who controlled the vines that killed Gun Boy says to me. She had been in here checking up on a friend as well.

"Thanks," I say awkwardly. "You did a great job with your vines... and stuff..."

"Thank you. Do you think you'll be able to stop the rest?" she asks.

"The rest of what?" I ask, but she gapes at me as if I, of all people, should know what she is talking about.

"The rest of the Duplicates who want to kill us," she answers.

"I, uh, I don't know..."

Her question caught me completely off guard. Personally, the idea of killing any more people, no matter how bad, makes me want to vomit profusely, but her question brings up a good point — something that hadn't managed to occur to me yet — there are still people out there who want to kill us.

More fights are bound to come our way. There have to be millions of people in this country who think we are terrorists and monsters, or at least they will think that when the government insists that we are. How could we possibly stop them all?

"We will all fight them and stop them together," Talia answers the woman after my lack of an enthusiastic response.

That chilling question has my mind spinning wildly, thinking about how big this could potentially become. I knew there was something extra-ordinarily wrong, running immeasurably deep into our society and government, yet somehow, I still looked at it in small scale. Escaping one place, defeating one team, would be the end of it all. But it's not. There is an army being held hostage in camps all across the country. They are being trained up to fight against us.

How far will they go to stop us? Can we stop them first? Could we convince them to give up the fight? I ponder these questions as I wander the corridors and end up running into the floating lady, so I offer my help to get my mind off of things.

Along with the floating lady and a few other volunteers, we set up the knocked over, bloodstained furniture no one wants to sit on, and throw away the tables and chairs that are too smashed, or have too many bullet holes to be useful.

One of the men who volunteered helps me set up a bunch of bunk beds in the crowded bedrooms, using our powers. He's a telekinetic who can move the beds back into place without touching them, and I let my forcefield do all my work for me.

Once everything is set back into place, the floating woman enlists us to carry out all the bodies throughout the building and take them outside to the yard, where those who were residents here will be taken to a nearby cemetery and buried. Those from the team of assassins will be burned.

The floating woman causes the bodies to levitate down the stairs. The telekinetic man uses his mind to move the bodies. I use my forcefield to carry the rest. All of these methods, however, scare onlooking children as we pass by and they run away in horror.

We lay the bodies in rows on the grass while a dozen other people are sorting between their families and Johnson's clones. They put all of his doppel-gängers into a giant burn pile.

"I need to ask a favor," the floating lady says to me after we lay out the last of the bodies. "I saw you speaking to one of our residents. You seem to know him — Thomas?"

I look out to the yard. The grass is wet with both blood and fresh dew. We had spent the entire night fighting and trying to clean up the fight. Now the sun is peeking out from behind the trees, casting a soft light on the harsh devastation around us, and renews my strength to face this next task.

"Oh, yeah," I murmur fearfully. I already know what she's going to ask, and I don't know if I'm pre-pared to do it.

"The girl — Hailee — needs to be taken away. She deserves to be buried with the rest of our loved ones, and her presence in the common room is frightening the children. Would you please convince Thomas to give her over to us?"

"I'll try," I regretfully accept.

I maneuver through the people in the common room, which is much easier now since most of them have settled down into corners where they hold tightly onto their loved ones, just like Thomas, who holds tightly onto Hailee.

Charity has returned from her private crying and now sits a little distance away from Thomas and Caleb. She is reluctant to sit too close, I'm sure because she, too, is disconcerted by Hailee's empty presence.

"Thomas," I whisper softly to him. "Can I take Hailee?"

I reach for her, but Thomas grabs my hand and looks up at me with puffy, red eyes.

"No, I can't leave her," he answers.

I hesitate to respond, and can only muster a string of the most cliché responses to death that I heard after Julie's passing. "Holding on won't make her come back. It won't make the loss easier to deal with. She deserves to be buried. She would want you to let go," I tell him, but nothing I say could truly suffice to fix how heartbroken he is right now, especially not this.

"No!" he screams at me, and his voice cracks.

A pang of both bitterness and sorrow resonate within my hollow chest. I'm frustrated with his unwillingness to let go of a rotting corpse. However, I can see the pain swelling in his eyes. I can hear it overcoming his voice, and I can't help but hurt for him.

The people sitting right next to us slowly back away after his outburst, and I am frozen for lack of response. How do I do this? How do I say a single word that could ease his pain, soften the blow? Is there such a thing?

"Alright." Caleb steps in, having been knocked out of his daze. "Let go of her."

"No!" Thomas screams again.

Caleb stands to his feet and reaches for Hailee, starting to pull her away from Thomas, who pulls back. I am sick to my stomach watching them fight over a lifeless corpse.

"No! No!" Thomas insists.

Charity, who had just barely begun to calm down, bursts into tears again and runs away.

"Let her go! This isn't helping anyone!" Caleb yells, clutching onto Hailee and pulling her away.

"No!"

"Stop it!" I scream over the both of them. Someone else in the distance yells the same words back to me. It's not until moments later it hits me. That was my own echo, but the voice is of someone completely different than me. Someone older and sadder. Someone screaming out in pain and confusion.

Caleb and Thomas both let go of Hailee and stare at me in concern. I can't see myself right now, but if I could, I'm sure I would be looking into hollow eyes resting on a blank face, covering up the shattered soul hiding underneath it.

"Please," I say, whispering now so I don't hear my own terrifying echo again. "I don't know what else to say. Please, just let us bury her. She's dead, Thomas."

Thomas says nothing, but his lips move, then he leans back onto the wall and buries his face in his hands.

Caleb and I grab Hailee before Thomas has a chance to change his mind. We carry her outside.

She's the very last body that has been laid out, so when we set her down, my eyes can't help but move to the rows of people along side her.

"There wasn't supposed to be any casualties," I mutter in agonizing defeat.

I expect Caleb to ignore me, or tell me some discomforting words of positivity like "you did your best," or "you can't change what happened," or something that a dad would say to his kid after he lost a baseball game. But he says nothing. Instead, he hugs me. I was never fond of hugs, but his offers me comfort, not the usual awkwardness. And with unfamiliar arms wrapped around me — as I come to the realization I barely know the person I am letting hold me — and my face leaning against his chest, I cry.

I cry for all of my friends, for all of my teammates who just wanted to escape, and all of the innocent people who died during the camp breakout. I mourn the woman who unintentionally lost her life when taking Madisen's dagger for me. I weep for all the people I have killed, and all the people who died for simply having the misfortune of knowing me.

I've had to suppress my emotions since the beginning of the blackout, though I have done the worst possible job at it. I've had to attempt to suppress all of the compunction that threatens to swallow my conscience whole and drown it in grief, because I knew if I didn't, I would undoubtedly break down. I've had to ignore how much of my own moral code I have broken, bashed into a million pieces, how many people I have hurt, and how many lies I've told so flippantly.

It has left me empty and dirty, and despite my best efforts to hold it back, the weight of it all is pounding me into the ground, farther and farther, but somehow never able to reach six feet under. But for just a moment, I allow myself to feel all of it. To release it. To let myself understand it. To begin to move past it.

I let my tears wash my face, and for the first time since my trial started an infinite amount of time ago, I feel clean. The sun shines brightly on my wet face. It warms my soul and dries my salty tears.

For a brief instant, I think I might be myself again. But eventually, the hug has to end, although I wish I could cry in his arms just a little bit longer. No amount of tears seems enough for all that I have done, or all that I'm going to do, because as the vine woman so morbidly reminded me — there are surely greater fights on the horizon.

Caleb and I return to the common room and sit down on the floor next to Thomas and Charity, who has, once again, returned from crying. Talia has made her way downstairs from the infirmary and takes a seat next to me. She swings her uninjured arm over my shoulder.

"I'm glad you survived," she says, and I smile.

A person who I know to be Sara, because of her uniform and unmistakable purple highlights, joins Talia on the floor next to us.

The sunlight shines in through the broken windows as I sit with what remains of our team of assassins, and what's left of the only friends I have in the world. Five people with war torn, but hopeful faces, who remind me I'm not alone in this.

"Listen up, everyone," the floating lady shouts. She stands heroically in the doorway to the common room, hands on her hips in a true superhero pose, demanding the undivided attention of all of us. "For those of you who may not know, I am Lena Tate. I, along with my colleagues, Ron Howard and Elizabeth Ashley, are the leaders of this place," she says, gesturing to the two people standing behind her. They are the ones who met me at the entrance, and they stand behind her like loyal bodyguards. "I have a few things to say about the events that have unfolded.

"We lost a great number of people here today, and that's taking a toll on all of us," she announces sorrowfully, and my eyes dart across the room. The girl who so closely resembles Lena Tate is nowhere to be found. "Mourn if you must. The lives of everyone we lost today were valuable. Every Duplicate and Disvariant life is valuable, but the people who came here to end our lives don't believe that to be true. They believe only their lives matter. They believe a simple variation between us and them makes us unworthy of life and basic human rights. We will not stand for that. They believe we are their polar opposites. They are the light and we are the darkness.

383

That is not right. The true variation between us —
what separates us from the ruthless murderers — is
not what nature has given us the ability to do, but
what we choose to do with what we have been given!"
Tate is yelling now. If anyone had slipped away to
their rooms upstairs they could still hear her speech.
"The ones who attacked us tonight were Disvariants
like us, but their actions were not justified, under any
circumstances. They were just as evil as the Duplicates who sent them here. They chose to use what
they had to hate and to kill, but we choose to love
and protect one another.

"We must not forget that the fight is not over.
More will come for us, no doubt. But even if they do
not, the battle still rages on. Our brothers and sisters
are still being slaughtered and silenced. The government wishes we continue to hide in the shadows, but
we can do that no longer. We must make it known
that we oppose them, and we must expose what they
are doing.

"We lost lives today, yes, but we won the fight,
and we will win the war. They want to take everything
from us. They want to take ourselves from us. They
want to break us apart and pit us against each other
until we crumble to pieces, but I refuse to let that
happen. We must fight *for* each other.

"We know what's right, we know what's good,
and we will fight for it. No matter the cost, we will
fight together. Carry on, and may the spirit of the sun

guide us through this treacherous path on which we must embark!"

Those who have energy cheer for her speech. Those who don't, sit in silent agreement with nodding heads but fearful expressions.

"What does she mean by the 'spirit of the sun?'" I whisper to Talia when the cheering stops. She gives me a baffled look, then turns to Caleb.

"He didn't tell you?" she groans in exasperation. Once again, Talia has snuck into my mind and seen my personal thoughts. She read through the pages of my life and found the chapter where Caleb told me all I know about Disvariants. She knows what information he held back from me that day on the road.

"Tell me what?" I ask.

"Now is not the right time to talk about it," she answers, then nods to Charity. Whatever it is Caleb hid from me, it's something Charity doesn't need to know right now. Though I don't see why that has to stop Talia from telling me. It's evident Charity is so lost in her own worrisome thoughts that she is entirely unaware of the conversations happening around her.

"Fine," I sigh. "But you *have* to tell me later. I'm tired of not having any idea about anything that's going on!"

I would demand immediate answers, but Talia is stubborn. I know I can't convince her to tell me anything if she doesn't want to, and to risk bringing up a potentially argumentative subject to Caleb in his volatile state, would be reckless, though it's admittedly frustrating. I finally accepted I must search for the answers no matter what horrible things I find, but now those answers are taunting me, existing just beyond my reach.

"Of course," Talia agrees. "If it had been up to me, I wouldn't have chosen to wait so long to inform you in the first place."

Talia shoots Caleb a quick, judgmental glance for his secret keeping. He doesn't register it, having zoned out once again. Talia then turns nervously to Charity, as if anticipating a reaction from her, but she hasn't been listening to a word we've said since Tate's speech ended.

"I don't want a war," Charity whimpers out of the blue, frantically twisting her curly hair with her fingers.

"The war has already started. It's unavoidable," Caleb says to Charity. Her loud whine snapped him out of his daze.

"So is winning," Talia assures Charity. "They have their weapons, but we have our conscience. They will stoop too low to stomp us out, and it will be their downfall. Good always wins."

"Good versus evil means nothing," Charity scoffs, tears forming in her eyes. "And Chadwick believed that, too. We're all gonna die, and not one bit of it will matter. Good, it doesn't win. It doesn't exist," she sniffles.

"Of course it does," I insist, though even my bones feel devoid of anything good or pure nowadays.

"The depravity of this world will come unceremoniously crashing down." Talia looks directly into Charity's glassy eyes. "And it will disappear without a trace. We will be here to witness that, I assure you. But until then, I refuse, for even a second, to let the demons who try to destroy us, get their way. You shouldn't either. Whether you believe in good or not, do not let the people who killed your brother take what's left of your life from you. Cling on to whatever hope you have left."

"I — I ca —"

"You can," Talia insists. "Do it for Chadwick. Honor his memory by not succumbing to the idea that will allow his murderers to win."

"O — okay," Charity whispers.

Without another word between them, they both hold out their pinky fingers and lock them together. An unspoken promise. Talia can read Charity's mind, and I would guess she has been this entire conversation. She must know that a pinky promise means something more to Charity than just a pinky promise.

With the conversation of impending war spreading throughout the room, our little group theorizes about the magnitude of it. I don't talk. I only listen as they discuss the widespread effects, and Caleb speaks in detail of what Disvariants have suffered through, something he kept locked up in himself until now. Though he makes no mention whatsoever about this "spirit of the sun" Tate had spoken of, he talks of things that send chills down my spine and only further confirms my fear that this fight will not be easily won. Threats, kidnapping, manipulation, and barbaric methods of torture are all weapons in the military's arsenal against us.

I shift in my seat, trying to find a way to be comfortable, but it's not how I'm sitting that is uncomfortable, it's this conversation. I glance over to Caleb, who has taken notice of how awkward and tense I am acting.

"But Talia was right. We will win. All of that will come to an end, because we will not have any more repeats," he says, and I know exactly what he means. No more running away because we're scared. No more compromising what's right. No more deaths because we were too afraid to fight.

This war is not something I want, but it's happening, nonetheless. No matter how long it takes, no matter what else happens, we will win, because morality always wins in the end. The truth will come out, the lies will burn to the ground like the cities they've torched, and only the good will remain. We will remain. We will be saved.

Desolation is coming, but so is deliverance.

END OF BOOK ONE

ACKNOWLEDGMENTS

Thank You to God, who instilled me with a love for literature, then gave me my own stories to tell.

Thank you to my Mom and Dad, who have supported my love for writing in every way possible. I hope you enjoyed this book.

Thank you to all of my friends who encouraged me and reviewed this story, but especially Haley Webber, who stuck with me through the entire writing process, tediously read through multiple versions of the same scenes, and gave me honest feedback each time.

Finally, thank you to the readers. Every person who reads this book holds a special place within my heart.

ABOUT THE AUTHOR

T.C. Joseph is a fiction writer, who has been fascinated by the dystopian genre for many years. She has been working on The Disvariants since 2016.

Born in 1998, Joseph has been writing short stories for as long as she can remember, but her desire to pursue writing didn't come until her teenage years. She is currently a full-time writer and a part-time reader, movie watcher, and artist.

Follow her on social media to keep updated about her future books.

twitter: @taylrokay

instagram: @tmliterary

Printed in Great Britain
by Amazon